THERE WILL BE BLOOD

E.C. HINRICHS

BEYOND THE FRAY

Publishing

BEYOND THE FRAY

Publishing

I dedicate this to my past, present and future family. I love you all and I appreciate you! To my son Janos for giving me a final push. And finally, to the teachers who challenged me to keep reading, thinking and working. Dr. Broffman, Dr. Mc Caffery, Jan Laville and Mrs. Rai—you've unleashed something terrible and it's going to be a blast.

PROLOGUE

The feeling had long gone out of my blood-spattered arms as I remained tied to a large marble pillar. In all my years working for HALO and stopping the bad guys, I never expected to meet my end like this. I figured gunfire or beheading, but death by human (well, almost human) sacrifice was not among them. Many thoughts ripped through my head: *How did I get here? Why is this happening to me?* I looked to my right and saw Damon's eyes flutter. I struggled against my restraints, gazing at cloaked people surrounding me. Should I tell them I'm deathly allergic to being sacrificed? Looking at the praying followers, I had the sensation that they wouldn't believe me.

I have worked for HALO far to long and after meeting the love of my life, I promised myself this was my last job. My wrist was tied artfully to Damon's. I could feel his heart beat through my skin. I swallowed the lump of futility that was growing in my throat. I promised myself that I could live happily ever after as a normal person. Sage smoke stung my eyes as the air became thickened with it.

The chanting became louder and more persistent. I didn't want my mother to have to bury me, and secretly I hoped that there would be nothing left so my mother wouldn't have to look upon a beaten corpse. I saw Damon's raven head move side to side. "Damon," I whispered harshly. "C'mon, wake up!"

His brown eyes flickered. The chanters' arms rose toward the sky, beckoning some invisible force. Their arms were swaying in a rhythmic motion.

A sharp breath beside me. "What the fuck…" Damon said with disbelief. The circle parted, and a tall figure cloaked in blue stepped his way through. The figure stepped in the center and raised his hands to the sky. A male voice boomed out over the chanting, reciting a separate incantation. Fear filled Damon's eyes.

"We're in trouble, aren't we?"

"Yup."

"This is going to be bad, isn't it?"

"Yup." The chanting got louder as if it were the thunder in the sky.

"We've had bad before, Trinity," he attempted to assure me.

"This is worse." Even through the thunder of the voices, I heard him gulp. I began to think about all the things I was going to miss out on, all the things I hadn't done. My eyes began to water. But then again, I had experienced the deepest love. *Oh, my beloved,* I thought sadly. *I regret nothing.* The chanting stopped as if frozen in motion.

"What's going on?" I felt Damon struggle harder. The followers lowered their arms and turned toward us. I stared at the darkness that hid their faces.

"Didn't you know?" I remarked wryly. His face turned to me, pale with fear. *I regret nothing, nothing.* Suddenly this was all so funny. "It's showtime." I giggled lightly. The man in the blue cloak started toward us. It was indeed showtime.

❧ I ❧

Here goes; you can do it, Trinity. I took a deep breath in. This was it. Exhaling, I shoved my hands in my pockets and looked out to the lapping shore. He was supposed to be my hubby-to-be, but as fate would have it, I was "undesired." I wondered if I had just faked I was quitting, maybe he would take me more seriously. Okay, deep breath. "I quit," I said quietly. My eyes flickered to the perfection that was Damon. He blinked his dark brown eyes twice. He tilted his head as the wind ruffled his brown hair. "I figured it's time for a change, you know?" I looked back down at the ground.

"Pardon?" he said as if he hadn't heard me.

"I quit," I said to Damon with a steadfast stare, watching his reaction. His face was blank as he looked at me. How I would have loved for some kind of emotion—any emotion—to cross the dead space of his face. I knew my face was giving my emotions away. I forced a blank and easygoing look to attempt to show that I couldn't care less. I wanted him to care. I wanted a warm smile and fuzzy embrace, but most of all I wanted him to beg me to stay. We were supposed to be each other's happily ever after, or at least that was what the mating specialist at HALO wanted us to believe.

He is going to disregard the rest of me like some sort of piece of trash, said a vicious little voice in the back of my head. I stuffed it back from whence it came and waited for a reaction. My heart flared with hope. *Maybe he is thinking of something sweet to say*. I took a few steps forward, shoving my hands in my blue jean pockets. *But what if he doesn't?* That was something I didn't want to think about. He would ask me to stay, make me feel important, or at least that was what I was secretly praying. What if he called my bluff?

That was something to consider. Maybe I have *had* enough. After ten years of constant training, torture and secret identity, maybe it was time that this little savior should hang up her red cape and start living. I looked at Damon with a half smile. We had been working together for six years in an organization called HALO. We had been inseparable when we first met, but for some reason he pushed me away. Both of us were working together toward a better world and a world of balance, at least that was what they told us. I listened to the beat of the lapping waves in the midst of twilight. I looked at his olive skin and longed to touch it. I wanted to run my fingers through his pitch-black hair and taste his cupid's-bow lips. I blushed and looked at the lake. Maybe I'd get lucky and he'd tell me I was needed or that I shouldn't give up so easily.

HALO had picked me as his "mate," according to our files, six years ago, and it had been six years of waiting for him to care about me. Most of the time, "mating" works out perfectly, and there will be a new generation of Reapers, Sentinels, Healers, Watchers, Seers or whatever people like us were before we were born. He was silent as he watched me walk beside him with a smile dangling on my lips. Maybe, just maybe, if he thought I was going to leave for good, he might wake up and smell the coffee.

It's funny how you never ever think that you will be that poor sap waiting for Mr. Right for years, yet here you are. I examined his darkened features, high cheekbones, cupid's-bow lips, thick black hair—he was like someone out of a bad romance. "I am sick of the games," I said, attempting to forget how good looking he was. Now that I was really thinking about it, it made me sick to look at him. Why should I wait around for him? He'd been dating other women ever since he found out we were supposed to be mated. He shoved his large hands into his pockets and strode slightly in front of me. "I think it's time for me to go live life for the sake of living," I said with a carefree shrug. He turned and looked at me.

A large grin danced over his face, and stars sparkled in his eyes. He was wearing all black, as most Reapers do, although this time he was wearing designer jeans. Dear god, his ass looked great in those jeans. I found myself thinking about what was underneath them. It was so weird to see him wearing True Religion jeans. I cocked an eyebrow. *Hold the phone,* I thought to myself. *This guy never spends money on decent jeans let alone designer jeans.* I started to examine anything else on him that seemed out of place. I noticed the watch he was wearing. It wasn't an ordinary watch. It was Cartier; it was a very expensive watch. *Holy crap, did this guy get another raise?* Goddamn it, Damon wasn't a job. I needed to stop examining him like this was a case. *This doesn't fit; none of this is right! Something is definitely up.* No, that wasn't it; I was just looking for something else to think about besides my heart getting crushed. God, he looked really good. His playboy smile spread widely across his face.

"Yeah, me too," he added with an upbeat voice. Okay, so maybe he didn't care. Maybe he was just messing with me and just wanted to see if I was bluffing. There were some days when I could read him like a fine Dickens and others, much like now like Russian literature, I wished I had just put the book back. "I got big plans for the future." He shrugged his sagging shoulders and kept an indifferent face, still hanging on to half a grin. "I'm going to build a new house with a pool in the back and maybe go to Cuba just to hang."

I swallowed my anger back. He must have felt pangs of joy as he watched me squirm. Why was the fact he came into some extra cash bothering me so badly? "I think Christie and I deserve it." Oh, yes. How could I forget about his beloved, 100% normal girlfriend? *That should be me,* I thought bitterly.

"Who doesn't?" I mumbled. It took all my energy to stuff my hands in my pockets and not grab him. I wanted so badly to scream, *"Why don't you want me?"* Our words only echoed off the lapping shore. He kept telling me about all of his remodeling plans, but I couldn't hear a word. I tried to think of a way out of this. Maybe I could say, "Psych! Gotcha! Didn't think I was actually serious, did you?" No, I couldn't do that. I tried to think of something more important. Maybe I needed to stay; after all, I was doing important work. We were top secret superheroes attempting to save the world, in a backdoor kind of way. HALO put us in situations before they occurred in an attempt to stop them.

They planted us in bad situations, and hopefully we stopped them from occurring. Sometimes we failed. We were a team and one of the best. We took down the bad guy in record time and celebrated. Okay, he celebrated. I moped. His version of celebrating was taking his recent girlfriend on a cruise or to some exotic place where they would screw for hours. Then he would tell me all about it. Maybe that should have been my first tip-off that the guy was a total asshole.

We talked, walking down the winding road while the world was waking up to rustic 5 a.m. *Let it sink in; give him a second—third —fortieth chance to see what he is missing.* He acted as if he didn't care. *This can't be happening,* I thought glibly. My "Big Plan" was turning sour quickly. He kept talking about all the wonderful things he was going to do because something had come along and made life that much easier.

I missed Rae. I missed her so much. Life hadn't been the same since she left for Paris. She was my strength, my spine and, most importantly, my best friend. I remembered the last time I had seen her. I had dropped her off at the terminal and walked her to the plane. She had spent the entire night before trying to talk sense into me. The hot air filled the terminal with muggy air, which made the passengers more irritated.

In the background of my flashback, I could hear. I tried to listen intently, as I always did to him. *"Be strong, Trin,"* Raeann had told me as she looked for her ticket to Paris. *"Be the bitch for once. Show him what he is missing and take it back."* Good advice at the time. It was the last time I would see her for a while. The airport became thick with disenchanted people when I told her, "I can't do it, Rae. Forget about it." I threw up my hands in uncertainty.

"You keep holding on to a man that, for one"—she held out a long slender finger—"is sleeping with the straights and doesn't want to be one of us *anyway*. Two," she said, flicking up her middle finger to join the first, "has been trailing you along like a pathetic puppy dog."

I crossed my arms and didn't like the taste of her words. I had the frown on my face to prove it. Knowing you're pathetic is one thing; being *told* is a completely different kind of hurt. She rolled her amber eyes and set her pouty lips in a frown as she rested her hand on her hip and shook her head. Damon treating me like crap had been on the agenda for years. She wanted to see it come to an end.

"He might change his mind," I pointed out weakly. I felt ridiculous cowering in front of this five-foot-four woman, but sometimes your best friend can frighten you with the truth. "He might!"

Rae threw her hands in the air with an exasperated sigh.

"You said that last year, and the year before that," she began. "Don't forget five years ago when you said you were fed up." She pointed her finger at me again.

I rolled my eyes and pushed it away from me.

"Hey!" I nearly shouted. "He took me out on a date!"

She ran fingers through her long chestnut brown hair in frustration.

"Oooo! One date!" she remarked with her fingers wagging in quotation marks.

"He has taken me on more than one date!" I pointed out.

Her eyebrow arched as she looked at me. A smile spread across her doll-like face as she rolled thoughts around her head. For a moment, her eyes grew wide as she asked me, "How many?" A look came across her face that told me she knew she was winning the debate. The classic Rae move, sealing the deal. "So?"

"Three." Goddamn it, I was being painted in a corner here.

"This year?" She was aiming for the kill shot of the conversation.

"Over the last six years," I said shamefully. I hung my head. I knew she was right, but something inside me clung on tightly. I really wanted that happily ever after.

"That's half a date a year. You realize this, right?" Her face turned to a sympathetic look. She put her pale hand on my shoulder. "See how he reacts when you say you are going to quit, and go from there."

I thought it was a good idea at the time. That was the idea, tell him I'm going to quit, and he would say, "Oh no! Please don't leave! I love you!" He would choose then to get down on one knee and propose to me. Pledge his undying love while sweeping me off my feet.

Flashing to reality, I realized this clearly wasn't happening right now; actually I was almost literally swallowing the backfire of the situation. I snapped back to hear him talking about how desperately he wanted to take Christie to Germany and how it was the "in" thing right now. I hid an eye roll. What an ass. But who was the big ass here? Him for rubbing it in my face, or me for thinking my "big plan" would work?

Maybe this conversation wasn't happening; it might be a hallucination. Or better yet, a dream.

"I really have to go to bed, so—later." He just turned around and started to leave in his typical casual stride. He was leaving already? That was it? No! this couldn't be happening. Crap! "Oh, good luck with—ah, whatever." It was like he wasn't even talking to me.

"Weren't you listening?" I heard Rae's voice in the back of my head: *And you're hanging on to him... why?* "I'm done." Final test, Damon, you still have time to take me back. "You are really not going to see me around."

He shrugged. I felt as if I kept digging myself in deeper with this.

"So? You got shit to do, so do I." He took his hand out of his pocket and swatted at the air as if to get rid of a fly. "You know, I really don't care what you do. Just have fun, you know? Get out, see the world." Ouch. He really *didn't* care, did he?

"What a coincidence, that's what I intend to do," I added nonchalantly. I threw in another word to lengthen the time we had together for just a moment more, but in my heart I knew this was the last time we would ever see each other. I felt the crisp burning in my chest as I began to realize that despite our history together, our files and shared interests, he didn't want me. I had time, I could run up to him and throw my arms around him, beg him to love me. No, that was pathetic. How could I ever tell him how much I cared about him or what he meant to me? He was more than just a partner, he was a friend. We were supposed to be together, but it seemed that he wanted anyone but me. For years, I had thought, *After the next girl, it will be my turn.* My turn never came.

Without another word, he simply walked away. Coldly as always, he left. He stuck his hands in his pockets and whistled a happy tune. I felt stupid just standing there watching him walk away with my mouth open. As I watched him, a chunk of my heart was ripped out of my chest and attempted to run after him like a desperate child, but I shoved it back into my pocket and walked back to my car.

I yearned for something better. Maybe someone would like me for me, or not. I can't remember a time when I wasn't a total romantic reject. I felt the sting of tears as I realized that Damon wasn't coming back; he honestly didn't want me. *Stupid! Stupid! Stupid girl!* I scolded myself. What was I thinking!? I slipped into my car, which was a block away from our showdown spot. I fished my keys out of my pocket grudgingly. It was over, it was finally over. Should I be happy? I climbed into my car and started it with a roar.

Lady Gaga's "Love Game" screamed at me. I hit the off button violently and hit my head against my steering wheel. I looked down at my hand and noticed a chipped nail. *Oh, horrid irony!* I said silently to myself, secretly wishing this song would shove *its* disco stick.

I took a deep breath in. Whether I wanted to believe it or not, Rae was right. This showed me the truth alright. He didn't care, and I had spent all these years wasting my time on someone who didn't love me. Hell, he did everyone BUT me. Why did I feel so awful? I needed to go somewhere. *I have some money saved up,* I thought. *Maybe I need a change.* I pulled out onto the road with the sounds of the lapping waves to sing me a lullaby. If there was one thing that could give me comfort, it was the fact the lake was still in one piece. Sometimes it is the simple things in life that keep me together. I pulled into my driveway and stormed into my house. I fully realized that stomping my feet like a two-year-old wasn't going to bring Damon running to my house, but at least it would keep me from throwing dishes at the wall when I got inside.

I unlocked the door and stepped into the darkness. My fingers felt for the light, and with a quick flip, my living room was lit. Then it hit me. I was never ever going to see the man I loved again. I felt a pain hit me in the solar plexus, and I crumpled down to my knees. I left him, and he didn't even care. I covered my face with my hands in a meager attempt to capture my tears. I couldn't tell what hurt worse, the fact that I left him and he didn't care or that I would never see him again. I got up and made my way to the bathroom. I looked like shit. My blond hair was stuck together and matted. My usually pale oval face was blotchy and stained with my mascara. My golden brown eyes were bloodshot, surrounded by black rings. I grabbed my brush and briskly brushed my hair. I caught something out of the corner of my eye and looked out my window. I opened it up and heard the waves lapping in the distance. A breeze picked up, and I smelt gentle wisps of sandalwood in the air. I shook my head and knew I needed to get the heck out of here.

I needed to get out of my house and get my life sorted out by taking some time off, but some things weren't as easy as they seemed. HALO wasn't exactly the vacation-giving type. There comes a time in every person's life when they take a big step back to examine things. If I saved up enough money and took a break, I'd have the chance to get my head all together. Aside from the whole "have-to-save-the-world" mess that I got myself into, I had normal people stuff to deal with.

I started to wish that I had been born like Bruce Wayne with everything intact instead of working a then full-time job while attempting to balance life, school and a dwindling pocketbook. I whipped out my suitcase and decided that I was going to hop on the next plane to France to meet up with Rae and hopefully a large tub of ice cream. I'd saved up six months, and maybe it was time to leave the country. I shoved another sweater into my suit-case. I had only been back two days, and it had been the loneliest two days of my life. All I wanted to do was crawl into a hole and die, but that was the easy way out.

This was the first day of the rest of my life; I would leave in a few days and make certain that I was never in the way of Damon's happily ever after. HALO had joined us, and here I sat like an idiot, waiting for him to come back to me, but all I got was a fistful of rejection. I started to pack piece by piece, suffocating the tears that threatened to emerge. I took a breath. *If he cared, he would have said "stay" or "no, please don't. I need you."* But those weren't the words, were they? I sat in front of the only suitcase I would ever need and started packing to head to France.

I started desperately looking for my journal. Nothing says "I'm getting over this" like journaling it out. I opened my night-stand drawer and shuffled the contents around. It had been a few days since I had written in it. The last time I had written in it was right after I had dropped off Rae. I went over to my beat-up old dresser and opened the top drawer where I kept my underwear. I shuffled around my underwear and didn't find my journal.

I doubted he would even notice I was gone. What was the point if he used me for what he needed and tossed out the rest? Was the rest of the non-superhero me so hard to accept? Was I not good enough? I went over to the closet. Locating a sweater, I bitterly shoved it into the suitcase while trying to shove back the tears. *This part isn't like the comics, is it? You don't see Batman crying, do you?* I tried to shove back my inner voice along with those flowing tears, but they weren't having any of it and started pushing back. I briefly shuffled through my closet, looking for my journal. A text message sounded from my forgotten cell phone that sat in my back pocket. HALO orders asking for a meeting with Phipps at 7 p.m. sharp. I stared down at my suitcase. I guessed the trip to France was going to have to wait.

I had to forget about Damon and move on. Six years was five years and 360 days too long to be chasing someone who would never love you. I rolled up and tied my underwear to make sure I knew which ones were clean, and tried to think of something else —*anything else.* Today was the first day of the rest of my life, yet I felt as if I were already dead.

❧ 2 ❧

I leaned against the tree with a cigarette dangling carelessly between my lips. I kept promising myself that I was going to quit. You know, the whole "quit for good because this is my last smoky treat." I watched the storm brewing in the distance over the lake. Sure, I knew smoking was bad for me, but what the hell did I care? After all, I was going to die anyway. I liked the way cigarettes helped comfort the numbness I'd begun to feel. As each cigarette slowly ebbed away my pain, I watched the smoke make curlicues as it wafted between the lake and the storm like a tornado ready to touch down. Damon kept popping into my mind. I tried shoving my thoughts back down. No need to think about him or the past, I had a job to do, and I could get it done without him. I had changed my shirt to a comfortable V-neck white tee shirt that set nestled under my white dress shirt. Something about the feel of fresh linen against my skin made me feel nestled in.

I looked down at my *Batman* vintage watch that was always three minutes behind and noticed that the middleman was late—again. His name was Phipps. No one knew where he came from or why he chose to watch over people or deliver these "SOS messages" to people like me. Despite what I had said to Damon, I knew I couldn't quit. Well, quit that easily. Maybe start slowly. I requested that my next assignment be kept quiet and make everyone think that I had quit. Would that even work? No, maybe not. All I wanted to do was find my journal and write it out, but I hadn't been able to find the darn thing for a few days. I tried to forget about it and turned my attention to the agent I was going to see. He could keep my quitting a secret, right?

And who was the most quiet in all of our underground society? Phipps. No last name that I knew of. They said he was a *seer.* They said that his superpower was to see issues ahead of time and to bring the news to the chosen. I always hated being called that, almost as if we were permanently marked away from society. Goodbye normal life. I flicked my cigarette as if to spite the cosmos that cursed me with this bloodied affliction.

"Curses... why do you always refer to everything as curses?" Phipps appeared behind me and startled my calm and cool façade. He crossed his long tan arms theatrically as the wind bustled through his silver hair. "It *must* be the Hungarian blood in you."

I glanced back at him, gathering the last remnants of my calm and cool, and gazed into the clear blue of his eyes.

"Of course a German would say that," I scoffed while I turned fully to face him. "And for God sakes," I shouted, "would you make some noise? Or at the very least put a fucking bell around your neck." He sported a smirk that proved to him that yes—he had indeed gotten under my skin. A thing I knew he *had* to relish. "So what's the story, morning glory?"

"His name is Frank Tennorman. He is forty-one years old, and he is a Sucker." Phipps started to pace around me, another theatrical trait he indulged himself in. "He moves in younger circles and singles out the most impressionable. Then he enchants them into believing in him and his 'healing' ability. After which he starts to feed off their energy until they are of no more use to him. Then he discards them when there is nothing left to take.

He prefers to feed on the addicted, the mentally unstable, and children. Think of it as his own personal all-you-can-eat buffet."

"Is he aware that he is doing it?"

"That is questionable, but given his age and the number of offenses, it is highly likely."

"Number of offenses? So this is definitely not his first time."

"Yes," he said with a thoughtful pause. "He has... a history."

"So why didn't you send one of us before?"

His smirk dropped, and the icy seriousness of the situation draped his eyes, making his face look like a mask of death. Something told me that there was something different about this assignment. Something dangerous—why else send the one with the savior complex?

"We did, and they couldn't handle it."

I looked up into his face with a questioning gaze.

"If they couldn't handle it, why not sic a Reaper on him and end the problem altogether?" I saw him shift uncomfortably.

"It's not that simple." His eyebrows gathered together. "We can't *just* sic a Reaper on him. If we do that, the Reaper turns into a Sucker, and then we have a Reaper-Sucker on our hands." I hated it when he made sense. He sensed my caving. "And would you want an assassin who can suck life out of people on the loose?"

"No, I guess not." I chewed on the thoughts that were spinning through my head. Why would you not dispose of someone so dangerous? Why not find some "natural" accident for them to get into? Reapers are the psychic assassins of HALO. I have only seen them have to kill seven times, and in their rose-scented attack, they were their scariest. I could never figure out why the smell of roses accompanied a Reaper's attack, but it did. Lord knows Reapers aren't very dependable, but the Impressers are. They could make him get into a habit that could kill him. "Okay, why couldn't you get an Impresser to take care of him?"

"Your assignment isn't changing," he said with a forceful glare.

"Your assignment remains the same: infiltrate, watch, and end the Sucker's damage," he said with a gilded eye roll.

"End it? End it so he can try to torture people in a physical sense? C'mon, Phipps."

He shook his head, and I could tell he didn't feel like talking about this anymore.

"Do you still take pictures and write?" he said, attempting not to answer.

"Okay, now I'm scared... what do you intend to do with me?"

His eyes sparkled with good-humored delight.

"You're getting a second job, princess." A grin danced on his lips.

"You're kidding me, right? I already have enough to do, AND I'm in my third year of my degree... how do you expect me to juggle another job?"

"Relax, it's when you're on summer break anyway," Phipps said as he brushed away my questions like he were swatting away flies. "You have some talent, and I would like to use it, and who knows, you could make a name for yourself."

"I don't *want* to make a name for myself! I want a normal white picket fence and a normal job and to be done with this save-the-world business!" Yes, this was it. I was finally going to stick up for myself. I had rights too, didn't I? Laughter started to trickle through the air from Phipps. For the record, this wasn't the reaction I was looking for.

"Yeah, right!" he roared. "As if you even had a choice in the matter, do you *actually* think you had a choice?" He laughed even harder, bending over, and my only defense was to cross my arms and shake my head. I was saving my tears for later. If there was anything I hated more than being mocked, it was seeing my futility thrown in my face. He started to bend over in massive laughter.

"Phipps, cut the shit. I get that you are mocking my dream, but can we stop the small talk and get down to business." I put on my best "don't fuck with me" face, hoping it wouldn't give away my insecurities as I had so gracefully earlier. "So what's the second job?"

"Photojournalist for a local paper." So he *did* know that I was leaving the country as soon as I could.

"You're joking, right? That's my cover?" I shook my head. Lamest. Cover. Ever.

"Do I look like a man who jokes?" he said, stepping back into Mr. serious German guy persona.

"You were laughing your ass off a second ago like a goddamn hyena," I pointed out.

"Well, that's the first time you ever said anything worth laughing at."

"Glad that my misery is *soooooo amusing*. You know, one of these days you'll wake up and think, 'Hmm, I wonder what the grass is like on the other side,' like the rest of us do."

He rolled his eyes again.

"I don't get nearly this much guff from anyone else. I was hoping that maybe you would just accept it and get over it."

"That's what makes me a fighter. Never getting over things I want to change but won't. One day maybe."

"Get over it. One day won't come because it has been this way ever since the cross, and something tells me it will stay this way until the cross comes down." We stood a moment in silence, staring at each other. For a moment I thought I saw him waver, and for one split second I thought neither of us wanted to be dumped into this situation. Yet here we were, humanity's last hope. Forever trying to save the lives and souls of people who would one day do a lot of good.

"So," I said, trying to end the mutual tension, "when do I start?"

"You go in for an interview tomorrow."

"Oh, joy."

He smirked at my exaggerated discomfort while he reached

into the pocket of his leather jacket and retrieved an envelope.

"Ah, *mien* orders, Herr Phipps!"

He rolled his eyes. At least I still had the German jokes to fall back on. He forced the orders into my hand.

"This is serious and no joke. You have to be careful with this one," he said as he pointed at me.

"What's the worst that could happen? C'mon, you worry too much," I said, waving away his worry. To be honest, his worried face made me start to worry. Phipps wasn't the type of person to show any type of emotion, no matter what the case. They should have called him "Stoned-Faced Phipps" because the house could be burning down with us in it and his eyes would remain that icy blue with a flat expression. "I've had worse."

"You won't be working alone. Since I have seen that you told Agent Damon that you were quitting, I'm guessing you won't want to work with *him* anytime soon."

I tried to open my mouth to complain, but a cutting glare shut me up.

"I'm sending a Reaper with you."

"Phipps! C'mon! I'll be fine!" Despite my half-assed approach at trying to be comforting, I knew once he let the words slip, there was no way I was getting out of having a bodyguard.

"Jester will call you tomorrow so you can brief him on the details."

My mouth dropped open. Oh crap!

"Oh, great, 'cause you know Mr. Fireworks is good at being inconspicuous."

"He is if he is a janitor."

"I'm not getting out of this, am I?"

"Nope. Good luck." Phipps shoved a black folder marked "portfolio" into my hands. He tartly turned on his foot and left. That was the second man to walk out on me coldly within five hours. Good God, this man drove me batty. I lit another cigarette and watched the smoke waft. Here we go again.

3

I decided to go home and cuddle up in bed. Sometimes all you need is a little downtime to do nothing, but did my mind ever shut off for one second? I guess that's all a part of existing. I don't think anyone can honestly shut down. I'd had a long night, and a hot shower was sounding incredibly good. I started leaving a trail of clothing to the bathroom and was relishing the idea of a nice hot shower; after all, tomorrow was a big day. I wasn't enjoying the idea of having an agent Reaper, code name "*the Jester*" (Jester for short), over for coffee.

We hadn't spoken in six years—a long six years. He wasn't happy with who HALO had paired me with. Then one day without a word to anyone, I up and left. I moved to another town away from everyone, desperate for a change. Regardless of my reasons, there were many HALO operatives who weren't happy with my leaving the area. I turned on the hot water in the shower in some attempt to drown out my own thoughts. We had stopped talking, for lord knows what reason. I'd take the blame on that one. Having someone get close to me and seeing my vulnerable side wasn't my idea of "romantic revelation." You know, having to disappear at all times of the evening without any explanations can really wear on a relationship.

I looked around the perfectly white bathroom, attempting to roll the idea around in my head of seeing Jester again. I flipped on the showerhead and eyed my worst enemy sitting smugly in the corner. That bastard, it had to know that it made my life hell. I figured it made every woman's life hell, and the saddest part of it all, we pay for it. That stupid, stupid scale was always mocking me, but nonetheless I stepped on the godforsaken thing, and guess what—I'd gained one pound. Sure, that didn't sound like a lot, but still it was very discouraging.

I stood five feet nine, and though muscular, I had love handles making their way into my midsection. Being tall and muscular is bad enough for a girl, but the extra pounds always add insecurities into the mix. I stepped off the scale. Wait! I still had underwear and my necklace on. I threw them off and stepped back on the scale. Okay, so not a full pound but a few ounces. I stepped off the scale and kicked it across the room. I walked over to the mirror, taking a good long look. At least I never looked my weight. Flat stomach, shoulder-length blondish hair, no chin roll, and—the only bonus to having a few extra pounds—a nice bust.

I gave up on studying my looks and stepped into the shower. In comic books they never mentioned the curse of the scale. Yet another thing that bothered me about the superheroes the media chose to look at. Ripped abs, tiny waists and always perfect hair. Most of the people who really saved the world didn't look like amazing supermodels; we looked human. I thought it was some joke or brilliant disguise, but there was one major downside. Our villains also looked normal, which made hunting them very difficult, and if it weren't for our abilities, we would never find them.

I stepped out of the shower and decided a nice nap would suit me nicely, and I'd at least pretend to sleep like a normal person. A thick noise sounded at my door, and I jumped for my gun. My trusty Walther PPK had never steered me wrong. I had my arms poised to aim. I was heading toward the door when the idea of a robe might be a good idea. "Who is it?" I said, making sure my body wasn't directly in front of the door. People didn't know we existed yet, but I didn't want to take the risk of some nutjob thinking I was the anti-Christ. I kept my arms steady and pointed at the midpoint of the door.

"Not who you want to see," said an all too familiar voice. Jester. How the hell did he find me? I waited a few minutes, hoping maybe for some sort of clever retort. "You're not going to find a clever retort in the silence, you realize."

"Goddamn it!" I whispered harshly under my breath. That was when I realized I was still very naked. "One minute." I scrambled to find some blue jeans, a bra and a tee shirt. I stumbled into them.

"You're not going to find a retort in any drawers that I know of either."

Dear god! Again with my failed retort! *Oh crap,* I thought, *I have only one clean tee shirt—whatever—fine. I'll deal with the tee shirt.* I threw it on and decided it was better than nothing. What about makeup? I tossed on a little bit of foundation and topped it off with red lipstick. Never underestimate the power of red lipstick. I opened the door with a reluctant demeanor, and there stood Jester. His olive skin accented his dark wavy hair. A thin yet perfect smile danced on his lips that led down to an angular chin.

"We were supposed to meet for coffee tomorrow, Jester," I said, leaning against the door. I crossed my arms and stared at him.

"I doubt that you didn't notice the fact that someone who should have been taken out a long time ago hasn't been." He leaned opposite me and gave a wide grin. Damn his logic. His dark almond-shaped eyes studied my face for a silent moment. "So you have noticed it."

I rolled my eyes. They didn't call him "Jester" for no reason.

"Yes," I said almost too weakly. "Come on in, Jester." I stepped back to let him through.

He walked in and took off his jacket. He turned around to face me and started laughing. He half bent over and started a raw cackling. At least his laughing habits hadn't changed.

I started to get irritated. "What?!"

He laughed even harder, pointing at my tee shirt.

"If I wanted to be made fun of, I would go into work early."

"Hello Kitty? A frigging Hello Kitty tee shirt? Sweet Jesus!"

If I knew this was going to be the reaction, I would have just answered the door naked.

"I'm not in the mood for this," I said grudgingly. "Why couldn't this wait until tomorrow?"

"Just wanted to say hello," he said with eyes that were too ready to avoid mine. His smile faded as he cleared his throat. "We haven't spoken in six years, and it occurred to me that I never said hello."

I narrowed my eyes. This wasn't the only reason for him being here.

"Not that I don't appreciate the gesture, but we were meeting tomorrow anyway. You couldn't have saved it for then?"

Whatever momentary lapse slipped out, he composed himself quickly back into his half-smiling persona.

"Because *that* was work. I like to keep my work and personal life separate, and both should be mostly peaceful." He shrugged as if to get out of my line of questioning.

"Our work relationship isn't suffering—"

He raised a hand and quickly cut me off.

"No, but seeing as we haven't spoken in six years over a dozen reasons." He paused and shoved his hands deep into his pockets. "I think we should at least get some of this out in the open or at least clear the air a little bit." His eyes flickered downward, then slowly gazed back up at me. And yes, it was the dreaded *puppy dog* look.

I attempted to give him a flat-eyed look, pretending I didn't care when I felt everything else but "not caring." I felt as if I was always hiding in my skin, hunting my divergent thoughts around my mind with slings and arrows. I had to, really, or else people I really loved would hurt me, and being a big tough superhero and all, I had to be strong for everyone.

"Alright, why? We don't need to talk anything out. We can be fine without discussing the past. I mean, are you really *that* hung up on it? 'Cause I am *way* over it, but since you are hung up on talking, I was just about to make a cup of coffee. Would you like one?"

He hated coffee, but he responded with a smiling nod. Honestly, what did I have to lose by mending a broken friendship?

"Funny, *that* part of you hasn't changed in the least," he said as he followed me to the kitchen.

"You're still a terrible liar." A grin spread widely like a cat looking for its next meal. "I know, all big and bad on the outside." He raised his hand as I began to protest. "For the record, only someone who has known you as long as I have would be able to tell."

"I'm not a bad liar. I've just changed."

"Is that what they call it nowadays? I call it a bad poker face. I'm wanna play poker with you, man," he said, pointing to me.

"So that you won't have another dime in your pocket?"

He cracked out a buckling laugh so joyous that even I had to crack a smile. "Yeah, you'd be mine, all mine." I shoved the coffee grounds into their trapped filter and pressed magical buttons to give caffeinated love. "So, what's up?"

"You expect me to start this?"

"You're the one who came to me, remember?" I threw my hands up and made gigantic quotation marks in the air. "'Our work relationship is suffering,' remember? In case you haven't noticed, you're sitting in my kitchen with me wearing no makeup in the late evening. So if you don't want to make this work relationship any more turbulent than it already is, I suggest you cut the shit and get down to the dirty." Ever say those words that you know you shouldn't say but do? Or even worse the words come out and cut deeper than you mean to?

His smile dripped off his face, forming ethereal puddles on the floor like childhood dreams lost within a moment of truth. I was an asshole. I turned around and filled his cup with coffee. He gratefully took it and looked up at me with aged eyes. I took cream and sugar to the table, hoping taking a few moments would take the sting away from my words. When I turned back, I saw tears dancing behind his eyes.

"Why did you leave?" His words sounded like a warrior's last cry to the dying light. What could I say?

"I had to," I said weakly as I took a seat across from him and took a big breath. "There was nothing left for me. I was watching everyone around me drown in the pools of addiction, I kept jumping in, but I—I—just couldn't take it anymore. I wasn't and I couldn't." How was I going to explain this? "You know I can't explain this. All I can say is I wanted, no, needed a change. I wanted a second chance that I knew I could only get here."

"So, what? You had to leave in the middle of the night, without saying goodbye to anyone? Without saying goodbye to me?"

"Why would I say goodbye to you? You hated me! You dated someone else and left me on my own!"

"You wouldn't let me close to you! I think you *wanted* to push me away. But I always thought that despite the fact we were never able to stay in a relationship, we were always friends. You were my best friend," he stated angrily. "Do you have any idea what is like to have your best friend leave and never EVER *think* to say goodbye to you?"

"I didn't think you cared." There it was again. The words that I didn't think were going to sound as awful as I thought they were. We sat there staring at one another. The hollow silence becoming deafening. Funny, how thick silence can speak volumes.

"Can't you just tell me you're sorry?" he whispered. His voice sounded like a sonic boom in the silence.

"Can you?" I retorted, mimicking his silence. He smiled widely.

"So, we reach an impasse, my delicate Trinity." He held his hand out. "Let's start over."

"You really think it was going to be that easy?" I pointed out skeptically.

"Not if you make it more difficult." I took his hand, and we shook on it. I raised my cup.

"To new beginnings?" He raised his cup to meet mine.

"To new beginnings." With a musical clink, our fate and friendship was sealed.

Dear journal,

You'd be proud of me, journal. I've gone a couple of days without talking to Damon. It's the hardest thing I've ever had to do, but I'm getting to the point where maybe this was meant to happen. I mean, how long can a girl just wait around? Granted, I know full well that I'm not some super-fantastic-looking chick with a sparkling personality (ha ha), but I deserve better than this.

I realize this is my first entry in you, and since my old journal went missing, you shall be my brand-new confidant! The best thing about you is you don't mouth back... Unlike Jester. There is something that is strange to me. Having him back in my life. I never ever thought that I would see him again. I'd never tell him this to his face, but I missed him a lot. I didn't realize how much love I have for him. A weird deep appreciation and affection.

I wish I hadn't blown my chance with him some days. He never did a damned thing wrong to me, and all I did was push him away. He was so sweet before he became incredibly sarcastic. I wonder what happened when we left each other. Where did he go? Will he ever tell me? Or will we just pretend that those six years didn't exist. So far, it's like nothing has changed between us.

I'm really glad I have a friend like him. It's been hard, but it is one step at a time. I wish Rae were here so I could tell her everything that is going on, but she is in a no-contact zone right now. Which means no cell phone for her! Whenever stuff like this happens, we go to some obscure mall with a Cold Stone Creamery in it. All I have been doing lately is going for two-hour walks at night. It helps me clear my head at night.

I remember when she had a bad breakup with Phil. Oh god, it was terrible. Want a see a woman who can throw things? I swear to god all the dishes in her house were smashed! I remember using my key to get into her apartment only to see a dish flying at my head coupled with the words, "I told you not to come back, you son of a bitch." It was only after she had thrown the plate did she realize it was me. I ducked, covering my eyes from the onslaught of flying porcelain chards.

It turned out Phil had been cheating on her with a guy name Peco. Peco was a stripper on the south side of Medosa. He specialized in belly dancing. Ever see a male belly dancer in action? It's freaky but pretty damn appealing in the right frame of mind. Phil was living with Rae and had no intentions of telling her about Peco. So, one quiet night, Rae saw Phil in the bathroom and decided to go talk to him (for what reason I have no clue). Apparently, Rae saw that Phil (the ever super masculine man he was) had started shaving... Not his beard. Yes, his junk. That was when she noticed the rash.

We are not talking about a mild irritation; it was big and ugly. No clue what it was, but whatever it was... WAS NOT pretty. That was when Rae started throwing things. Did I mention she was an all-star pitcher in high school? So there I was ducking flying plates of death while she was screaming like a banshee. With the whole Damon thing, I guessed it could have gone worse, but then again, I was nowhere near any plate, was I?

❧ 4 ❧

I sat up straight in the executive editor in chief's office. I wore a big smile that screamed hopeful applicant. My white fresh-pressed dress shirt offset the black pencil skirt I wore. I felt even more confident in my black knee-high boots. I sported my black-rimmed glasses that gave an intellectual touch to the outfit. Thankfully, Phipps had put together a portfolio on short notice. Ah, the perks of short-notice infiltration. I had been dealing with his secretary, who gave him my portfolio and had a stick so big up her snotty German ass. "Herr Larson will be mitt you soon," said the straight-backed supermodel secretary. It didn't seem fair that broads who looked like that had to be mean to everyone. Look at me; my battle with the scale hasn't made me any worse for wear; if anything, I'm nice. Unlike Mrs. Snitze the secretary.

I wished that I had my cell phone to screw around on, but the last thing I needed to be doing was messing around on my phone during an almost interview. I looked over at Mrs. Snitze, who was eyeballing me strangely, like she was waiting for me to do something. Wait, I thought as I snapped away from her gaze. Did she know who I was? No, that was not possible. I felt her stare bore into the back of my head. I was starting to feel uncomfortable. No way did anyone know about my assignment, yet she stared. No, I was getting paranoid. This was why I want to quit; it was on my mind—*This is the last job. Do this and you are done for life.* The door opened and drew my attention to the five-foot-nine hunk of man that was striding my way. He was no Damon, but hot damn, I could melt butter on the heat he was generating. Pure fever baby.

"The name's Tim." The man who stood in front of me reminded me of a poster boy who would work for the brawny. The editor in chief came in the door, heavy footed, and stopped in front of me, offering his hand. I took it and shook it. His lightly tousled hair offset a pair of kaleidoscope green eyes on a canvas of reddish tan skin. "Your portfolio is lacking. Mediocre at best," he said, waving me into the office with his large hand.

Ouch! That was a dig. Was it a dig?

"But since you're a student, it means you can learn."

I tried to hide my shock. I had been an award-winning photographer when I was in high school. I had all my own equipment, but what can you do? Some people just want you to play dumb.

"But I see you have potential. I'm going to give you a chance. You have potential, kid."

Kid? Was he serious? I had to be HIS age or older! I pretended to be excited and thrilled.

"Really? WOW." I gave him my best shit-eating grin and dazzled him. I "impressioned" him and made him think that this was the best decision of his life. It was a wonderful trick I'd learned from the impressers I met while I was in training. "Impressioned" is when we stretch out our aura and make wrap it around whomever we want to and use our emotions in our aura to impress on their aura. We reach way down into our happy spots or sad spots to make what we want you to feel. I stood up abruptly and reached out my hand to shake his. "You won't regret this."

He gushed more, how generous he was.

Still got the "get hired" touch despite my "mediocre" talent. I would have to get a hold of that stupid portfolio. I turned and gave him a dazzling baby-Gerber smile. "Won't let you down, Tim! You can count on me!"

He opened the door to let me loose. My eyes grazed over Mrs. Snitze, who looked to be eavesdropping with raised eyebrows. She looked shocked; it was okay because I didn't think I should have been able to pull that off, either.

Tim walked over to his desk to scoop up an envelope. With a large smile, he passed back my portfolio along with a secondary manila envelope. "Thought you might want this back, and I added some comments into the mix," he said with a happy wink. I resisted the urge to roll my eyes. "Also in the envelope is all of our policies, keys to the office, and just kind of get-to-know-you types of thingies. Oh, a map of where all the offices are so you won't get lost. Oh! And a parking pass."

I smiled, I couldn't help but be happy with a parking pass.

"How thoughtful." It always pays to compliment the genius of your boss. "I really appreciate this."

He beamed, proud of himself.

"I'll send you your first assignment in your email. Good luck." He turned and walked back into his office.

I made my way to the ground floor. As I walked out of the building, I let out a gigantic sigh of relief. Part one taken care of and now on to coffee. All I wanted at this point was to get out of this monkey suit and into something far more comfy. I really wanted to slip into a pair of jeans and flip-flops. I turned on my cell phone while walking to my car. Two new text messages and I held my breath. It was Jester telling me he was waiting for me, and the other was from Phipps telling me that my employment had been confirmed and that part of my assignment had been completed or as the message had so coldly phrased it: "Employment: confirmed. Objective one: Completed." I quickly deleted the messages. For a moment I thought that it might have been Damon. No, I wasn't hoping—okay, yes, I was. Stupid, stupid, stupid! I needed him off of my mind.

Dear journal,

So I just got back from my new boss's office. I'm sitting in my car, and I thought I would jot down a few words to you. I don't know how to feel about this new assignment. I mean, why is everyone so weird about the Frank thing? How often does steely-faced Phipps go silent? I've rarely seen him speechless.

One time we were on a mission in his hometown of Triberg in the heart of the Black Forest. It was when I was still training. I had found what we like to call a changeling, or supernova, roaming through the woods. I separated from the others; we were on a training exercise. A changeling is someone who finds a "host" whom they like, eventually taking on their form and killing their host. They do horrible things in the guise of what used to be a good person. One famous changeling goes under the name of H. H. Holmes. I hate those things; it's like seeing two of the same person.

I bet you are wondering why they are called supernovas. The reason why they have the nickname that they do is their attraction to setting things on fire. If you don't stop them, they will start exploding things. Think this is a joke? No, they use so many explosives that it looks like a supernova. I was just thankful that we'd been in the middle of the woods at the time.

I didn't believe anyone about it at first, there had been rumors of an actual case being in progress while we were there being trained, but no one ever had any proof. So there we were on a training mission in the middle of the Black Forest. I was in a tree waiting because we were training in evasive maneuvers. I was so high up that I could see everyone and everything. Phipps allowed us to all be "hunted," and we had to run or do whatever we could to hide. I, of course, dressed for the occasion. I was wearing dark green everything and brown boots, with a dark green hat covering my head. I sat there playing with my knife while watching the chaos.

I felt pretty good about being in this tree. It was a comfortable tree to sit in. I was watching everyone scramble around trying to hide from their chasers. The air nearly sang with giggles. I blended in pretty damn good. Damon was "my attacker," and I watched him scramble around like a crazy person. I felt pretty damn good about myself considering he stopped to take a leak on the very same tree I was hiding in. I tried so hard not to start laughing. So I looked away, and what should I see? A man wandering through the woods with a wheelbarrow and what looked like cement and a crowbar. Damon scuttled off to some area where he thought I ran off to.

I watched this man; he looked normal enough. Twenty-something, five feet eleven, brown hair, husky build... he looked like a man who had a life well lived. He stopped for a moment and stuck a bunch of black sticks in the cement. I had no idea what he was doing, but something didn't seem right. I slowly climbed out of the tree and followed the man. He went deep into the forest. I was far away from the other members. He looked behind him, and although I hid from him, I saw his eyes. I couldn't believe his eyes.

They were red and gold end to end. There was no iris or anything. I pressed my back to the tree and breathed. It was the scariest thing I had ever seen. I tried not to whimper. But I had to keep following him. I didn't know why, but I had to. Finally he stopped at a hidden church in the middle of the woods. I could no longer hear the laughter of my friends and workmates. He dumped the barrel of cement at the back of the church. It clumped out like it was plastic. The man's demeanor changed. His shoulder hunched, and a hoarse voice whimpered out of his chest. "Burn," he said coarsely. He laughed to himself.

I took out my knife and kept it behind me. "Mister." I walked out of the shadows carefully. "What are you doing, mister?"

He jerked up straight. He paused as he tried to think of something.

"What are you doing?" I stated louder. He turned around and came at me with the crowbar. I ducked and took swipes at him with my knife.

If we could pause a moment, I never ever had fought before in this type of situation. Sure, that schoolgirl, hair-pulling crap... no problem, but having some overweight motherfucker come at you with a crowbar. This was definitely my first rodeo. I tried my best to remember all the training videos we watched. Or should I say the ones I paid attention to instead of counting the hairs on Damon's neck.

I blocked him with my forearm, he hit me in the center of my chest, and I went flying backward. Pain seared through me as I coughed up some blood. I got back to my knees; staggering, I raised my knife and plunged it into his chest. He hit me upside my head with his fist. As I attempted to wrestle the crowbar out of his hand, two zipping noises whooshed by my head. The man went slack. Red splattered my vision, and before I knew it, I was covered in blood.

I whipped around to see a very quiet Phipps holding a gun. He lowered his firearm and stared at the body that now lay dead. He looked at me and stared. Phipps had always been the witty one. Always a remark handy at the right moment, but all he could do right now was stare at the body. He blinked twice and looked at me, as I too was silent. I had never seen a dead body before let alone seen one dispatched in front of me. He asked if I was alright as I heard other people approaching. All I could do was nod and collect my thoughts. Something seemed more personal, more monstrous, yet all I could do was stare blankly, drifting in and out of my humanity.

We stood there staring at each other until others arrived; then without another word, he turned and left. I never understood his silence until three weeks after we had left Germany. Apparently, the changeling had been under his nose the entire mission. It chose his brother as a host. I learned a valuable lesson that day (aside from stain guard everything) that no matter what your feelings are, you always have to do the job until it is done. Always follow it through no matter what the cost.

Phipps and I never discussed what happened that day, for we both carried scars from it. This is what scares me. Silence from Phipps is never any good... so what kind of monster am I dealing with?

J ester sat propped up against the café wall with his cowboy hat tipped down ever so slightly. It made him look like a sleepy cowboy. He was seated in a brown leather armchair with his arms folded over his chest. I knew it was the one way that people would disregard his presence while he was keeping an eye on everyone in the room. He was the best, although I would never tell him that to his face. The guy would eat it up like a starving man eating his first cheeseburger. He strangely blended in with the wilderness setting of *Demeter* café. The café had twisting trees wrapped around the support beams. The floor was brown and green marble, with throw rugs near their couches. The lamps hung from the ceiling were decorated with stars. My work packets were stuffed underneath my arm tightly while I made my way across the café. It was hard not to notice the people swirling about like an out-of-control dust bowl. He kept glancing at the newspaper he had in front of him, barely noticing the words on the paper.

I highly doubted the coffee zombieswould notice him sitting in plain view while they sipped their mocha green tea low-fat soy lattes and barely lifted their heads from the view of their Blackberries. Great, this was what I was trying to save—a world of people so busy trying to be connected that they were disconnected from life. Was it really life that they were living? I made my way past the zombies to a seat across from Jester. A steamy brown cup sat neglected across from his own. "What's this?" I pointed to the cup.

"You had a long day. I thought you might like a steaming cup of your favorite."

"Holy sweet mother of god, is that what I think it is?" I leaned over and took in a giant breath of clove. How sweet it is!

"That's right, kitty! Chai!"

I swallowed the "kitty" comment and settled into the chair. After all, he got me the coveted chai latte I loved.

"See? I didn't forget much these last few years."

"Alright, you got me there." I lifted the glass to my lips and reveled in the delicious taste.

"Hate to jump right to business here, but do you have your package?"

I passed the packages to him over the table. His eyebrow arched as his eyes danced over the black folder.

"Wanna see my so-called portfolio?"

Both of his defined black brows arched in speculation.

"Normally I wouldn't because I have seen enough of your award-winning work, you ham. But then again, you never offer... so I would love to."

I passed him "my portfolio" and sat back, looking at his face.

His face twisted in a look of disgust. "This sucks."

"Your kind words bring me so much comfort in my time of need," I sarcastically remarked.

"Alright, Ms. Surly, allow me to rephrase. This sucks so bad that this work couldn't possibly be yours."

"Thanks. I think." I paused and took another sip of my chai. "It's not mine. Phipps put it together for me so I wouldn't have anything to worry about, and since you came over last night, I never had a chance to look over what he had given me."

"Phipps, eh?" He paused and comedically turned the portfolio upside down. "That explains the obsession with contrast."

I grabbed it back from him. He tried in vain to read the newspaper that lay in front of him.

"My question is why?"

A smile spread on Jester's face, revealing his tooth-filled smile.

"Alright, spit it out. What do you know?"

He started laughing.

"If you don't tell me, I'll enter your mind and make you a blubbering babe!"

He laughed even harder.

"A trip back to our short-lived relationship!" He roared in laughter.

I simmered in my own angry juices while I suppressed bubbling amounts of laughter. Our relationship was a good one but a lacking one, no connection whatsoever, but it was my fault. We saw each other briefly before we knew that both of us were members of HALO. Back then, I never let anyone close to me. I guessed I still didn't, but how many people could understand that saving the world was a full-time job?

"You ever think that if you looked overqualified for the job, they wouldn't want you. At least with this monstrosity of a portfolio, it looks like you can do the job but can take direction."

I crossed my arms over my chest and attempted to pout. I guessed it made sense, but was my work really that bad to begin with? I stared at my tea. What if I didn't do that well? Or I did too well?

Jester went back to glancing at the newspaper and flipped the page, then stared at a group of leather-clad men with looks of rugged determination. Their metal studs glistened against the photographer's flash. Above was the very large lettering: "HEARTACHE PLAYS AMPHITHEATER TONIGHT!" I felt as if I had been drawn into the lead singer's eyes. I supposed that was the intended image by the photographer. With all the chaos that had been going on, I hadn't been able to purchase any tickets for the most popular band in the universe. Go figure. And now a second job was on my plate to go with saving the universe.

"I take it you weren't able to get tickets either?" Jester said while lifting his coffee mug. I could tell his eyes were studying me, but his eyes suggested a lingering worry. "So when do you ever get a break?"

I snickered. "Break? What is this break you speak of?"

"You seem even more stressed out since your so-called vacation. And don't even think about pulling that long-trip-home and jet-lag nonsense."

Somehow it seemed unfair. We hadn't spoken in a long time, and it was if nothing had changed. It was as if he knew me too well. His eyes bored into me with an honest probing. Reapers were also trained to bring out emotions or track the enemy. Suddenly, this coffee date was becoming very awkward. Something in the back of my head appeared in my vision like a forgotten shadow emerging from a nine-foot grave.

"I told an agent I was quitting."

Jester jerked forward and nearly spat out his coffee.

"Dare I even ask what or rather who the agent was whom you chose to tell this to?" There was old trusty Agent Jester, all business.

"I told Agent Damon."

Jester started shaking his head.

"You told a high-ranking Reaper that you were 'quitting.' So you can what? Live a normal life?"

"I don't know what I was thinking." I shook my head. I wished I had never even blurted it out.

"You know better than I do, we don't have a choice in the matter."

"I know," I remarked bitterly. "But who says we don't have a choice in what we want to do?"

"That isn't going to stop me from asking you why," he said, pointing to me.

"Why? Why what?" This was going to be more difficult than I wanted it to be. I hated talking about my emotions or motives. I was hoping it wasn't the fact that it was all about—

"What is it with you and revenge?" Goddamn it.

"I was hurt, I was spurned, I felt like I was rejected, and I'm sorry if I reacted badly, but I couldn't help it, okay? It is not like this halo of mine gives me much room to date as I wish or love as freely as I want. No, we have only set partners we can mate—*not love*—mate with. And just because he has rank and duties doesn't mean I have to sit around and wait for him to fuck every—"

He winced at the words. I noticed a very shocked-looking individual who was eagerly eavesdropping gasp at my words, and I turned to her, continuing with my angry tirade. "Yeah, I said *fuck*! What the fuck are you going to do about it?"

The woman stormed away. I turned back to Jester with a pointed finger. "Fuck his way through the tri-county area while I get the leftovers of whatever love he has left over for me. Because he might turn around and love me? No, because he *has* to mate with me. And I have the misfortune of being head over heels in love with him. So, yes, I told him I quit because I thought if I told him that I was quitting, maybe he would turn around and convince me not to!" I sat back in the chair and let out a long sigh. I guessed the forgotten shadow in the back of my mind had a voice after all.

Jester didn't move a muscle; he just stared at me, which was worse than saying nothing at all. He tilted his head slightly and reached his hand over to my cheek. With a quick movement, he picked something off of my face. A tiny tear sat glistening on his finger. He wiped it off and shook his head. "Seeing you cry is as if the sun would stop shining." He took a deep breath in. "I understand why you did it, but you have to understand that sooner or later he'll find out that you lied."

"Phipps agreed to keep this very quiet, and he even went above Agent Damon's head to keep him in the dark. It's not like he cares anyway."

"How do you know that he doesn't care, Trin?"

"He basically said 'oh well.'"

"Ouch."

"My point exactly." My text ringer sounded in my purse. I tried to think of something witty to say, but I couldn't come up with anything. The text was from Tim: "Call me immediately if you are free tonight." "Well, this looks promising."

"Oh?" Jester said as his eyebrow rose.

"Tim sent me a text to call him immediately."

"What are you waiting for?"

"Fine, Mr. pushy." I flipped open my cell phone and called Tim, and in two rings, he picked up. "Hi, Tim. This is Trinity. You called?" I grabbed a pen and a piece of paper off the table that was next to me.

"Thank God! I know I just hired you, but an emergency came up with one of my photographers, and I have no others to cover the assignment. Are you free tonight?"

"Yes, of course."

"Okay, well, this is a two-part assignment, and don't worry, you'll receive ample pay. The first part of this assignment will take place at six o'clock. You'll meet a reporter named Autumn at the Hilton, that's on Main Street. They will be getting into makeup, so I want you to be getting into doing test shots and just a few fun ones. Get them at the happiest, zaniest times. These are five of the hardest and biggest atheists you'll ever meet. I want you to get them at their fuzziest. Then you and Autumn will make your way to the stage, and you'll be set. Oh yeah! I almost forgot, all the expenses will be taken care of. You even have hotel rooms taken care of. I want you two to bang out the entire article by the time everything is wrapped up. That includes photo editing. I want you to send all the photos—well, good photos—to me, and that should be about it. If I have forgotten something, Autumn will catch you up on it."

My pen scribbled every word to make sure I got every important detail. Every detail but one.

"So Tim, what exactly am I covering here?"

"I didn't mention it?"

"Nope," I said with apprehension.

"You're covering Heartache."

Dear journal,

You are not going to believe this! I actually get to go on assignment but not just any assignment. I get to cover... Now hold on to your shorts here... HEARTACHE! Can you believe it? The biggest band in the world and I get to meet them! Score! I can't believe this.

I just got home, and I'm getting things together for my stay at the super swanky Hilton. I think I have everything together that I need. I'm taking a break to look at my weapons bag and write in you to tell you my good news. So I guess there is an upside to this whole situation. Call it a glorious perk.

I'm glad this is happening because I think it is symbolic. I remember Damon (I know you are probably sick of hearing my bitching giving me the CD after I had a bad breakup. Long before Damon and I became "mated," we were pretty awesome best friends.

I thought Derek was my dream guy. He had longer hair than I did and beautiful eyes and the soul of a poet... If poets were full of total shit. Sorry, I guess I'm still bitter. He was a smooth-talking Irish man who played a good guitar. I thought he had good hands because he played me like he did his guitar. Hard and fast. Everything was great, he was always gone for gigs, and I was on training missions. It was the first relationship I had in the agency that was going so smoothly.

I was ecstatic! I always had a bounce in my step and a good attitude. I'd go out places with him, met his friends and parents. They loved me.

We'd go out shopping and chat on the phone. Life was going pretty well. It was nice to have a man who didn't call you at all hours of the night and ask you were you were, what you were doing or even who you were doing. I was trying to kick some bad guys' asses, not have sex with them.

After they would get crazy and try to follow me, it began to become a major risk, so I had to break it off. The relationship with Derek was perfect for those reasons. So one day I came home early with a brand-new acoustic guitar all wrapped up in a red ribbon. I went in his house with the key he had given me. I heard loud Dido playing the song "Thank you." How funny, I thought to myself, a guy who plays metal listening to the ultimate chick album. I opened his door and was about to razz him about his music choices when I saw him going to town on some Goth chick.

Motherfucker! I should have known! Now before I continue with this tale, I should let you know that when I was younger... I kinda sorta had a bad temper. Maybe just a little bad temper... Okay, I was pretty bad. Not homicidal bad just disconcerting bad.

So here I was watching my beloved pound a girl through the bed we shared and saying the same beautiful nothings he once whispered in my ear into hers. Without thinking, I tapped him on the shoulder, smiled once terror filled him, and smashed the guitar over his fucking head, knocking him unconscious. His girl screamed. He flopped over on his fucktoy, pinning her with his dead weight. I collected my things and waltzed out the door to the Goth chick's screams. Ah, memories.

I never did take these "breakup" things well.

Am I rambling? I think I'm rambling... sorry.

Anyway, needless to say, Derek was not the one, and I suppose neither was Damon. I have really bad luck when it comes to dating men. For some reason they think I'm attractive and think... lord knows what they think. I get grabbed and dry humped, which I guess is a boost of confidence for an overweight gal like myself. I just never knew how to pick them, you know?

Before Damon became... whatever the hell he is now, he used to be very sweet and kind when we were friends. I mean, after the whole Derek ordeal, I called him, and he was there for me. I called him shortly after I walked out the door and drove three miles away from Derek's house. It hit me, and I started bawling. I was so racked with sobs that I didn't think Damon would make out all the words I was saying. He asked me to come over to his house, where he had a warm cup of coffee waiting for me.

I pulled in his driveway to find him waiting on his porch with two cups of coffee. Mine was just the way I liked it, pinch of cinnamon, a teaspoon and a half of sugar with some cream. I still wasn't finished crying. How could I have been so stupid? I always let the biggest assholes in my life, and here I was thinking I had found my dream guy.

Taking our cups of coffee upstairs, we went to his bedroom. I lay down on his bed, still crying, as he put some music on. He gave me the Heartache "Heartbreak" CD. As silly as it sounds, that CD helped me get through the entire Derek ordeal. We sat there talking about everything that had happened. He laughed at my bad temper.

I think I'm beginning to deal with everything that is happened a little bit better. But as I embark on a new chapter of my life, I can't help but feel that maybe I need to leave him behind as well.

6

I juggled my camera bag, my chai latte, car keys, reporter's notebook, overnight bag and cell phone while attempting to put an extra two pens in my ponytail and attempting to lock my car. This was like mission impossible. "Fuck it," I said out loud, and I set everything down and put all the things I needed for the actual reporting in my camera bag. I fished my weapons pack out of my back seat. The basement parking was a blessing some days. The cold and quiet was very comforting. I shoved all the other crap in my overnight bag, and that was when I noticed that I'd left my freshly baked chocolate chip cookies on the passenger's seat. Chocolate chip cookies were always a good way to meet someone you would be working with. Besides, if you said something strange or blunt, it would all be okay because you had cookies, and you were a sweetheart for bringing cookies. Everyone loves cookies.

Two bags on one shoulder and one bag on the other, I made my way to the hotel. A tall muscular man near the door saw me in all my clumsy glory. "Need a hand?" he said while he opened the door. A black "KISS" hat adorned his head while doing little to cover his charming sparkling blue eyes and perfect white smile. I couldn't help myself, I blushed a little. He had that kind of face.

"Thanks!" I said sheepishly as I walked through the door. The elevator would take us to the main floor. I pressed the button for the elevator while attempting not to drop everything. He smirked at me. My black-framed glasses slid to the tip of my nose. I rarely wore them, but since I needed my vision at its best, I thought today I could pull it off.

"Do you need help with your, uh, bags?" he said.

There was pity in his eyes, which wasn't a turn-on, but then again—he was really cute. Wow, if that wasn't a heaping chunk of girly knowledge. I smiled again and decided maybe just for one day I didn't have to be super girl—after all, I WAS undercover. I handed him my overnight bag.

"So, I hate to use this line, but you come here often?" He snickered; it was so musically beautiful that a part of me was melting inside.

"'Fraid not." I shrugged. "I just use my excess luggage as a cheap way to meet new friends."

He started laughing.

"I'm doing a photo shoot for a job I just got hired for and pretending to know what I am doing."

"I do it all the time! It's the only way to be!" He reached out his hand that wasn't juggling my ginormous bag. Was it a bad idea to mention that the bag I was holding had a supernatural arsenal in it? "My name is Jake, what's yours?"

I reached out and shook his hand. It was firm—I liked that in a man.

"Trinity. It is very nice to meet you. A Good Samaritan is hard to find. So what brings you to this dank little burg?" He released my hand but not before giving it a gentle caress. If this kept up, I was in trouble. A mysterious smile flickered on his face.

"To be a Good Samaritan and bring pleasure to the masses," he said with a wink.

44

I giggled like a schoolgirl and snorted slightly. My eyes grew large with embarrassment while I pushed up my glasses and stared straight ahead. Oh dear god, did I just do that? *Please don't notice! Please don't notice! Please don't notice! Please don't notice!*

"I never say this out loud, but that was frigging cute."

Damn it.

An awkward silence filled the air. *Say something!* I repeated to myself. "I'm usually very witty!" I blurted out loudly. Oh, great word vomit. Yeah, that was effective.

He started laughing and kept laughing until tears streamed down his face.

"I really am," I whispered while trying not to laugh at myself.

"I'm sure you are." The elevator door opened, and we stepped in. Great, we had to go up four floors. Of course this had to be right after I made an ass of myself. "So," Jake said with a clever smirk, "aside from being witty, what do you do for fun?"

I shook off my embarrassment; no point in wasting a conversation with a cutie.

"I like to hike or sit on the beach. I love nature."

"What a coincidence, me too. Are there any good areas to enjoy the scenery?"

"Yeah plenty. You should definitely check it out." The elevator doors opened, and we stepped out. The hotel décor was typical Hilton. Cold marble with warm lighting gave a mausoleum feel. The head desk was a few feet away from us. He turned to me with a grin.

"Wow, I'd love to, but I don't have anyone to show me around. Whatever am I to do?"

Was he coming on to me? No way! No frigging way!

"I'm sure there would be more than enough people to show you around," I replied with a half smile. Okay, it was a leading question, I realized this. But how often did a normal cute guy with no supernatural abilities hit on me. Let's try none, and the last time I had sex was when flare jeans were in style. So, yes, it had been a long time.

He leaned in to whisper in my ear. I felt his hot breath on my neck.

"None as genuine as you."

My body shuddered, and then I stopped to think. He leaned back to his original position.

"You just met me," I pointed out to him.

"I meet a lot of people on a daily basis, and some of them I have known for years. You showed me more honesty—" he looked down at his watch "—in about ten minutes than most have in five years. So I'm going to ask you for your number, and I won't be free until after about midnight, but if you aren't doing anything, I would love to take a walk with you on the beach."

I felt my knees want to buckle, and I blushed.

"I don't know what to say," I mumbled.

Jake whipped out his Blackberry and leaned in while gracefully setting my overnight bag beside me.

"You can tell me your number." He smiled.

Okay, he won. I prattled off my number, and he called my cell phone. "That's my number. Please save it." He started to walk his cute ass to the elevator. Oh boy, I *was* in trouble.

"I'll see you later."

"You have no idea."

"What's that supposed to mean?" I replied to the ominous phrase, and he smirked. It was then I noticed my forgotten chocolate chip cookies. I tore open the plate while I walked over to him and fished out a yummy cookie. "Wait! Payment!" I shoved a cookie into his hand, and a thought occurred to me. "Aren't you going to check in?"

"I checked in a few hours ago." He leaned in. "You smell good, like, really good."

I childishly shoved the plate near his face while the elevator chimed open.

"Sure it's not the cookies?"

"I'm sure," he said as he stepped into the elevator and the door closed behind him. My knees melted, and I felt all warm and fuzzy. I tried to snap myself back to reality. What was it about him that made me weak in the knees?

7

After checking in with a giggling receptionist, I made my way back to the elevator. I thought things were looking up. A hottie had hit on me, and he was beyond cute, but I couldn't help thinking that he was familiar in some way. With a smile like that, I guess I recognized the kind of tooth paste he was using. Maybe this was a sign that my life wasn't over. Tonight I had a date and a romantic one at that. Yes, I did realize how cheap a walk on the beach is, but on the other hand, the memories are priceless. Honestly, all the priceless memories I had of Damon were ones that I needed to replace.

I always felt that I was on some sort of mission to remember something, but when I finally remembered what I had forgotten, I went through an entire process to forget it. How redundant was that? As my mother used to say, "Remember to forget what you remembered." Ah, the power of mom logic! I started going through everything I had done today, and I felt waves of exhaustion pass over me, but with the power of my mind, I refocused and pushed it out of my way. The weight of my overnight bag began to weigh on me. What the hell had I packed, anyway? Oh yeah, concert gear.

When in Rome, do as the Romans do. In this case when at a metal concert, dress like you're ready to kick ass or look really hot. Can't a gal have both? I'd packed a black silk dress that had a bodice sewn into it. A gift from Jester when we were dating once upon a time. The bodice had secret compartments that allowed for not only weapons such as knives and guns but for things to fight the supernatural baddies. With fishnets and my knee-high boots, I was sure to blend in with the crowd. Thankfully, I'd packed several kinds of outfits just in case I lost the gall to wear the fishnet man-eater dress. One fuzzy white sweater, two pairs of jeans, flip-flops, my favorite AC/DC tee shirt, and one motorcycle jacket. Yeah, I get the jacket was worn nearly to the hilt, but the thing had been faithful. When I got thrown against walls, dragged along gravel roads, had to run into burning buildings, the thing held together and took the brunt of the punishment. The elevator doors opened to the eleventh floor. The Hilton décor was very typical Hilton: creamy beiges and whites with plushy carpet that was chocolate brown. Even for the nosebleed section of the hotel, this was pretty plushy!

Down the hall, I saw a girl who looked like the mirror image of my bags, jacket and jeans. She was juggling a plate was some sort of baked goods on it too. She was struggling with her laptop bag and an overnight sack. Both bags were fighting for space, and both were losing. Her ponytail was in the same sloppy mess mine was, but her hair was black. As her heart-shaped face turned toward me, I noticed that the same black eyeglasses adorned the tip of her nose. She looked like a normal everyday Snow White. She looked at me quizzically, and then her kaleidoscope blue eyes widened. She knew who I was, and she smiled. "Are you Trinity?" she said, attempting to fight a hand free to outreach it to me in friendship.

"Maybe putting the bags down would be a good idea." We both set down our bags and shook hands.

"I'm super nervous. How about you?"

"I would be if I weren't so good at running on adrenaline," I said with conviction. One of my greater talents, I assure you. "I figure even on my first day, I'd better ride the high." I went to the door beside hers. I put down my bags and slipped the key card into the door. It opened with a quick click. I peeked inside. "Adjoining? Fancy." We walked into my room. It was a beautiful white-filled room.

"Wait, it's your first day too?" she said with panic as she followed me in to my room. Jesus Christ, this couldn't be happening. I saw worry flicker through her eyes. I had to get her under control before a panic attack ensued. "Oh, God, this isn't happening," she said with a hand to her forehead. I gave her an assuring smile while she pushed her glasses up on her nose.

"Don't sweat it. This isn't my first rodeo," I said with a sparkling smile.

Her chest stopped heaving, and she sighed. She shook her head in a daze.

"Sorry for the meltdown," Autumn said as she gave me a sheepish smile. "I was barely expecting to get 'you got the job' let alone an assignment on the first day. I mean, I was only a few feet from the building when I got the call. Apparently, both the writer and photographer came down with West Nile virus and mad cow disease."

"You're joking, right?" I started laughing because what was the chance that would ever in a million years happen? "There's maybe one-in-a-billionth chance of that ever in a lifetime happening."

"Then chalk it up to coincidence, weird and bizarre, but coincidence nonetheless." She got the adjoining door open and shoved her things inside. "Well, it could be worse. We could be covering a major story involving the largest band in America." She raised her finger as if an invisible light bulb raised itself above her head. "Oh, wait a minute!" We both started laughing. At least my new partner in crime had a sense of humor.

"We had better get a game plan down and ready before we

head to the top floor." There was me alright, typical leader type. "Don't sweat it, pretend you know what you're doing, and rock it like a star. If you gush, they'll know!" I said ominously.

She grinned. "Don't worry! Together, we can do this." She seemed renewed and reassured. It was always how I like my audience. I looked down absently at my watch and noticed the time. I had an hour.

"After all, I know this is going to be a good day," I mentioned with a reassuring wink.

"Oh? And how do you know that?"

"I have a date tonight with a hot guy, and I know that has to be a good sign."

"Oh god, seriously?"

I nodded with a smile.

"He helped me with my luggage at the elevator."

She giggled.

"I'm going to go get ready." She left, shaking her head.

I dressed in an artsy tee with a fishnet tee shirt underneath and my trusty jeans. I lay down on the softer than soft bed and relaxed. After all, what was a few minutes of R & R before I attempted to prove myself against the firing squad?

8

A dull knock sounded on my door. I looked over at the clock with a curse. I had slept for fifteen minutes. Oh well, at least I got some sort of sleep. I straggled up to the adjoining door to see a smiling Autumn holding up a plate of scones. "Scones?" she sang with a huge smile. "Since it's getting close to showtime, I thought we could enjoy some scones before we head up." Her purse had the armory of a typical journalist. She might not be a journalist, but she could be a hell of a writer. I thought I'd mention that later.

"Only if you'll enjoy one of my homemade chocolate chip cookies." I smiled, trying to mimic her chipper nature. I shook off the rest of my sleepiness and got the plate of cookies.

"So, are you nervous?" She unwrapped her plate to reveal apple scones. They smelt like grandma's kitchen. I was in heaven. I fixed my makeup quickly and put on my glasses.

"Not now, but I will be later for maybe a minute or two before I snap myself out of it." I offered her a cookie. She took it and popped it into her mouth. "I guess I start running on autopilot or something and just go with the flow." I took one of her scones and chewed on it. It was lovely. I found myself wondering when the last time I had enjoyed one of these was. I'd tried making them before, but they were far too dry. Wasn't that my luck?

"Wish I had that talent!" she mumbled between bites.

"Everyone does, whether you believe it or not."

She shot me a skeptical look mixed with a "you're joking, right" smile.

"I'm serious, it's like you know when you're dreaming and you think you can do anything." I peered down at my watch while I grabbed my gear. "It is time to go, but let's continue this conversation on the way." We started toward the elevator after making sure the door was locked.

"I don't understand. When you're awake and when you're asleep are two way different things," Autumn said as we reached the elevator. "I mean, there are only two different states... awake and not." She pressed the button, and the doors opened. I smiled at her and gracefully stepped in. She looked at me sideways like someone who was about to sign a blood pact. Uncertainty rolled off her, and it was delicious. It was as attractive as the moment Alice starts going down the rabbit hole. I leaned in like the grand Mad Hatter.

"Says whom, exactly?" I leaned back and started to laugh.

Her eyes grew wide in wonder.

"Everyone, like doctors." The doors closed as if to seal her fate to go further down the rabbit hole. "It's a fact."

"Is it now? You have all these people telling you what the world is really like, yet when you get out into the world, is everything exactly as they said it would be?"

She gave a gentle shrug.

"Yes and no, I guess."

"Okay, here's a perfect example, when you were in high school, they claimed that everything was going to change, yes? They claimed they were preparing us for the real world, were they?" A light flickered through her eyes. "I am under the largest assumption that no one has any clue what they are doing, and if they were ever to admit it, their heads would explode! Ka plow!"

She started laughing.

"Okay, you have a point, but that doesn't show me how I can run on autopilot and forget stage fright."

"It's like dreaming once you know you are in the dream. Just go with it, and maybe, just maybe, you'll enjoy yourself."

"I don't know how you can do that," she said as she shook her head.

"It's like living outside yourself from the inside of yourself." Silence filled the elevator. I could almost feel her chewing on my words. Her emotions ranged from panicked to understanding to happy to sad. I wished I didn't know what people were feeling, but I couldn't help it. Sometimes it was helpful, especially if someone was lying or was going to kill me. But most of the time it was a real pain in the ass. Nine times out of ten, I could feel what people thought of me except for underlying attraction. If they were jealous of me, mad at me, or even getting ready to backstab me, I'd know about it. Phipps always said I should be grateful for that ability on top of the others I had because most of the people with those abilities were hermits. Boy, I couldn't imagine why. Because most of us thought we were freaks. Most of the other gifteds could reason themselves out of it by thinking they knew for certain, but we knew and we would always know.

I had been in this society ever since I was in high school. They said the electrical shortages gave me away. I suppressed it all because all I wanted to do was fit in like everyone else. I remembered sitting in the back of the cafeteria, looking around at all the normal students. I was feeling so alone and helpless. With my arms hugging my legs, I felt the worse feeling of all, jealousy. How wonderful it would be to be normal and to have normal things to think about. I wondered what it would be like to kiss someone without feeling like I was going to suffocate in the energy of their aura. I wondered what it would be like to drink without my gifts getting out of control. One day, a man in a black suit found me sitting in the back of the cafeteria with tears in my eyes. They were tears of pain, tears of jealousy, tears of plump emotion growing fragile yet stronger with every thought. He handed me a card and walked away. On the back of the card, written in Sharpie, was: YOU'RE NOT ALONE. I watched the man known as "Phipps" walk away. I thought all my problems would be over, and I could be normal. BING! sang the elevator as it pulled me out of my memories. The elevator doors opened, and we stepped out. "I wish I could do that," she whispered lightly.

"Do what?" I said, pulling my head together. "I'm sorry, I started thinking about something else!"

"I meant be able to get past everything."

"Yeah, me too."

"What were you so deep in thought about, anyway?"

"Banana-flavored, octopus-shaped bubble gum on a stick that plays the theme song from *Cheers*." I grinned; sometimes honesty isn't always the best policy. She looked at me and started to laugh. Her laughter filled the hallway like wind chimes as we made our way to the only room on the floor, better known as the executive suite.

"You've got to be kidding!" she said in exasperation as we reached the door.

"Nope," I said with conviction. "Wave of the future."

I reached up my hand to knock on the door when it whipped open to reveal one very intimidating six-foot-six, topless black man. His bald head led the way to a body rippling muscles on muscles, which I assume led throughout his entire body if it weren't for those pesky leather pants and shit-kicker boots. His chocolate brown eyes settled on us with fiery intensity. Autumn beside me started shaking. She felt as if she had the wrong place or she had done something wrong. I, on the other hand, couldn't help wondering what was hidden under those pants. I looked at his face, noticing his pouty lips, and continued to meet his eyes. A large smile spread across my face. I thrust my hand nearly into his chest. "Hi! I'm Trinity!" His tough demeanor started to crack until he revealed a large smile. "I'm your friendly neighborhood photog, and this is the reporter Autumn. We're from *Banner News*."

Autumn weakly waved; she was feeling as if he were going to bite.

"Yes, we are expecting you," he said with a thick French accent. "My name is Stephan." He looked at Autumn as she shrank back from him. "Don't worry, I don't bite." He leaned toward me. "Hard." He let out a thick and throaty laugh that felt like velvet coating my skin.

"Darn," I said with a wry smile. "Looks like I'm out of luck."

"I wouldn't be too sure of that," he said as he grabbed my hand and took it to his lips. "For you I would be willing to change," he whispered onto my hand. His lips gracefully grazed my hand while he breathed in my scent. A part of me did a happy dance. Two cuties in one day? What IS a girl to do? I smiled sheepishly.

"Stephan?" a disembodied voice hollered. "Are they here?"

He let go of my hand and turned toward the voice.

"Yeah," he shouted toward the voice. "And they are pretty."

I started to laugh. Autumn swallowed an "oh god." I was pretty sure she thought she was going to get eaten alive. I felt like leaning over and asking her what she thought of this side of the rabbit hole, but I thought she would be too scared to say anything.

"Tell me that in the morning," I mused.

"If you gave me the chance," he said with a raised eyebrow.

"Not before the first date, hot stuff," I said, bumping my hip against him. We started laughing.

"Stephan, come on! Bring them here before Darth Fred gets back," said a young male.

"Darth Fred?" I inquired.

"Fred Draft, their manager. He's an egotistical prick. Follow me."

I leaned near Autumn as waves of fear were rolling off her. She was going to get eaten alive unless... "How about a good luck hug?" I smiled.

"Okay," she said weakly.

I gave her a hug and took some of her energy and replaced it with my own. I wrapped her up in a bubble of my own happy self-assurance. I made her feel warm and fuzzy. I pulled away and swallowed the energy she gave me.

"Ready?"

She blinked a few times and smiled. She straightened her shoulders and stood tall. She walked with a confident swagger.

"Ready or not, let's do this shit."

I didn't think my personality would transfer, I thought humorously. Maybe her life would improve if she kept growing a pair. Stephan looked back with a half grin. I winked at him, returning his smile. We walked down a long hallway until we came to a corner.

We turned the corner, and it revealed a large sunken crème and beige living room with a white wraparound couch. It looked dark in comparison to the setting sun filtering through the wraparound window. A man who looked like only a silhouette against the light, with his hands clasped behind his back, looked over the city. He was silent and still while three men sat on the couch, relaxed and bantering. All were dressed as if they'd walked out of a Calvin Klein's with their assorted jeans and black and white tees.

A tall man was mixing drinks behind a bar. His long black hair was disheveled, and a cigarette dangled carelessly out of his mouth. "Fucking finally!" he said, raising his hands in exasperated joy. I recognized him as the lead singer, Daniel. He eyed Autumn and smiled. "Stephan, you're right, they are pretty." I knew he wasn't looking at me, and I got some joy out of seeing her blush.

"Autumn Pearson, *Banner News*," she said proudly.

"Ah, the local paper!" said one of the Calvin Klein boys. He was sandy blond with a surfer smile. His skin was tanned from numerous days on a beach somewhere. "I'm Rick. I play the drums," he said with a jerky nod.

"I know." Autumn smiled politely. "I did my research."

"Oh?" he said, giving her his undivided attention.

"Yes. Your name is Rick Tons. Before you got in this band, you were a surfing champ and spent hours on end teaching preschool."

He started laughing.

"Ooo! Ooo! Do me next," said the pale brunette. He sat beside Rick with a magazine spread across his lap. He was built like a football player and had the crew cut to prove it. *Good girl*, I thought to myself. *Show them confidence and wow them.* I slipped my camera out of the bag while their attention was on Autumn. A thrill settled through me as she gave him a wink and a smile. She skipped him and kept talking. I felt as if I were a tigress on the hunt. I noticed then how round the room was. It didn't have a single corner. It was the only part of the hotel that didn't look overly trendy. Autumn continued to throw around different facts about the band; then she finally settled on the football player,

"Johnny Rickles, a onetime telemarketer, sought fame and fortune at the young age of eighteen, and two years later you gained that fame when you joined up with Daniel and Jake."

Jake? I thought to myself. *No, it couldn't be.* My eyes turned to the silhouette looking out the window. I looked at the man who stood at the window. He was in a black suit with a black silk shirt. He looked tall and stocky and not like the man who asked me out on a date. I watched his black hair nearly touching the collar of his shirt as he breathed in. That led the way to dress slacks, where his hands rested. A silver Rolex peeked out. This couldn't be the same person.

I reached out with my invisible self toward him. He leaked remnant flavors of pleasures that became nearly aromatic, like tendrils of power mixed with nutmeg and sandalwood. The voice of Autumn melted away, and all I could see was this man. The sun appeared to melt around him, and in turn I felt my aura grow brighter as if the sun were feeding me and he was the spoon. For a fragment of a second, I felt the world spread open like a delicate lotus opening itself for the first time. A cloud drifted across the sun. The silhouette turned toward us. The prattling of Autumn echoed back into my ears. The others were musing with her, and he looked at me and smiled. The clouds spread open like a delightful Venus, and for the first time since I'd met Damon, all the pain burned away like the first fire ever lit by men. His icy blue eyes seemed to glow, creating a blend of strange and strangled energy between the sun and the shadow. Everything stood still for a fraction of a second. I felt normal and free. I returned the smile just in time to hear Autumn ramble off just one more fact.

"Jake Fortinbras, former executive and still owner of Ark International, aged thirty-two, but... there wasn't much else I could find out about you."

He finally turned his eyes to her. It was definitely Jake. He winked at me with a playful smile. He walked over to the bar and sat down on one of the stools. He seemed relaxed. Daniel poured him a shot, and Jake denied it. I felt so embarrassed. How could I not have known?

"Well, Ms. Pearson, I'm a very private person. If people knew what I did all the time, where would be the mystery? Someone has to be the mysterious one!" He laughed. I felt intoxicated with his laugh.

"Yeah, no kidding!" sounded Johnny. "We've known him for years, but do any of us know anything about him?"

"Pure mystery," Daniel said as he removed the cigarette from his mouth and downed a shot. "He thinks chicks dig it."

"They do," Jake said as he gave a playful shrug of his shoulders.

"You mean they would if you'd ever date," Daniel pointed out with a grin.

"Unlike Daniel, *I* have standards."

Daniel threw up his shoulders and hands in defense.

"Hey! I'm as picky as the rest of them!"

"Yeah, right," said Johnny. "A clean STD test is about as *picky* as he likes to get, and sometimes not even that much!" Everyone started laughing.

"C'mon, guys!" Daniel said, not attempting to dispute the claim. "Can you keep that off the record?"

"I can promise the paper won't print that," I said. "But I don't think *we'll* ever forget that."

Autumn let out a musical laugh.

"Autumn," Daniel said as he lifted his hand to mimic a phone, "call me!" Everyone started laughing. I started shooting it all. Just the way Tim wanted. Cute and fuzzy.

"I will if you let me interview you all," Autumn said coyly. They all let out a roar of laughter. Looked like I was not the only one who might have a date.

Between questions and shooting, my eyes flickered to Jake, and every glance I stole, I met his gaze. He watched me carefully. While his counterparts seemed distracted with the undeniable beauty of new and improved Autumn, he barely muttered two words. Mysterious indeed.

❧ 9 ❧

The interview was very typical of interviewing most musicians. Blah, blah, blah—tour dates. Blah, blah, blah —future music projects. Blah, blah, blah—controversy. I snapped an easy 350 photos of them being cute. Autumn soaked it in and exchanged flirtations with the not so subtle Daniel. She was adorable when she was flirting. Autumn had the kind of essence that was like a child with an ice-cream cone. Happy, innocent and carefree. It looked like Daniel fed on it. I didn't say a word while I was taking apart my camera or during my entire time there for that matter.

I messed around with different lenses, filters and flashes. The good thing about my camera bag was that there was an extra bag hanging off my camera bag that allowed for easy access to a flash when I needed it, but luckily I wouldn't need that flash for this part of the project. Autumn, being always polite, thanked them graciously for their time. Richard and Johnny sat on the couch to play video games while Daniel went back to the bar. To me, it looked like Jake had disappeared, and a part of me was thankful for that. I was uncertain how I felt about the entire situation.

On one hand, he hadn't told me that he was the guitarist from

Heartache, but then again I didn't ask. Before in the elevator, I didn't feel what I felt in that room. It was almost as if he were inside my skin. I could smell his cologne from across the room. It smelt like hot vanilla, with notes of sandalwood, nutmeg and lavender. It was nothing I ever smelt. I took a deep breath in; the scent reminded me of hot sex on a bearskin rug in a cabin in the middle of nowhere in the middle of a snowstorm. I couldn't help but wonder if one day I would find out what that was like with him, but as I walked down the hall to the exit, I shook the thought of him out of my head. Jake was charming, sexy, intelligent, successful and not to mention rich. Wouldn't Mom be proud? I packed up my equipment and started for the door. Autumn saw me start for the door and followed me.

Come to think of it, money and men was never really an issue until I found out how much they owed on their credit cards. Somehow, I would get taken for a ride for the next three months. Mediocre sex and an empty bank account were all I was left with. This was too good to be true; what would he ever see in me? After all, he was in the biggest band in the world, and hot chicks were never in short supply. My equipment felt heavy.

Stephan came up from behind me and whispered in my ear, "So what do I have to do to get your number?"

I stopped and turned around to look at him.

"How many backflips can you do?" I laughed.

"As many as I have to. What do you say?"

"I have plenty to say, but rarely does anyone want to hear it," I said with a sigh.

"I would love to hear all about it." He let a tooth-filled grin spread widely across his face.

"Yes," a voice said behind him. "I'm sure you would."

Stephan glanced behind him at a very comfortable yet intimidating Jake leaning against the wall, examining his nails. "Stephan, if you can be a doll and go get Dan's wardrobe? He is trying to find the best possible outfit. He's so vain, you know." He winked at Autumn.

"After I see the ladies to the doors," Stefan said as he kept his eyes on me.

"You needn't bother. I'll see them to the door, and don't worry, Stephan, I'm certain Trinity will be shooting later on tonight at the show."

Stephan turned with a grin and left.

"Shall we?"

I looked at him and shook my head. Autumn smiled and nodded. Jake walked behind us as we made our way quietly down the hall. I kept thinking about how heavy the quiet was. It was like the hallway was its own silent universe. We finally got to the door after what seemed like an eternity.

Autumn turned around to face Jake.

"You guys are so nice! Thank you so much for everything," she said as she extended her hand.

"You're very welcome, Ms. Pearson."

"Okay, we will see you tonight." Autumn gave him a wide smile and turned out the door.

"So long, Mr. Fortinbras," I said curtly while I turned to leave. An almost hurt look crossed his face, and then a smile spread on his face. "Thank you for your time."

"Oh dear, Ms. Trinity! Didn't you have a little bag attached to your camera bag?" he said with exaggerated vigor. That frigging drama queen. "Well, I guess we'd better go back and look for it."

"Do you want me to come with you?" Autumn said with a worried brow.

"No, it's alright. I'll be down in a moment. Do you know how to upload photos?"

She nodded.

"Okay." I handed her my camera. "Can you upload these for me? My laptop is on my desk, and I left it unlocked."

"Yeah, no problem. If you need me"—she eyed Jake suspiciously—"you know where I'll be."

"Don't worry, doll. I'll be right behind you."

Jake put his hand on my shoulder, gripping it tightly.

"Yes," Jake said. "She's in good hands."

Autumn twisted her mouth in a concerned frown.

"Yeah, I'll bet you have *good hands*," she remarked as she exited.

Jake clasped his hands together with a loud whack.

"So, let's find that flash, shall we?"

I crossed my hands over my chest.

"So," I said, mimicking his enthusiasm, "let's cut the crap, shall we?"

"What?!" he said, shocked and surprised.

"I know you have my flash. May I have it back?"

"I don't know what you are talking about," he claimed innocently.

"Listen, I'm going to close my eyes, Mr. Fortinbras, and put out my hand. When I open my eyes, I expect *my* flash to be in my hand." I closed my eyes and lifted my palm toward him. I heard him sigh. I felt something weighing down my hand. I opened my eyes to see the flash in my hand. "Thank you." I turned to walk away.

"Hey! Wait a minute. Where are you going?"

"I'm going to get ready for your concert. Like you should be."

"You're mad at me." He looked down, looking almost boyish. "Why are you mad at me?"

"Why didn't you tell me? Like, I realize I have no right to demand honesty from you, but it makes me reconsider our date tonight. *And*," I pointed out angrily, "you took my flash."

"I just wanted to talk to you, and I know you're mad at me... so I thought this might be my only chance."

"Two strikes against you for dishonesty," I said, pointing my finger at him.

"I didn't lie," he said with honesty.

"You're absolutely right, you didn't. I'm sorry I wasted your time." I tried to turn to leave, but Jake grabbed my hand.

"Please don't go," he said, almost begging. "I meant everything I said. If I had told you who I was, would you have still been as honest, and I don't know... you?"

I took my hand back.

"It's a good thing you don't know me too well or else I would be *very insulted*. I would have treated you just the same. I don't care what title someone has. I take a person at face value and go from there."

"Please, I'm sorry. I guess I just wanted to see if you like me for me."

"Listen, it's not like I don't understand because I do. But I'm not certain I want to go on a date with you tonight. Besides, I just got burned yesterday, and I'm not sure if it would be fair to date while my heart is on the mend."

"So, the man who hurt you so badly," he said with concern, "is he taking the same measures?"

I shook my head. I knew damn well he wasn't because he didn't give two craps about me.

"I know I'm coming on strong, but I would really like to see more of you." He reached his hand out again to grab mine. This time I didn't pull away. "Give me another chance." I had to look away from those beautiful blue eyes.

"You are... a very, um—" Everything I want in a man and more? I want to bear your children? No, maybe marry me? "— wonderful person, and I have no idea why you are interested in me, but I don't know if we should get this started or not."

"I see something in you that I have never seen in other people, and if you give me this one chance, I promise you a night you'll never forget." His hand grazed my chin and tilted it upward, giving me a front-row seat to those eyes. "Please?"

"Alright." I gave in, but what would the harm be? "But you only get this one chance."

"Seal it with a kiss?" He grinned hopefully as he leaned in and pulled me closer to him. Was this guy serious? But I figured why not? I was going to give in just this once. His hands started to massage my back. I could barely control myself when I felt his feathery-soft lips touch mine. I felt my body grow hot with desire. He crushed me into him while my hands started to explore his body through his clothing. I wanted him. My tongue grazed the inner sanctum of his mouth. His tongue greeted mine like an old friend ready for a dance. He pinned me against the wall, and his hands started traveling up the back of my tee shirt. I cursed my clothing for not melting away at his touch.

I felt his heat engulf my being, threatening to sweep me away or, worse, burn me alive. I felt myself start to drift with the waves of heat. I wanted to feel him inside me and melt into my body. It was as if our blood, our essence, our souls were mingling back and forth. As much as I was enjoying this, I pushed his hands away. "Um, I am sorry. I got carried away." When I pulled away, I still felt his energy inside me. With each thud of my heart, I felt something pumping through my veins. It was something better than the blood that was there before; it was power.

"That was one hell of a seal," I whispered breathlessly. I was buzzing from the energy, and I wanted more. My logic bitch slapped me back into reality. *What are you doing? Get yourself back to normal!* I steadied myself and smiled at him. He almost seemed surprised I was still standing. I couldn't blame him; I was pretty surprised too.

"Could you blame me? You smell really good, and you're really soft, and... I'm going to shut up now."

"That's okay," he said, straightening himself. "So I guess I'll see you after the show?"

I started to walk away.

"I'll call you shortly after midnight."

I left him staring after me as I walked away. He crossed his arms and smiled a boyish smile. Dear god, if this kept up, I was going to be in worse trouble.

⚜

Dear journal,

I'm having some relationship jitters. What if Jake's a dick and I don't know it yet? If I could just accept the fact that he wasn't everything I may want in a man, this whole thing might be easier to handle. A good-looking, financially stable, polite... good-smelling... hot... warm... soft... where was I going with this? Oh yes, Jake. I have a lot of problems, and I realize that maybe I shouldn't take it out on Jake.

What should I do? Should I go with it? I remember when I dated this guy named Harry. He was charming and funny. I thought he was so perfect. I worked a lot of nights, so we met every day for lunch and had a few evenings where we chilled out. You know what? I just really need to start getting suspicious when the guys I date enjoy the fact that I work long nights. I mean, if I had any common sense at all, I would start asking questions about what they did at night.

So, Harry was this British guy from somewhere in Liverpool. We spent long nights enjoying the best of Monty Python over pizza. How many guys really enjoy the true subtlety of British humor unless they happened to live in Britain? I guessed so few that I had one imported. Ha ha. Eventually things got a little strange. There were some people who started telling him how much they adored his performances. When I asked him, "What performances?" he rambled off a reply that I couldn't understand.

I sometimes wonder if Harry did that to me just so I would smile politely and not ask any questions. I mean, it wouldn't be the first person to go into a whole slew of unintelligible jargon in some meager attempt to confuse me. I usually end up getting this from lawyers, doctors, IT people and the British. I don't know why, but it happens to me more than I would like to admit.

As usual, I ended up getting curious about what or where he performed, and I followed him to his "performance." It was a shady area with red neon lights. I walked into a room that looked like it fell out of a '70s velvet painting. Actually I thought that most of the walls were covered in red velvet. The stage curtains parted with a heavy sigh, and what should I see, dear audience? A tall willowy blond in a feather boa and sequined heels. I almost thought I had walked into a burlesque show until the blond opened her mouth. Unfortunately I found out Harry's moonlighting activities. Or should I say "Susanne's"?

I honestly don't think I would have minded that much if he would have been honest with me. Or if it hadn't been my dress. I thought it came down to the fact that he looked better in it than I did AND wasn't honest with me. But that makes me wonder, what if Jake isn't completely honest with me, or worse, he's hiding something?

I might be freaking out over nothing. Damon has shattered my trust beyond anything I ever thought possible. I like him! Regardless, I have had a good amount of time to rethink the too-good-to-be-true aspect of things. Will Jake turn out to have a problematic secret, or can I take him at face value?

🕸 10 🕸

I tried to catch my breath from the intensity of Jake's advances. My skin was almost electric, and for some reason I felt stronger and healthier. Why did I react like that? If any other man had done that (with the exception of Damon), I would have decked them, but then again, with Damon it wasn't exactly a choice. Funny, HALO always said that mating was in the interest of protecting the human race. They say by keeping the bloodlines going, we stand a better chance of fighting evil. They systematically chose who would be the perfect match for whom. They never force mating; usually the people who are chosen for one another fall in love and live long and happily together.

Why did it have to be Damon? I could have been happy with anyone but him. He had a smug and cocky attitude that graced his masculine features. Six feet one, brown eyes that sometimes almost seemed like a whirlpool of emotions and pain. I wanted to soothe his pain so bad that I could taste it. I wanted to run my fingers through his dark hair and make all his pain go away. Why was I a sucker for the beaten puppy? No, it wasn't the beaten puppy that made me a sucker; it was the fact that he, too, was a survivor. I understood his pain more than even *he* knew.

Wait, I'm romanticizing what happened and how he was. It was *never* me he wanted; he wanted "normal" women. He wanted the white picket fence and children and no HALO. He always decided to live the double life because "it was easier that way." I, on the other hand—take me as I am, universe! You created me, now deal with me! Screaming matches constantly ensued with us, but it wasn't like it was all bad, he just never wanted me. He once told me that we were "stuck together." Not anymore, sucker. I quit. Well, not really, I just quit him. He had someone now, someone who was *not* me. Sometimes I can say such stupid things. Instead of saying "I love you; please stay with me," I ended up saying "go fuck yourself." Why is it so hard for me to just give my heart over to someone I love so much?

I had to admit, I wanted to run to him and throw myself at his feet and beg him to love me, but who was I kidding? I sure as hell wasn't going to allow myself to bang on his door and say "let's get married and live happily ever after," or what would really end up coming out of my mouth would be "you can treat me like crap as much as you want, just love me." No, I was done being his personal doormat. After all, my heart didn't belong to him as his own personal shit rag. I wanted something deeper than this electrical love-lust. I wanted to love and beloved. Was that so much to ask?

The elevator doors opened and disrupted my reverie, but even more disrupting was Autumn standing right in front of them. "Tell me everything!" she said, nearly shouting in girlish excitement. She grabbed my hand and started dragging me to the hotel room. "I totally ordered pizza and soda and cake! I want details!"

Wow, I'd never had a friend to be girly with, with the exception of Agent Rea, but they'd sent her to France on a mission. Autumn was beaming with excitement and happiness.

In that sense I couldn't blame her, the interview went very well, and she'd scored the phone number of the world's most wanted man. I was happy for her! She deserved every moment of praise she had coming. Shy, panicked and she'd gained some guts. I really liked her.

"You want details about me? What happened between you and Daniel?" We were in my room, which was perfect because I had not that long to get ready.

"Me? You know what happened; you were there, remember?"

We had a little bit of time before the show, and that left me just enough time to eat and get freshened up. I also had to punk up my makeup.

"I saw the way Jake was looking at you. I could have sworn that the way he was looking was the way a diehard Catholic would look at the statue of Mother Mary."

I'd never noticed, but then again I was focusing on everyone else to try to get the best shot.

"I almost felt the heat coming off of him toward you. My god! The fever!" she said, fanning herself with excitement.

"You can't be serious," I said. I couldn't believe he kept seeing me in tee shirts and jeans with sloppy hair; where's the justice? I scooped up a pizza slice off of her dresser. "Yummy, mushroom and tomato pizza."

"I hope you like it. I was seriously craving some."

"Yeah, this is just what the doctor ordered." She offered me some Coke, but I shook my head. "Sorry, if there isn't sugar in it, I'm not interested."

"Okay," she said, putting the Coke away. "But I'm still waiting."

"Waiting for what, my sister-in-arms?"

She shot me a pouty and skeptical frown.

"Oh, that!"

"What happened?"

"Well, I don't suppose I told you that a certain cute gentleman helped me to the ground level with the luggage."

"Oh." She raised her eyebrow in anticipation.

"He was wearing a baseball cap, and I didn't recognize who he was." I shrugged. "I was struggling with my baggage, and he helped me. We talked a bit, and he gave me his number. I didn't think that, actually... scratch that. I have no idea what I was thinking."

"That explains *your* cold shoulder."

"I guess I shouldn't have been so cross, but I thought he was being dishonest, and I kind of just got out of a thing. Not a relationship or anything, just a mistake."

"Maybe he was just trying to be cute."

I shot her a look.

"Okay, or not."

"Maybe he is a sucker for yanking my chain."

"I meant it when I said I didn't really know much else besides his name and company."

I opened my mouth to reply, but she raised her hand to cut me off.

"No, I'm serious. I ran extensive background checks and cross-references of other interviews they had done in the past. Jake doesn't like to talk about himself at all. Never. No woman, no marriage records. I mean, anyone he has ever dated, they all give the same response when anyone talks to his exes about him. 'Wonderful man' and 'we're still friends' but other than that, nothing."

"Really?" I wolfed down the rest of the slice and started on my makeup.

"So what did you guys talk about?"

"Well, he loathes the fact I called him '*Mr. Fortinbras*,' and he was the one who took my flash."

"Really?" she exclaimed.

"He claimed it was so he could talk to me. He knew I was pissed," I admitted.

"You know, he doesn't need to go chasing after women."

"I noticed," I said with a cutting edge to my voice. "But I have had enough of dishonesty."

"Technically he wasn't being dishonest," she reminded me. "I mean, look who he is. How many man eaters do you think go after him in any given year? There *are* women out there who make a literal career out of this." She watched me finish my makeup. I used black eye shadow to give my eyes a smoky look with a touch of lavender. I applied a silver eye shadow just for some fun, and this time if he saw me, I was going to look smoking good! "So what else did he say?"

"He was really insistent," I said with a smirk. "He told me if I go on a date with him tonight, he will make it an unforgettable evening." I started debating whether or not to tell her about the hot and steamy kiss. My knees felt weak just thinking about it. I wondered if the rest of him was as delicious as his lips. I shook the thought from my head.

"So are you going to do it?"

"I'm still thinking about cancelling," I said, fixing my hair.

"Oh, why?"

"He seems really eager, and I don't know," I said, pausing in thought. "I guess this is too good to be true."

"Go for it!"

My cell phone started ringing, and I automatically knew it was Jester. I chose his ringer as the "Humpty Dance." Autumn started laughing and I rolled my eyes.

"Hey, J man. What's up?"

"Are you alone?" Shit. Business. I have to keep my game face on.

"No, no, of course not. Can you hold on a second?" I turned to Autumn. "Hey, I have to change, and I'm sure you want to freshen up before we head out."

"Oh yes, is it that late already?" she said as she made her way through the adjoining door. "What should I wear?"

"I don't know, it's a metal concert, so go metal."

"Okeydokey!" She closed the door behind her, what a relief.

"Alright, we are alone. What's wrong?" I said, slipping out of my calm and cool.

"I just heard from Phipps. We've got a major problem."

"I haven't had enough time to infiltrate yet. We can't have a problem."

"No, no. This just came off the wire," he said with an edge. "Phipps said a rogue Reaper is planning an attack at the concert."

"A rogue Reaper? Since when do Reapers go rogue?" I said angrily. Someone had to be kidding. Reapers were typically so well taken care of that they didn't go rogue. If one did, it could mean the deaths of many people.

"You know HALO, never one for details."

"So what attack? Who is he targeting? Why?" I sighed lightly. I could feel a headache coming on already.

"I have no idea. They are arranging tickets for me as we speak. You won't be able to see me, but I will be your backup."

"Do I need a gun?"

"No, people will go insane if they see a piece. Bring your knives. I'll shield you when it comes down to the dirty." A shield is a fancier word for glamour. They were always a good thing. Since we didn't want the normal people in the world figuring out our existence, shields make us nearly invisible. If you are completely normal with no ability whatsoever, all you will see is a clear blur, but if another gifted is around, incognito is out the window. The stronger the gifted, the better they can see us. The funny thing is, the larger the crowd, the better we hide. That was a small relief in an otherwise crappy situation.

"Alright," I said, giving in.

"Be safe, Trin. I mean it this time. This guy is dangerous."

"I will, Jester." We both hung up without saying goodbye. We'd promised a long time ago that we would never say goodbye to each other unless we thought it would be the last time we would ever see each other. I'd said it only once to him, but he never said it back. I started to put on my outfit, and I was hoping that it wouldn't turn into the one I would be buried in.

❧ 11 ☙

It felt good to know that despite my black minidress, fishnets, knee-high boots and excessive black makeup, I wasn't the most scandalous-looking person in the amphitheater. The best thing about going to a metal concert was that no matter how short the skirt, there was always one other person with a shorter one. Backstage was the perfect example. I fit in perfectly. Autumn, however, stuck out like a sore thumb. Her idea of "going metal" was black eyeliner and a black tee shirt. I shook my head while she shuffled her feet and looked down.

"I didn't know. I listen to Anya."

That just killed me. I doubled over in laughter but not too far or else I would be flashing the entire backstage.

"This is your idea of metal?" I roared with laughter. I couldn't help it.

"I thought I looked badass."

"For a kindergarten teacher, yes!"

The band members filtered through the doors. First one through the door was Daniel, then Richard, Johnny and finally Jake. He stopped the moment he walked through the door. His eyebrows knitted together as if he had known something was up.

The scandalously clad woman approached the men and fawned over them. I saw many of the women slip their phone numbers into their leather pants. I had to half wonder if they forgot about them being in there and got paper cuts.

"Oh god." The poor girl looked mortified. "I can't wait for this to be over." Autumn had begun to pale.

Daniel saw her and was making his way over but taking his sweet time.

I leaned over to her and whispered in her ear,

"Hey, remember, you were the one who wanted a last minute quote." I kept seeing Daniel's eyes flicker back and forth to her. I didn't think she picked up on it, but I did. He looked like a glowing beacon against the blackness of the backstage.

"Oh, yes, a quote."

I raised my eyebrow. Yeah, I'm *sure* it was a quote she was after.

"If you want to see Daniel, just go and talk to him."

"Really?"

"Go for it." I kept looking around for Jester, but I guessed it was safer if he wasn't seen with me. If one of us got caught, they'd know our weak spot, or worse, they would start to know our associates. I watched Autumn bounce off to meet her would-be boyfriend. I kept scanning the crowd. I closed my eyes and started to scan the energy. Sometimes I could see better in darkness. There were many colors drifting around until a flash of white nearly blinded me. I blinked to try to adjust my eyes.

"Just because you can't see us doesn't mean we can't see you," a velvety gruff voice whispered in my ear. I felt tremors make their way down my spine as I opened my eyes to see Jake standing beside me. "You look good enough to eat," he said with a smile. I wasn't certain whether he was kidding or not. I looked into his eyes and saw a hunger. He looked at me like a thirsty man looks at a glass of water. His embroidered vest clung tightly to his muscles. The vest looked like it had been taken off a seventeenth-century mannequin, chopped up, and died black. He had on tight leather pants that left little to the imagination. I guessed it was safe to say he wasn't wearing any underwear. I gazed at that area long enough for him to notice I wasn't disappointed.

"Hi, Jake. How are you?" I turned my body toward him and tore my flickering gaze from his groin.

"I'm doing well. I must say that I am glad you're here." He looked me up and down. "And may I say you look absolutely breathtaking. I mean that most literally." I saw a group of women he had to have waded through to get to me nearly burn holes into my face. He raised his voice enough for the group to hear. "And may I say that you are also the most stunningly beautiful woman in this room." I was very thankful that looks couldn't kill.

"You're going to get me beat up, you realize this, right?" I said as my eyes flickered from the group of very ticked-off women to him.

"Not if you stay by my side, or better yet, you could give me a kiss."

"And here I thought you were a private man."

"Good point, I am. So if you will gracefully take my arm, we can go somewhere a little more private."

Great, he thought I was going to have sex with him. Not that I wouldn't give in if he ended up giving me another seal with a kiss. It was the most powerful sexual energy that I had ever felt. My knees grew weak at the thought.

"I'm not going to sleep with a man I just met today," I pointed out.

He smiled when he heard me say that. I knew that if he really pushed it with me, there was a really good chance I would give in, but I was still going to fight it. It was the strangest thing, even though I had just met him today, it was if he was someone I had known for years.

"Not that I expected that of you," he said, putting his arm

around my waist, pulling me toward a door that Stephan was attempting to protect. "I just like talking to you."

"Good because I have some questions for you." That slowed him down a little. His eyebrows started to knit.

"Off the record?"

Oh, great, he thought I was going typical reporter on him. I rolled my eyes. I couldn't help but feel awful. I just wanted to know more about him than his name, his band work, and his kissing style.

"I promise." The tension melted away from his face. I stopped and wrapped my arms around him. I gauged his reaction, and he seemed comfortable with the rather couple-like gesture. He actually seemed *really* happy with it. Flashes went off around us while the other bandmates took pictures with fans. I pulled him closer. "I just want to know you better." I gave him a small smile.

"That's not a lot to ask at all." He looked into my eyes with a smile. "Let's go somewhere a bit more private. Stephan?"

"Yes?" his voice boomed.

"Can you make sure not to let anyone but the band members through the door? I'm going to take a walk with Trinity. If Autumn asks about her, could you make sure to tell her she's with me?"

"No problem." I could feel twinges of jealousy as Jake ushered me through the door.

"Is he going to be alright?" I asked with concern. I liked Stefan.

"I think he wanted you all for himself."

Himself? I wasn't a toy. We walked up a few staircases in silence until we reached a door.

"Roof exit."

I didn't know what to say; after all, it wasn't like we were a couple or anything. What did he mean by that, anyway? He reached into his vest pocket and fished out some keys. "I like heights," he mused. When he opened the door, I saw the night sky spread across the city lights. The full moon trailed behind the twinkling stars. He moved near the edge of the roof and sat down on a metal box that looked like it had been an air compressor at one time.

"I didn't mean that the way it came off."

I shrugged to try to pretend I wasn't offended. I sat across from him on a pile of bricks.

"I mean that..." He reached out to touch my hands but stopped. He stared at me for a moment and tilted his head sideways.

"I told him that I was, uh, I don't know how exactly to put this or how not to come off insulting."

Insulting? Oh, sweet Jesus! I knew there had to be some sort of flaw especially if he was attracted to a freak like me. I hugged myself slightly. It had to be too good to be true. I mean, nothing this good ever happened to me without having some horrible sacrifice.

"What?"

"I didn't want to imply that you were anyone's property. I'm just very picky in relationships, and I kind of, maybe told him that you and I were dating."

Okay. Dating wasn't so bad, but

—"We haven't had one date yet. Not that I don't appreciate your enthusiasm," I pointed out to him.

"Yeah, I realize that. I'm sorry." He looked down at the ground. He looked innocent. He looked like he felt genuinely guilty. He looked away at the skyline as if attempting to find something to say.

"What's your favorite color?" I blurted out.

"What?" He looked at me, suddenly confused.

"Your favorite color, what is it?" I wanted to know more about him, and this was my way of getting to know him. Maybe if I got to know him a little better, I wouldn't feel as if I was violating my morals if I gave in too quickly.

"Black, red and blue. Why do you ask?"

"I said I had some questions for you, remember?"

He looked baffled again, and then a smile spread across his face.

"I'll tell you what, whatever questions you ask me, you'll have to answer as well."

"Okay."

"Okay, what are your favorite colors?"

"Red, black and white. What is your favorite food?"

"Pizza, alfredo, spaghetti, pretty much all Italian food."

"Me too! Except for pesto sauce on penni... that's kind of gross. What about your favorite song?"

"You're asking a musician what their favorite band is?"

"Yeppers."

He shook his head and pretended to think really hard.

"Okay, not favorite song but bands. AC/DC, Halestorm, Rammstein, Oomph, Elvis, Breaking Benjamin, Mozart and, you know, most of the classical artists." He looked at me, waiting for my answer. I wasn't certain if he would believe me if I said the same thing, but I was going to try.

"I agree. That is some awesome taste although I don't think I would agree with you on the Elvis, but he had his good sides. I think I would like to add Linkin Park, Moist, David Usher and Pink."

"Pink?" His eyes opened wide.

"Yeah, punk! What are you going to do about it? Where is your favorite place to visit?"

"The middle of nowhere."

"Me too, buuuuuuut there would have to be a lake of some sort."

"You like to swim?"

"Love it," I said with enthusiasm. "I could swim before I could walk."

"Same here, I was born in Oregon, and I spent most of my

time hiking and swimming. I like my privacy because in the middle of the woods, you don't have all that clutter that people bring in, you know?"

"I understand all too well. Nature doesn't go out of its way to hurt anyone or try to emotionally wound."

We looked at each other, and we had an understanding. I smiled at him, and he smiled back at me.

"I would love if you would join me in a hike one of these days."

He nodded and took a deep breath. He shifted uncomfortably.

"I have something to ask you, I know this will be forward, and you don't have to say yes or anything, but if you ever want to..." He cleared his throat and shifted again. "I have a house in Alaska, and after the tour, we decided to take a bit off before hitting the studio again, and if you were ever..." He coughed again and shifted.

I wanted to ask him why this was so hard for him, but I thought this was hard enough for him.

"If you ever had some time off, like a weekend or week or something, I think you would really enjoy it there." He looked at me, slightly pained. His shoulders were hunched as if he was anticipating rejection. Honestly spending more time with him sounded like fun. If we did start dating, it would be nice, but if we didn't, it might not be so awesome.

"That sounds wonderful. When is your tour done?"

He relaxed slightly. You would think that he'd never asked a woman out before.

"In about two weeks, I know it's a long time, but..." he said uncomfortably. "You know, I'm not really good at this part."

I felt his pain. Who was good at this part? The wooing was usually the easy part, but after that, what comes next? One of the things that ever kept me from sleeping around was the after-sex conversation. When I first talked to a guy, I thought *"hey, he's hot,"* but then I started to think about what it would be like with him, and then I got to the aftermath. I always came up with the thought that they looked better when I was horny. Maybe Jake was worth the extra effort. He seemed sweet enough.

"I'll wait for you. It's no big deal." When I said that, he almost looked shocked. "I have plenty to do. I now have a second job, and I'm going to school. So there is a lot I get busy with."

"What are you going to school for?"

"Writing. I really just want to spend the rest of my life writing. But I'm thinking about adding another major. Maybe education or something that is really useful." It would be nice. No HALO or other constant havoc. Just me and my computer.

"It sounds nice."

"I figure when I have children, I could stay at home and write until they go to school, but that is way in the future."

"It's weird how many women don't want to have children."

"Really?"

"I guess it's been a while since I have been away from the industry. People there are much different. Sometimes, I wonder if they live in their own universe."

"Tempting, isn't it?" It would be. That way you didn't have to worry about anything outside of that universe, but then again, those people drove me absolutely batty.

"Yeah." He looked back at the skyline as silence engulfed us again. "I have a question for you. What is your absolutely best memory?"

"Seriously?"

He nodded, still gazing at the skyline.

"I was four years old, and I was with my grandfather, driving to his farm."

"Not at the farm? To the farm?"

"Yeah, my grandfather died a year later, and all I could remember was the car ride there. It was like knowing you were with someone who would keep you safe forever." Looking out at the skyline, I remembered my grandfather very well. That was the last time I ever remember feeling happy and safe. He, too, had been a member of HALO. He kept me away from HALO when I was little because most operatives were taken after they were born. He was one of their greatest operatives; he had a grand reputation for being able to stretch his abilities to almost every section of gifteds. He could see things before they would happen and be able to intercept the bad guys before they even assigned agents to the cases. He was able to harness his telekinesis to cross over to not only controlling the physical matter but that of fire and air.

I remember that ride to the farm, after he had long quit HALO after he refused to have his three daughters join. He told them that it was an archaic practice to force people into a secret society. He gave his daughters a choice on whether they wanted to join or not. Riding in his beige truck on that perfect sunny day, he told me, "Trinity, you are very special, and one day you'll be something great." Shadows clouded his eyes with the weariness of a life well lived. His sad Germanic blue eyes were filled with the memories of awful things. "Trinity, you never have to do anything you don't want to do. Promise me something."

"Yes, Opa?" He looked almost like a god to me. I saw his blond hair growing messier in the fresh air filtering through the open windows as he drove. Small silver tears welled in his eyes. "That one day you'll live your own life." I remembered smiling a smile that only a child could smile, and I nodded. How I wished that moment could last forever.

Like lightning had hit my brain, another memory came out of the blue. When we had gotten into the farmhouse, the telephone in the kitchen was ringing. He had run through the front door to answer it. He pushed me to the living room to watch cartoons, but eventually I got thirsty and made my way to the kitchen. His voice boomed with a temper I had never heard before. "No! You can't have her!"

Jake snapped his fingers in front of my face.

"Are you still here, Trinity?" Jake's voice brought me back to reality.

"Yeah, I just remembered something."

"What did you remember?"

Just then Stephen opened the door and barely fit through it. He struggled to fit his shoulders to go through the frame as I choked back a snicker.

"The people are taking their seats. It is time to get onstage."

Jake looked at me as if he wanted to say something and then swallowed his words. He got up to leave and then turned around to look at me with a look as if he thought this might be the last time he ever saw me.

Stephan got the hint. "I'll see you down there."

I got up from my makeshift seat and headed toward him. I had forgotten how to walk in heels and stumbled slightly. What barbaric kicks we get from making ourselves put on constant balancing acts. He came a bit forward as he thought I was going to fall, but I waved him off with a hand.

"I'll be okay, I promise," I said as I steadied myself. "So, I will see you tonight?"

He smiled sadly.

"Yes, of course. Wish me luck?"

"Isn't it bad luck to wish luck before someone goes onstage?"

"Yes, I suppose you're right."

"How about this, don't die."

He laughed a little.

"As long as you promise not to die."

I drew an invisible X with my finger over my heart, and he held up the Boy Scout promise sign.

"Showtime," he whispered to himself as he turned and exited down the staircase.

I couldn't figure him out.

❧ 12 ❧

It was ten minutes to showtime, and the crowd was buzzing with anticipation. I had checked everywhere with the little time I had. I went into the sound booths to make sure there were no weapons or bombs that the Reaper could have hid. I filtered through the crowd to try to feel any out any animosity and came up empty.

The voices molded together like hot oil bouncing off cold water, loudly and anarchic. Autumn and I were standing in a twelve-foot area in front of the red-curtained stage. We were swallowed in muddled sounds, and screams sounded around us as the lights began to dim. In my left boot I felt a small and short vibration. Flipping open my phone to see a text, I got confirmation that Jester was in the audience. "You look smoking hot," was the response I got from him. I guessed it was better than Phipps's "Subject confirmed." I turned around and searched the crowd. He blended in so well that I didn't see him.

Autumn's pen posed on her paper, ready to observe the spectacle. She was going to make a great reporter one day. She was really a sweet person, and I was getting quickly attached to her. My camera posed and ready to shoot. I liked this part. It was as if I was hunting a poor and unfortunate soul. Like a ghost capturing a moment in time. The curtains started to part, and the audience grew to a dull hum that was more vibration than sound. The four men, backs to the audience, were facing a screen that was stretched over gothic columns topped with angels reaching toward god. Silver confetti started to fall like tears from heaven. With an apocalyptic burst of light, flames from the pits of hell covered the screens, and the show began.

Guitars and violin on heavy distortion roared as if they were the battle cries of a generation. Drums thundered to progress the battle with Daniel to sing its hymn. The crowd responded like demons being exorcised. Writhing, grinding and fists flying into the air like judgment day had arrive to punish the wicked unto hell. They frolicked with their instruments like pagan children paying tribute to their gods, and the audience gluttonously devoured it.

Autumn seemed nearly outside the spell, furiously scribing away another universe's tale of the night. The thunderous crowd lost no energy as one song turned into their top twenty hits. The night blended in sparkling pyrotechnics that wowed the crowd into a chaotic subdued trance. Autumn ignored the pandemic of contagious energy and kept writing; my lens never left the stage. My ears and my senses were filtering out into the crowd. Clean. There was no malicious energy but most importantly no reaper energy

Daniel's arms spread out toward the angels with a scream, and the crowd went wild. That was when I noticed it. Shit! The stage! I had not been paying attention to the stage! Everything flowed in slow motion as Daniel's eyes became glossed over and his hands remained suspended in the air. Fear flickered across his face, as it does with all people who see the Reaper. I threw my camera at Autumn. "Catch!" I shouted at her. "I need a shield! NOW!" I screamed into the audience. With a strength I didn't know I possessed, I jumped on the stage to Daniel just as he collapsed to his knees. I lifted him just enough to get his back to my chest. His face started to turn blue. Shit! A heart attack. I put my palm over his heart and put my energy into his heart. Beat... please beat.

I heard his thoughts enter my head. "Please, don't let me die, God. I'm not ready; I'll do anything, Mother... I'm not ready. I'll never do coke again, God." His head flopped back, and he saw me. His eyes bored into mine with pleading. If he got out of this alive, he might remember me; for his sake, I hoped not. "Please, God, I want to have children... if you let me have children... I'll be a good father... I promise..."

I hugged him tighter and turned his head. Just touching him wasn't enough. I shoved my mouth to his and pushed as much energy as I could into him. Light started to beam out of his skin, and his heart regulated. The purple drained out of his face as I pulled away from him. He remained staring at me as I started to back away from him. His bandmates started toward him, and I knew I had to make my exit. If I didn't now, my cover would be blown.

"Don't worry, my darling," I whispered low enough for him to hear. "Your work isn't done yet." With that, I ran off the stage, and I felt the cover recede.

I grabbed my camera from Autumn, who looked at me with a mask of horror. She started to tremble looking at me. It was strange that she wasn't looking at the stage. Her eyes grew wide, and she retracted from me like I was a monster. Her voice became like a wave in the chaos.

"WHAT DID YOU DO?!" she wailed. "WHAT THE FUCK WAS THAT?!" Like a wave too big for a surfer, a realization washed over me. She'd seen everything.

❧ 13 ❧

I needed a plan and quick. They even train us for this kind of situation. Autumn started hyperventilating, which was a blessing. You couldn't scream when you were trying to breathe. With my camera slung over my shoulder, I had bigger fish to fry. The crowd was in chaos while the paramedics tried to help Daniel to his feet. He looked stunned but alive, and that was the important part. The curtains closed, and I grabbed Autumn by the waist and dragged her through the crowd. Everyone was frantic with concern for their beloved singer. She began flailing her legs and arms, fruitlessly attempting to free herself. This was where superhuman endurance came in handy. Thankfully this was going to give me a better cover than anything else. I pulled her into the backstage area. Oh dear god, she felt heavy. This was very difficult to do in heels. What was I thinking? Why didn't I just wear running shoes?

Stephan had been directing paramedics onto the stage area.

"Stephan, Autumn is freaking out. I need privacy."

He nodded and pointed toward the roof door. I carried her through the door, and she started kicking and fighting harder. Might I add that this carrying a flailing woman up a flight of stairs was a chore? My leg muscles were burning, my arms exhausted. This would be a lot easier if she could walk and *not* run away from me screaming. She was still hyperventilating too much to say anything. Thank God for small blessings.

We reached the door, and finally she was able to whisper out a word.

"Pardon?" I said casually.

"Let," she gasped.

"What?"

"Me," she gasped again.

"Let you?" I opened the door to the roof. I was thankful for the fresh air against the beads of sweat coming from my body.

"Down."

Ah, of course.

"Alright." I dropped her flat on her face with a flop. The thunk of her face plant left her moaning. I walked a few steps forward and felt a million pounds lighter. Autumn started to recover but just decided to sit up. I took in a big breath and leaned close to her face. "So, are you done freaking out now? Or do I have to drop you from a higher height?"

She let out a small whimper.

"Okay, good. What exactly did you see?"

"I didn't see anything." She whimpered. Her eyes looked down and refused to meet my gaze.

"You're lying, and please don't lie to me. I was trained to be able to tell. When you really begin to think of it, it is really rude to lie." She started shaking. Oh, sweet god, she wasn't going to— "Please don't cry." Autumn's body started racking with sobs.

"Please don't hurt me! I swear I won't tell anyone! I promise!" She sobbed.

I was coming off pretty intimidating. I sat beside her and put my arm around her. I could feel her tremble with fear. She thought I was going to hurt her or worse. If she were the bad guy,

I'd feel great about it, but she was some poor girl who saw the wrong thing at the wrong moment.

"Autumn, I'm not going to hurt you. I don't hurt people. I'm the good guy." I felt her relax but not entirely. "You weren't supposed to see anything... I need to ask you what you saw."

"I saw you jump on the stage and attack Daniel." No wonder why she was scared; she thought I was trying to kill Daniel.

"No, no, I saved his life."

"But I saw him—"

"The Reaper got to him before I could stop the attack."

Her eyebrows started to knit, and she looked up at me with confusion.

"Reaper? Like Grim Reaper?"

"Reaper is a nickname." I paused in thought. *You know what, I'm gonna tell her.* "I work for an organization call HALO, and we try to save lives."

She peered at me, wide eyed.

"A Reaper is an agent who is trained for the last line of defense. If we can't intercept things in time, and it gets close to a high casualty count, we call in a Reaper. They give the final solution and eliminate a target."

"Eliminate?"

I started to laugh.

"It's a polite word for kill." Whatever color she had in her face drained. "Before you start to get scared again, it is a rarity that it ever comes down to that. Reapers do other things as well. They can make other gifted, like myself, almost invisible. That's why no one else saw me jump onstage."

She looked confused.

"Why was I able to see you?"

"There are several explanations. Um, one, you are immune to Reapers. Two, you are gifted, or three, Jester never gave me a cover, which means I could be screwed."

"I gave you a shield, so you can scratch number three."

I turned to see Jester standing behind us. I cursed under my breath. I hated it when he snuck up on me. He wore black silk pants with accentuating off-white pinstripes.

"Did you acquire our target?" I said with all seriousness, but in all honesty I was more concerned about Daniel.

"He came out of nowhere, and he left just as quickly." He sighed and sat down beside us. "I didn't even get a bead on him. It was like he came out of nowhere. I checked the entire audience and nothing."

"Did anyone see me?"

"No one that I scanned. Except for her." His almond brown eyes started to dive into her. She started to shudder. I could feel her need to run away. I was not into this today.

"Knock it off. She's had enough," I said, smacking him in the shoulder. I took a moment to pause. "Did the Reaper see me?"

He looked away from me, a dead sign that something was amiss.

"Crap."

"What's going on?" Autumn said with genuine concern. Was this a sign that she wanted to be friends? I guessed I would really find out when she was done writing the article.

"The Reaper knows who I am." I started getting swallowed up in thought. If he saw me and knew who I was, I might be in some serious trouble. A Reaper could kill you very easily.

"Is that a bad thing? I mean, look at you." Her eyes widened as if she realized what she just said was an insult. "Not that you look bad or anything, but you look almost completely different from earlier today. So maybe he might not be able to find you."

"The Reaper can track her down and kill her just by her energy alone if he suspects she's an agent of HALO." Jester tilted his head sideways and reflected for a moment. "You know, then again, maybe that chick—"

"Her name's Autumn." I scowled.

"Whatever." He waved the scowling away. "She has a point." I wasn't certain if he thought that she was a liability, but I wasn't going to allow him to do anything to her. I wasn't certain whether or not he thought about the fact that not only had she seen me save Daniel, but she'd seen me. There were only very special people who could see through a Reaper's shield. One is Reapers themselves, or people like me. I looked at her sideways. Yes, people like me.

"Is Daniel okay?" I muttered while studying Autumn. I didn't know her all that well, but I felt comfortable with her. I usually didn't feel comfortable around anyone. They taught us don't get involved, and don't get attached. I had been too reckless most of the time.

"Yeah, he's fine, but the manager is going to make a statement soon to all the reporters who were there. You guys had better get back down there. Do we need a wipe?"

"Absolutely not."

Jester stood in front of me like a dog standing up to his master. He didn't like it; he didn't like it at all. I was waiting for some sort of sign or debate. I was hoping that he wouldn't argue this with me.

"A wipe?" Autumn asked with notes of fear. She started to back away from us as if she'd just learned that we were the devil. There were some instincts that could never be censored by our polite ways. In some ways I suppose that's what keeps us alive.

I stared at Jester, telling him to back off. The poor girl had thought I was killing her potential beau, and then saving him, and who could forget the top secret underground that changed history. All in a day's work? The poor girl deserved better than this.

"I need your word that you won't tell anyone what you saw tonight. If you tell anyone, it could mean my death warrant." I turned my eyes intently on her. "I'm serious, Autumn." I grabbed her arm. "Please."

Her clear blue eyes met mine, and somewhere inside them, I thought she understood. I released her.

"I promise," she said with determination. Jester stood with his big arms crossed over his chest with all the silent force of a wolf. Her eyes flickered to Jester and then back to me. "I'll say nothing." She looked Jester straight in the eyes. "I mean it, Jerko, nothing." She turned around and started toward the door.

Jester smirked. "I like her. She's got spunk."

Autumn looked at him with confused eyes filled with thoughts. She shook the thought free. Good idea. Attempting to understand Jester was a head-hurting task alone.

"I knew you would, and she's my friend, Jester."

He smirked even wider.

"You look very nice. What are you doing later tonight?"

Now it was my turn to smirk.

"Wow, tempting to go down that dusty road, but I have a date."

The smirk dropped, and the moping ensued.

"With whom, might I ask?"

I rolled my eyes and crossed my arms like a deviant teenager caught in a car. I felt as if I had "but, Dad" dangling on my lips.

"Oh God, you're not going to go all shotgun dad, are you?"

"Not if it isn't necessary. Who is it?"

"It's Jake Fortinbras."

"The guitarist? You're joking, right?"

"She's definitely not," Autumn said with zeal. Back to the happy-go-lucky self. I bet she was thankful to have the spotlight taken off her.

"Holy shit. How perfect is this!" It was if a light bulb was lit above his head. "The Reaper is targeting the band. Obviously."

I rolled my eyes. Oh great, a plan was roaring in those eyes of his.

"Yes. Date him. Get as serious as you can because if you stay close to them, you can point out who the Reaper is."

"You jerk face!" I pointed to him. "I will date as I please. This will not be some mission. AND! In case neither of you noticed, his band member and friend nearly died today."

"He'll be fine. No one knows your little secret like me, darling. A little shaken but he will be just fine."

I shook my head.

"You ever think that this is a fling and nothing serious or intense?"

"You guys are looking pretty intense for one day," Autumn said as she shrugged.

"Autumn," I moaned, "you're supposed to be on my side, 'member?"

She pantomimed zipping her lips.

"Get off it already; we have work to do." I turned and walked toward the door, motioning toward Autumn behind me.

"I'll be watching."

Of course he would.

"Don't be watching too close, I might get lucky," I said with a wink. I loved getting the last word. Now for the hard part... life.

❧ 14 ❧

The press conference went by like a blur, and like Jester said, yes, Daniel was fine. They said it was a stress-related collapse due to the excessive touring. What bull, but I was thankful for it. If they delved any deeper, they would see something was amiss. Autumn kept it calm and cool, even after we got back to the hotel room. I thought she wanted to ask questions, but since the article had to be done as soon as possible, we just pretended that everything was just fine. We worked together and got the article done. We emailed the article and the photos to Tim with much relief. Shortly after that was done, Autumn got a call from Daniel. He needed to talk to someone and wanted to be around someone warm. Not that I could blame him. He had just been through a situation that I wouldn't wish on my worst enemy.

As I sat alone in my hotel room, fixing the last of the pictures, I started to wish I could go with Autumn to make sure that he was alright. Yes, alive, but was he alright?

It was starting to get past midnight, and I decided that maybe it was time to give up on Jake. I threw my phone on the bed. It had been a nice fantasy while it lasted, but now I was tired, and I wanted to get out of these sick clothes. I slid off my knee boots, and I felt nearly 90% better already. Then I took off my stockings, and there was the last ten percent. It was amazing to feel free after so many hours being incased in man-made garments of oppression. I slipped off my bra in one final movement and let out a sigh. The bed looked inviting, and I crawled in the cottony goodness in the sea of cotton.

I breathed in the clean linen and felt refreshed. I knew I had to get up and take a shower, but this was too nice. I eased into complete relaxation and sleep slowly. Frothy white warmth and happiness washed over me. I swam in it.

My ringtone ripped me from my enjoyment. I fished out my phone from the sea of white cotton sheets. I looked at the clock and it was 2 a.m. I had been sleeping for an hour and a half. "Hello?" I should have looked at the number.

"Trinity?" I didn't recognize the voice.

"Jester? Do you any idea what time it is? Couldn't you have waited?"

"Jester?" the voice said. "Who's Jester?"

"I'm sorry, who is this?" I felt all sleepy headed.

"Jake. Um, this isn't too late, is it? I'm sorry I got caught up with something, and with Daniel and all it's been quite a night. Are you still free? I could really use some company." It was late, but then again he'd had a bad night, and I'd had a nap already.

"Yeah, no problem. I just woke up, so I'm a little groggy."

"Oh, God. I'm sorry, really, it's just that—"

"Jake, there is no need to apologize. I mean, look what you have been through."

"You don't happen to have anything planned for tomorrow, do you?"

"Aside from turning in the pictures from the concert, not really, unless Tim has something planned for me, which I doubt."

I was very happy about getting the top twenty finished, photo-shopped and ready to be dropped on the page. So my schedule was pretty much free until my next assignment. If every job was this independent, I was in heaven.

"Oh, wonderful. Dan decided to postpone the tour for a few days, and I have some spare time. Would you like to do something?"

"Sounds nice. What do you have in mind?" A normal relation-ship? Me? Heck yeah! I would enjoy something nice. Hell, the guy liked nature, good food and great music; what was the big deal if I wanted to spend time with him.

"If you allow it, it will be a surprise.

Yup, and may I finally make it up to you tonight?"

I didn't say anything. I wasn't sure if I'd had enough sleep to involve a surprise.

"Please."

"Okay, where do you want me to meet you?" I needed some deodorant, makeup, and there was no way I was going to pour myself into another outfit like the one I had been wearing earlier today. I muffled a yawn and stretched. I *really* didn't want to get out of bed. Was it possible to make a hotel bed this comfortable?

"Well, I will come and get you. Are you hungry? Personally I could dig some breakfast."

I forgot about food. I didn't remember when I had eaten last, aside from the slice of pizza earlier today, and let's face it—that was awful. With a loud growl, my stomach agreed.

"I will take that as a yes."

"You're joking. You didn't actually hear that, did you?"

"I have great hearing. So breakfast is safe?"

"Yes, but give me fifteen minutes."

"Wonderful, I will see you soon." He hung up the phone as I tried to pry myself out of bed.

I padded my way into the bathroom. My reflection in the

mirror screamed washed-out rocker. My mascara had run down my face, and my formerly smoky eye look became like a washed-out Picasso painting. Fishing through my overnight bag, I found my cleanser and washed my face. Scrubbing away the night's chaos off my face made me feel incredibly renewed. I felt even better after I had brushed my teeth. I flipped up my hair with a few clips to create a sloppy but stylish do.

As for my makeup, I figured something brief and simple would be fine. Some basic cover up, followed by some blush, bronzer and black eyeliner with mascara. I figured maybe this time around, I would just wear jeans and a sweater, but before I could don any clothing, a knock on my door sounded. He was five minutes early. I grabbed a complimentary robe and answered the door. Instead of the expected Jake, an elderly gentleman stood with a wide square box tied with giant silk ribbon.

"Can I help you?" I said awkwardly. He probably had the wrong room judging by the way he was shuffling his feet.

"Miss Trinity?"

"Yes?"

He looked instantly relieved. He smiled and held out his hand.

"My name is Billy Comdin."

I shook his hand, and he was a very warm person.

"I am here to give you this package, and I am going to escort you to where Jake is waiting." He handed me the package and stepped back. "I will wait for you here."

I closed the door, and I had to wonder if there was a bomb or a dead monkey hand, but I had to figure it was only the first date. I mean, my dates never got creepy until the third date. I pulled the silk ribbon slowly and noticed it was scented with lavender and vanilla. I lifted the box lid and became washed over in shock. I had never seen a more beautiful dress. I looked at the label. Oh my god, it was Vera Wang. It was a white country cream light silk gown that had tiny sparkles in the fabric. It was an off-the-shoulder number with long layers of silk that looked as if the dress itself wasn't a dress but a light silken aura. I didn't know what to do. Should I call him and tell him there was no way I could wear it because it was too nice for me? What if he was insulted? I decided to give him a chance, just this once.

I donned the dress, and when I looked in the mirror, I was amazed to see that the dress looked like it was made for me. Not to mention it was incredibly comfortable. There was still more in the box. There was a wrap that went with the outfit, and as I wrapped it around me, I noticed there were shoes to match, but thankfully the shoes were gold flip-flops. I couldn't help but wonder why flip-flops, but then again, I was going on faith here. I applied some of my favorite perfume, *Noir*, and went out the door, carrying my cell phone and key.

Billy seemed pleased with the sight of me and walked with me in silence to the limo waiting in front of the hotel. Outside was quiet and calm. The full moon hung fairly high considering it was nearly three in the morning.

He opened the back door. "Before I forget, Jake asked me to give this to you." He reached inside his business suit and retrieved a thick white envelope. I stepped into the car and wondered briefly if I really knew what I was getting myself into.

I opened the letter, and a blindfold fell out. With anticipation, I opened the letter.

Dear Trinity, I'm glad you decided to go further down the rabbit hole and trust Billy and me. I know you are probably wondering why the bells and whistles, but I told you that if you trusted me and gave me a chance, I would make it worth it. I need an act of trust from you in order to properly follow through. Enclosed with this letter is a blindfold. Put it on until the vehicle comes to a full stop. If you at any time feel like you are uncomfortable with this, just tap twice on the driver's window, and he will turn around to take you back to the hotel. I will be waiting.

—Jake

In blind trust, I put on the blindfold. I wanted to go further down this rabbit hole, but for what reason? I couldn't say. I was beginning to wonder if I was truly stupid enough to follow through with this. I didn't know this man at all, yet I was trusting him now. My mother always said that the truest love was the truest trust.

❧ 15 ❧

After a half hour of being *literally* in the dark, the limo came to a gentle full stop. I felt Billy get out of the driver's side. I removed the blindfold just as my door opened. I stepped out and waited for my eyes to adjust to the surroundings. I was surprised to see that I was in the middle of nowhere. I heard the crashing sounds of waves and realized that I wasn't just in the middle of nowhere; I was in a place that was always comforting to me. I took a deep breath in and felt the waves in my soul. I noticed that the moon still hung pregnant in the sky, and I smiled. Right, a walk, I thought to myself. "I have another envelope for you," Billy said as he handed me yet another white envelope.

Trinity,

Thanks for trusting me. Now there is one more thing I would like you to do for me. There is a trail of rose petals. If you follow it, you will find me.

—J

This kept getting more and more, well, romantic. Rose petals, blindfolds, I wasn't certain if I'd ever had anyone ever do anything this romantic. The most romantic thing that Damon ever did for me was take me ring shopping for his new girlfriend. How awful was that? Tonight was about starting a new relationship, not dwelling on the past. I was already too far down this rabbit hole to turn back now. Slowly but surely I followed the delicate petals by moonlight. The soft wind floated off the waves; I reveled in the moisture as it moved through my dress. As I followed the path, I came to a large lit white votive candle. I picked it up and continued to follow the path.

It slowly turned into a hill, and I watched my footing carefully. I found myself surrounded by a beach. The sand was a dazzling white against the moonlight. A few yards away was the sound of the waves lapping against the beach. The sand was being swallowed by a kingdom of stars. I saw lights that looked like they were floating above a round table that had another large votive candle on top of it. The table had a cloth on it that looked like it matched my dress to a tee. Rose petals surrounded the table, and I couldn't help but think that this was the end of the road. The chairs were wrapped in similar silk.

I got to the table a mere few feet from the shore. There was another envelope sitting on the table. I smiled and opened it up. Was this guy for real? In HALO they train us not to be surprised, but I couldn't help it.

Trinity, turn around, please.

I turned around to see Jake as fresh as if he just woke up. His black hair was slicked back and his face clean shaven. I was shuffling through my head for something clever to say, and all I could come up with was, "Are you for real?" Smart, Trin. I guessed it was better than the "wow" and "gee" I was really feeling.

"Yes, I am," he said sheepishly. "I know that all this may seem extreme, but I had a feeling you haven't been treated very nicely, and I wanted to do something special for you."

I paled slightly. Was this wounded heroine that obvious?

"I'm sorry, I've insulted you."

"Um, it's not that." I felt a pain in my neck starting to emerge, and I rubbed it to attempt to keep the pain at bay. "I was just hoping that I wasn't so transparent."

He smiled and walked around the table to pull out my chair. Pulling out my chair!? Who did that? I guessed he did, but this was something incredible.

"You're not transparent, but how do I put this..." He paused. "It takes one to know one."

I sat down as he took the seat across the table.

"I was burned too, and let's just say I know how you feel."

He looked at me a little closer and then shook his head. "Okay, maybe not entirely."

"I guess I missed the punch line." The waves crashed against the shore, and a wonderful smell floated through the air. Like a lightning bolt hit my stomach, I suddenly felt unusually hungry.

"Mine is old, and *yours* is recent. So I guess it's similar but not quite the same." Jake looked off in the distance as if to watch for something. "I hope you like Italian," he said with a wink.

"I love it. I didn't think I would be hungry, yet... whatever the case, I blame you," I said with a laugh. He smiled, and it was the most beautiful smile I had ever seen. "I'm sorry if I seem insulted; it's just that it was really recent."

Jake's eyebrows furrowed, and he picked up his chair and moved it beside me. Not uncomfortably close, just close enough to be cozy.

"Are you going to be okay?"

I felt my lips tighten instantly as I suppressed tears. No one had asked me that. I held my breath in my chest and tried to will the pain away. I felt his warm hand wrap softly around mine.

"It's okay to be upset, you know."

There was no way I was going to let him see me cry on the first date. I swallowed the open hole into my chest.

"In all honesty, usually I don't date until I'm entirely over someone. I find it horrible that I was barely in a relationship with this man. It just went bad."

"Why did you decide to go on this date with me if you weren't ready to?"

I looked at him with a crooked eyebrow.

"I'm saying this outside of my attraction, although I would like to know what makes me so lucky."

I turned my head down. I wasn't sure if I was ready to get to this part. Would it be so bad to try to open my heart to someone so beautiful? Out of all the women he could have taken out on a date, he chose me. Not only did he choose me, but he put a lot of thought into it.

"Firstly, it didn't look like you were going to take no for an answer."

"What gave you that idea?"

"I'm wearing a designer dress that you picked out, enjoying a five-star meal on a beautiful beachfront. Last time I checked, no one ever goes to that much trouble on the first date."

He tilted his head as he thought about it.

"Okay," he said with a smile. "This is pretty out there, but I did tell you I was going to make it up to you, but that couldn't be the only reason."

"You were sweet and kind when I met you. Would it kill me to date the good guy for once?" I said with a smile. "I just want to forget all about him."

His fingers found my face and tilted my chin upward.

"Give me a chance." He pointed at me. "And I will help you forget every second of it."

I met his eyes as a flurry of emotions flittered through me. He placed a delicate kiss on my cheek. It felt so wonderful that it was like a fresh blanket out of the dryer wrapping around my soul. I felt dopey and engulfed in a very happy-go-lucky way.

"I hope you're hungry." When he leaned back, there was food on our plates, and it was the best thing I had ever smelled. Spaghetti and meatballs! I didn't remember when the last time was I had that. I looked at our glasses filled with red.

"How did you do that?" I said with wonder in my eyes. That was one impressive trick.

"Magic trick that they taught me in Hollywood." He grinned as I shook my head. "I hope you like Layer Cake Shiraz."

"You're joking, aren't you?"

He looked at me with wide eyes.

"It's my favorite wine."

"Mine too, I fell in love with it when we were touring in Australia. It is wonderful, isn't it?"

I lifted the glass to my lips and breathed in. Delicate violin notes floated through the air and clashed with the percussion of the waves. I took a sip of the wine and almost instantly relaxed. I leaned back and smiled.

Jake took a bite of the dish and smiled back at me. "I would give anything to know what you are thinking right now."

I looked off into the distance of the shore and smiled back at Jake. It felt as if we had been dating forever.

"I was thinking that I don't remember the last time I got to go by the beach and enjoy a really good glass of wine." I took a nice sip of wine and let the warmth fill me.

"When was the last time?" he asked curiously.

I put the glass down and rolled the thought around for a few minutes while I took a bite of the pasta. It tasted even more wonderful than it smelled.

"I think the last time I was able to do this, it was maybe approximately five years ago, and I believe I was alone."

"Alone?" He gulped down another bite. "I never thought that you would be alone."

"I needed to go and be alone to relax."

"You can't go out with friends to relax?"

I let out a small giggle between bites.

"I didn't mean to be funny."

"I'm sorry; I guess I should let you in on the joke." I took a sip of wine. "When I make friends, a good chunk of them are friends for a while, and then they turn into DIDs, and then, well, I never get any rest." I took a deep breath and another drink.

"DIDs? What the hell are those?"

"Damsels in distress, the type of person who is constantly in trouble." We both started laughing. I guessed I always thought about this as a job.

"That's terrible!" He managed to choke out between gulps of laughter. "You refer to all your friends like that?"

"No, not at first, anyway." I took a bite of the pasta. "They always seem to end up that way. It starts well, and they get into some trouble, and I help them out."

"That doesn't sound so bad; friends help friends."

"It wouldn't be, but eventually it becomes an over and over habit. I mean, if it's a major issue, I have no problem. But before I know it, they get in way too far with whatever it is, and I can't do anything about it." I took my last bite and nursed my glass. "I wish that I could help them—"

"But you can't help everyone," he pointed out as he finished the last bite of his meal, "especially if they are self-destructive." He wiped his mouth with one of the glamorous napkins and started sipping the wine. He started to look more relaxed than ever. "I bet it wears you out."

"It does, but I can't help myself, really. I wish I could but—you know."

"It's one of the reasons I started being a recluse. It just gets easier that way."

I smiled and I felt better. At least I wasn't alone. His smile grew wider as mischief twinkled in his eyes. "I hope you are ready for dessert."

"I'd like to see you pull that magic again."

He started laughing again.

"Would you like to join me for dessert," he said as he stood up and held out his hand. I'd trusted him this far. I put my hand in his, and it was wonderful. His skin felt so wonderfully warm. Together we walked around the table to find yet another path of rose petals. I smiled lightly as he slipped his hand around my waist. "You have the most wonderful smile I have ever seen."

"Now you are trying to sweet-talk me," I remarked, slightly suspicious of the compliment.

"No, I'm serious," he said, defending himself. "It's honest and pure. I like that."

I blushed. No had ever said anything that nice to me.

"I have something to show you." We walked toward a dock toward the end of the beach. I opened my mouth to ask and then closed it. I almost made a golly gee comment but thought it was safe just to keep my mouth shut. He smiled at me, and I hugged him tighter. He smelt like warm vanilla and sandalwood. I pressed myself closer to him just to feel the warmth of his body. I'd never felt this warm and safe before. I felt his hand brush the ends of my hair, sending tremors up my spine. Music floated closer as we made our way to the boat. "I hope you don't get seasick," he said with a smile.

"No, never." We made our way through onto the boat. "I love being near the water."

"I was hoping you would." The interior of the boat was the most beautiful thing I had ever seen. It was hardwood everywhere with a cherry stain. Candles lit the deck with orange splashes. A long silken couch sat watching the moonlight. The music remained gentle like the wind that was surrounding us.

"I'll be back in a moment." Jake disappeared for a moment,

and the boat started to move into the middle of the lake. He returned with another bottle of Layer Cake and two glasses. "Will you join me for another glass?" he chimed in while he poured.

"I would love to," I said while I received a glass.

The moon was at its fullest as twilight hung high. He motioned to me to hold on one more moment, and he disappeared. The music was turned up a little more, and Jake returned with a plate of hot molten chocolate. It was then that it occurred to me that it was a miracle that the dress was still perfect. He produced two silver forks.

"I'm sorry, but I am very full."

"No problem." He moved the dessert aside. "I was hoping that you would join me for a dance," he said as he took a swig of the wine.

"Sure." Now it was my turn to take a swig. I stood up from the couch and joined him near the hull to slow dance. I wrapped my hands around his shoulders while his hands found my waist.

He pulled me closer to him, bringing our faces inches apart. "You're right, you know."

I felt his breath on my skin. "About what?"

"This was worth it."

I smiled, not a fake smile—a real smile. He planted a kiss on my forehead, and I felt wonderful. I didn't think I was ever this happy before. I laid my head against his chest.

"I'd like to tell you something."

"Oh?"

"You're good enough. I know after what happened with the person who hurt you, I would think you probably feel less than dirt, but you're good enough."

I was familiar friends with that feeling.

"What makes you say that?" I said curiously.

"Just a gut feeling. I wanted to say something more romantic or sweet, but I'm not really good with that kind of stuff.

I know this is only our first date, but would you be willing to maybe start dating... more often?"

I lifted my head to meet his eyes. I used my senses to stretch out over him as I felt him sigh. I scanned him for any sign of deception, and he seemed entirely honest. As I put my energy on him I felt him relax almost with a sense of ecstasy. He pulled me closer. If there was any hint that he might *not* have found me attractive, it would be betrayed by the growing hardness between us.

He hugged me tighter, and we danced in silence. I felt as if I'd known him my entire life. I wondered if this had been another life, in another world, maybe we could have met each other earlier. I wondered what it would have been like. A life without Damon, a life without HALO and just simply a life. I felt his swollen manhood press against me. I debated throwing off all my clothing and taking him right here and now. He brought his lips close to mine. I enjoyed the smell and feel of his soft lips.

"I'd like that," I said, smiling.

I felt myself sinking into his safe and warm being. I tried to pull back my energy, but it started to pulse with a life of its own. His energy started to merge with mine, and I let out a sigh. I surfed on the edge of something I'd never experienced before. The twilight started to disappear from the sky with the threat of the sun. My skin tingled with hunger for his lips. My tongue reached out and grazed his lips. He allowed a delicate moan to escape his lips. His hands traveled up my back and cradled my head. He brought his lips to mine with a furious crushing hunger. I couldn't control myself anymore. I forced him closer to me, my body melting into his. My skin was on fire, begging for him.

My hands traveled under his shirt, and I wanted to explore every inch of his body. His hands moved over my naked shoulders. As his lips crushed into mine, I wanted to give in more than anything. I put my hand to the top of his chest and gently pushed him away. "I meant it when I said I don't give myself so easily." For a moment he looked hurt. "Not that it isn't *very* tempting."

He wrapped his arms around me, pulling me closer. We continued to dance with the rising sun, not that we needed the extra warmth. After all, we had each other.

❧ 16 ❧

I tried my best to tiptoe down the silent hotel hallway. I took off my shoes and carefully padded my way to my room. I was hoping that even the near silent swishing wouldn't give me away. I fished out my key as I crept closer to my room. I was relieved that despite the nine a.m. rush hour, approaching the hotel had been as quiet as a tomb. I paused at Autumn's door and listened carefully. Silence. Thank God. I tiptoed past her door to my own. Just as I lowered the key into the lock, Autumn's door swung open, and she jumped out as if to catch me in the act. "I knew it!" she shouted, breaking the silence.

"Knew what?" I said, hiding my shoes behind my back.

"Cut that out! You went out last night!"

I was about to comment that I had done no such thing, but having on a long Vera Wang gown and tiptoeing with sandals in my hands—I knew that arguing this was futile. She looked me up and down with knitted eyebrows. Even though this outfit was comfortable, I hated being stared at.

Her eyes grew wide. "Did you go out with Jake last night?"

"Yes." I started to rub the back of my neck. I chalked up my fatigue to night two of no sleep. Although I did have some sort of sleeping on my mind, just not the kind that involved rest. "I didn't think he'd call me, but an hour after you left, he did." I stared at her. Why the hell did I have to explain myself? She looked at me with wide blue eyes, secretly pleading with me for details. I guessed this was what girl friends were supposed to do.

"And?" She prompted me with her hands.

"And what exactly?"

She threw down her hands in exasperation.

"You don't have many friends who are girls, do you?" she prodded. I knew I spent far too much time at the shooting range and not enough doing normal people things.

"Hey now!" I said in an attempt to defend myself. "I have one! We meet once a year to go to the shooting range."

Autumn shook her head lightly and put her hand over her face to hide a giggle.

"Alright, do you mind filling me in on the joke? What am I missing?"

"Okay, this is the part where you tell me everything!"

I looked at her, and then I looked at the door.

"Alright, get changed."

I let out a long sigh. I wasn't certain if I wanted to shower. I smelt like Jake, and I wasn't exactly eager to wash away the memory. I slipped into my bathroom, carrying a pair of pants and a maple leaf jersey.

Autumn followed me into my room as I filled her in on the details. "Oh God... how romantic!" She plopped down on the unmade bed.

"Is it?" Between weapons training and hand-to-hand combat, I guessed I wasn't given the option of romantic thoughts. I looked at the dress on my arm, and I wondered why anyone would go through so much trouble to charm me. I resisted the urge to smell it again. My body began to melt just thinking of him. It was difficult to suppress the feeling, but I had to. This was all moving too quick and too soon. I felt my knees go weak.

"It is!" she squealed. "And I was talking to Dan, and I thought maybe we could go on a double date!"

"A double date? Oh god! Jake and I went on *one* date. I don't even know if he will call me again." Just then a soft rapping sounded from the door. I wanted to shout *now what?* As I got to the door, I looked back to Autumn. "No one treats a girl that good without some sort of sex. Sorry, but it's true."

She crossed her arms and visibly pouted.

I opened the door and had a giant vase of red roses shoved in my face.

"Trinity?" The voice behind the giant bushel.

"Yeah, that's me," I said, attempting to look behind the roses.

"Flowers for you... Here!" Whoever was behind the vase shoved the flowers at me and scuttled away. The vase was almost too heavy for me to hold on to. I tottered over to the dresser to try to set it down but not before getting a nice smug smile from Autumn. She looked cute even when she was smug. I lifted out the card before Autumn could come out with a smart-ass comment.

Trinity,
I had a fun time with you, and I would like to see you again.
Love, Jake

I slipped it back into the white envelope and shook my head. There was no way I was getting out of this. Just then I received a text from Jester. *Lucy... you've got some explaining to do!* Great, make that definitely not getting out of this. I set down my cell phone on the nightstand. Would it be so bad? I mean, a nice guy wanted to date me. Was it too soon? A thought of Damon with bimbot number forty-five on his arm. Okay, maybe not. I turned to Autumn and said the words I never thought I would ever hear come out of my mouth, "What do you think I should do?"

Autumn raised an eyebrow.

"Really, you want to know what I think?" she asked suspiciously.

"Yeah, I'm not very good at this part. Thoughts?"

"When was the last time you were in a relationship? Like how did it end?"

"He started avoiding me, then started saying he needed his freedom—"

"He wanted to sleep around?"

"Yeah," I remarked reluctantly.

"He didn't even want to touch me... like I was unclean or something. Then I just thought *okay, if I let him go—he will come back to me.* Then we grew apart, tried friendship, and then... well, it didn't end up going out with a bang but a whimper."

"Ouch," she said as she shifted uncomfortably. "So, in that case, give him a chance. Apparently, he was talking about you to Dan." Now, that got my interest. I wanted to play it cool and not be interested. A smile spread across Autumn's face. So much for my poker face.

"Alright, I'll bite. What did he say, oh-new-girlfriend?"

She beamed as I sat down beside her.

"When he saw you, he was smitten."

I looked at her with rolling eyes.

"Smitten? Come off it. Who uses that word? Besides, hello, one date."

Her lips drew in tightly. Great, she was hiding something.

"What is it?"

"Jake doesn't date."

I wanted her to tell me something I didn't know.

"I thought you said that even Jake's exes gave him a clean slate."

"Yes, but something had to happen to break them up."

Crap. She was right. I looked at her again as she held in her breath. She knew what it was.

"All the women told Dan that Jake just wouldn't let them in. He loved them, doted on them, but never opened up to them."

Great, another Damon.

"I'm not interested in this roller coaster again." I got up off the bed and picked up my cell off the stand. "I'm calling him and telling him I'm sorry for wasting his time."

"Wait, Trinity. No—put down the phone. There's more."

I sighed and sat down beside her again.

"With the other women, he only came to visit them. Never invited them to stay with him or never stayed overnight or anything like that."

So I was the exception? He invited me to Alaska.

"Dan was really shocked when Jake began to talk about the plans he had and *has* for you two."

"He seems so sure of himself, doesn't he?" I said with contempt. Why was I looking for a reason to be mad at him? I knew why. I wasn't ready for this. Yet, on the other hand, I *needed* this. I felt as if I needed him. He made me feel so human. He made me feel normal and loved, but I just couldn't help but be suspicious.

"According to Dan, when they are on tour; they call him 'the priest' because he doesn't sleep with anyone, doesn't indulge even once. Apparently, he goes back to his hotel room and spends all of his time with his books and papers."

That one caught me. "Books and papers," I reflected. "What kind of books and papers?" Why was I so apt to put this man on trial? *Tone it down, Trin. He's a civilian. See? You get one taste of the normal life and BOOM! You go all agent on him.* I shook my head.

Autumn shot me a puzzled look.

"Business, I guess."

Of course, duh!

"Anyway, you apparently brought something into his life that Dan has never seen before."

"Oh."

Autumn gave me a twisted look.

"You know, most girls would be happy—not suspicious."

"I can't help it, you know!"

She twisted her face to frown.

"Listen, he does nothing wrong. He's sweet, kind, thoughtful... listen! The guy doesn't even fart, okay!?" I started laughing. "No one, not to mention—no man is that perfect all the time! So damn right I'm suspicious!"

"So what? He has a flaw that he hasn't shown you. Not everyone is like you." She then lifted up her hands to mock me. "Oh, here I am, world! Take me as I am." She rolled her eyes and threw down her hands. "Give him a chance."

"Okay, fine. No jumping the gun," I promised.

"Besides," she said, letting her glance slide sideways.

"Oh crap, a catch. Spit it out!" I yelled at her, pointing.

"We already planned a double date... kinda."

"Kinda? What do you mean kinda?"

She shifted again.

"Well, on Saturday we are going to meet up here and go somewhere that Jake has yet to choose." She made her eyes wide and flashed those baby blues like a dog begging for scraps. I thought she sensed my apprehension. "Pllllllllllleeeeeeeeeeasssssssssseeee!"

Oh, dear God. Is this what other people go through?

"If I do this, you owe me."

Her face lit up, and she bounced up and down, giggling. I couldn't help myself, I started laughing too. I looked at the roses and thought maybe it was time to enjoy myself for once.

❦ 17 ❧

I collapsed all my crap in my living room and let out a very large sigh. I placed the huge vase on my fireplace. Finally home again. I kicked off my shoes to the beat of someone pounding on the door. I was hoping that for once I could get three seconds of peace. Turning to the door, I was faced with the giant shit-eating grin of Jester. Whenever I saw that grin, it meant trouble. Self-satisfaction sparkled in his eyes. The problem about having him as my best friend was knowing when the shit was about to hit the fan. His hands were clasped tightly behind his back as he rocked back and forth on his heels. "Dare I even ask?" I asked with my hands firmly set on my hips.

"What a beautiful and glorious day, isn't it?" He took in a deep breath. "Change is in the air, I reckon." His smile got wider, and my fears got deeper.

"Cut the crap, Jester. I know that smile."

"May I come in?" I opened the door wider and let him through. "Ah, you just got in, didn't you? Well, maybe you should kick up those feet; you look like you have been up all night," he said as he started to rub his chin.

"I'll bite. What's going on?"

"Well, you see, I'm tired, and since I don't feel like talking." He then produced what he had clasped behind his back. One guess it wasn't his hands. A magazine entitled *Hot Topic.* "I'll let the pictures speak a thousand words. Mind telling what thousand words they are telling you?" He handed the magazine to me, and I gently unfolded it. "Word is that they recalled all their issues after they got that shot."

It was a picture of Jake and me looking really intense. He was whispering in my ear, and I was looking down, blushing. His boyish smile hung on his lips. Despite our metal clothing, we looked very much in love. I quickly flipped to the inside story about our top secret date, which, thank God, was only rumor and no pictures.

"The great and witty Trinity... speechless?" He plopped down on the couch and waited for my response.

Half of me wanted to keep the issue and study his body language to see how sincere he really was. Apparently, he was very sincere. Yet, on the other hand, I wanted to throw the magazine in Jester's face.

"You know, I'm allowed to have a life too," I said, plopping down beside him. "Listen, I'm not thrilled about this," I said, looking down at the magazine. "But I really like him. He's nice to me." Out of the corner of my eye I saw Jester's smile drop.

"I'm sorry, Trin. I thought it would be funny." He took a deep breath. "It's not like I'm not happy that you are getting over Damon, but I don't know anything about this guy."

My eyes flickered to his face while I tightened my lips. I shook my head; I was ready for this kind of talk. "But I'll tell you what. If he continues to make you as happy as I see you on that cover, then I won't say a peep. I would even give you away if you got married."

I smiled, at least he cared.

"Thanks. I appreciate the support." I put the magazine between us. "It was really nice last night."

"Oh?"

"He planned a special date for us, which involved us dancing while the sun rose."

"Dancing? *Just* dancing?" The smile returned. His eyebrow rose in a lewd manner.

"You know me better than that," I said, pointing at him.

"Okay, no whoopee?" He saw a smile spread across my face. "Ah... But there was something."

"Yes, it was very tempting." I laughed at the truth. It was so truthful, and it had been a long time since I felt this good. "I don't know what it is about him, but he just sweeps me off my feet, and he makes me laugh."

"Well, I like the blush he is giving you, so I will bask in your —" his phone went off, and his smile dropped "—happiness. I have to take this." He took a breath. "Yeah. Hi, Damon, what do you want?" There was a brief pause. "Yeah, I thought as much. No, I think she's still on a date with him." Jester let a wide grin flicker over his face as an unhappy sound sounded from the phone, and Jester jerked it away from his head. "No shit, buddy. Listen, you couldn't have given two shits about her, you treated her like ass, now eat your crow pie, you prick." I wanted to stand up and applaud. Another burst of noise and another jerk away from the phone as I smothered a giggle. "I don't care that you outrank me, but don't sit there and pretend that she's still yours after you trampled on her heart." More noise came out of the phone. "She quit, and now she's gone." He rubbed his head. "Hold on." Jester lifted a finger to his lips to tell me to be quiet. He hit the speakerphone button on his cell phone. "Why are you so upset?"

"She was supposed to be mine," Damon said mournfully. "I wish that she hadn't picked him. *Anybody but him*," he finished bitterly.

"What's so bad about him? He makes her happy, and you don't. So quit getting angry."

I smiled, and I was thankful for Jester's bluntness.

"'Cause I still love her. I'm just not ready to settle down yet." Okay, that hurt. I wasn't ready for those words coming out of his mouth.

"No, you're ready to settle down. Only with someone who is completely normal. A human. You don't want her."

"Don't presume to tell me what I can and cannot do."

"A girl like that doesn't wait around for long especially when you are engaged to another woman."

Damon fell silent. Tears filled my eyes, he proposed to her? Great, now I really felt like chopped liver.

"I don't know who you are kidding, but it's not me, and she's already found another person who loves her."

"Hey, I'm just being honest!"

"Honest," Jester snorted with contempt. "I highly doubt you even know the meaning of the word. Get over yourself and go back to your fiancée. Why are you calling me anyway?"

"I had to know if it was true. I'm staring at *Hot Topic* right now, and I wasn't sure if it was her, and then I read the article." There was silence for a beat. "I'm your commanding officer. I heard you guys were talking again. I want you to tell me everything you know."

A giant bark of laughter sounded from Jester's mouth. The laughter rolled around my living room until tears streamed down his face.

"*GODDAMN IT, THIS ISN'T FUNNY!*" Damon roared.

"It has to be if you think I'll tell your sorry ass anything." He continued to laugh, and I had to smother my own laughter.

"You don't want to make enemies with me."

"Well, I think you have that one mixed around. Listen closely to *me*, Reaper, if I go to Phipps, or anyone higher than him, and tell him that you are attempting to bully me into giving you any information *that doesn't have* to do with a case but your *own* personal interests, I don't think I need to tell you what will happen to you."

"So you're not going to help me?" he remarked as darkness crept into his voice.

"Maybe when you pull your head out of your ass and quit trying to use your rank against me—"

"I should have figured as much," he grunted quickly. "Fine, I'll take this up with her personally."

"Leave her alone and go back to your fiancée."

Damon snorted.

"Goodbye, Damon. You wanna call me to talk sports, I will, but you leave Trinity and Jake alone."

"Fine. Goodbye."

"Oh, one last thing. Just thought as a *friend* I should let you know that Jake isn't going anywhere. They are getting serious and fast. So get used to the idea that she isn't yours anymore."

"Thanks," Damon spat. "I'll keep in touch." The cell clicked off with the ring of what sounded more like a threat.

Jester turned to me with worried eyes.

"I guess you should consider yourself warned."

I received a text message on my cell phone. It was Autumn telling me that we were needed at the office because Tim wanted to see us.

"I don't think you should be going out alone until he cools his heels," Jester said, noting the text message.

"I have to. This isn't just a new job, it's a case. Lives depend on my success with this mission."

"I'm not talking you out of this, am I?"

"No." We sat in silence for a few minutes. "Can I keep this?" I said, pointing to the magazine. "I'd like a picture of us together."

He smiled and nodded.

I got up and walked to my bedroom and slipped on some dress slacks and a frilly blouse. I hated coming in and out like this, and frankly I was beginning to miss my own bed. I opened my dresser drawer and fished out my waistband holster with my Walther PPK. Not that a gun would do me any good if Damon tried anything. Reapers had a really good resistance to bullets. They weren't bulletproof, but their bodies could push them out with a lot of ease. I walked back out into the living room to see Jester reading the magazine. "Well, I'm off to the office. Wish me luck?"

"Luck," he said as he started out the door with me. "You're gonna need it, kitty. You're going to need it."

❧ 18 ❧

Autumn and I sat side by side in Tim's office in silence. Neither of us knew why we were there, but I figured it wasn't good. Being called into the office by your superior is never a good thing. His secretary sat us down and told us he would be with us in a few minutes. We had been sitting here for over 20 minutes. I felt her anxiety growing with each passing minute. It was just then that I noticed how much I hated white walls. Funeral homes had white walls, hospitals had white walls, HALO rooms had white walls... all the places that made me miserable had white walls. Tim's office just made that list.

Tim threw open his office door and quickly strode to his desk. "Good! I'm glad you two could make it."

Autumn and I exchanged looks. We had one job at this paper, and I was pretty sure that we were about to be on the chopping block. "Alright," he nearly shouted as he plopped down in his chair. "I'm glad my gamble paid off. This was the best concert issue we have put out in years," he said with a giant smile.

Autumn's jaw dropped as her eyes grew wide. I pushed her jaw closed with one finger.

"Thank you," I said.

"Here's the thing." He threw his feet on his desk, leaning in to a slump. "My photographer and reporter are still in the hospital. I need you two to cover their latest beat."

"We were just a quick fix," I said suspiciously. I couldn't help it, but putting newbies on another's beat was in poor taste. "Are you sure you want us to cover it?"

A smirk dangled on his lips. "You two are now officially the dream team. Now, don't deny the story until I tell you what it is."

"Alright, let me have it." I looked at Autumn. Her eyes were still very wide, and I was beginning to wonder if she was catatonic. She just blinked, so I was going to assume she was okay.

"There are a lot of religions around here, and all the heads of these religions have been talking to one another. They decided that they want to put together a 'Fair of Faith' to show the public those connections of faith between them. Sort of a way to tell people we are here and we stand united."

"Wow, that is intense," I remarked.

"So," he said, taking his feet off his desk. He leaned forward in a dramatic manner. "Will you do it?"

Autumn nodded silently.

His eyebrow rose, and his gaze shifted to me. "And you?"

"Bring it on."

He started laughing.

"What do we need to know?"

"Well, for the next week there is a lot of legwork that Autumn is going to have to do. The fair is in two weeks, and we have several interviews lined up. One with Father Reinhiem, Rabbi Stein, Tao master Chang and Reverend Tennorman."

Ding, ding, ding, ding, we have a winner! There we go, that was why I was here.

"So, Autumn, I got an agenda that is sent to your email, and, Trinity, you will only need to be at the fair itself, but if you want to accompany her, you are welcome to."

I nodded.

Autumn found her voice. "I would like to have her come with me, and I am glad that you enjoy our work, and I hope that we can continue our work."

"Good." He stood up with a great burst of energy. "Autumn, there are some things I would like to brief you on. I had a press kit put together."

I stood up and felt a lot better.

"Is there anything else that you will need from me?" I said innocently.

"Nope, you are good. See you next week."

I nodded and started striding my way to the elevator. I felt a million times better. My target was in view, and with any luck this would go off without a hitch. But let's face facts here, I was never that lucky. Standing in the quiet of the elevator, I leaned against the wall when I realized that I was hungry. Not hungry for food but hungry for Jake. That was strange, I never recalled being hungry for anyone. Not even Damon made me feel this way. I played the kiss over and over again in my mind, and I felt as if I was whole. I never knew I wasn't. Not until Jake.

The elevator doors opened to the parking level, and I strode to my car, tottering on my high heels. I felt warm and confident. It looked like life just kept getting better. I slipped into my car and was about to put my keys in the ignition when something *thwapped* against my driver's door window. With a groan I was faced with the cover of *Hot Topic*. Damon's face appeared beside it. "Out! NOW," he yelled as his breath created a mist against the glass.

Great, just great.

❧ 19 ❧

I pushed opened the driver's side door, and Damon stepped back. "What do you want?" I said, crossing my arms. His dark eyes bored into me. One of the reasons Reapers are never allowed to go out on missions solo is because their eyes change with their moods into extremes. His face looked gaunt and hollowed out. Somehow, this made him more frightening. His eyes were the pitch black of sulfured hell. The black started to leak into the whites of his eyes. He paced back and forth like a tiger preparing to pounce. He kept staring at me and pausing.

"What?" I said, this time demanding an answer. He came at me, grabbing my shoulders and holding me close without our bodies touching. His body pressed into me. I felt his every muscle press against me like a well-trained animal.

He leaned in and smelt my neck. I felt his tongue brush against my neck, licking my jugular. He melted his tongue into my pulse. I shuddered and began to squirm. I didn't want to hurt him. He took a big breath in, and his hands dug into my flesh. I let out a small whimper. "Let me go, Damon." I heard him grunt, and he shoved me into my car, hard. He started pacing again; this time he was angry. I felt the metal dent, colliding with my body, and I flopped to the dirty ground. I felt the world swerve. One thing I didn't like to do was fight, but my need to survive was overpowering my moral complex. I glanced up at him as he was pacing.

I steeled myself for a blow. Unfortunately for Sentinels like me, we really didn't have defenses against Reapers. Damon looked as if he were lost in his own world. I knew I had to get out of this as quickly as possible. I drew my gun out of my waistband and drew back the slide. I aimed it his kneecap, and with focus, I pulled the trigger. With a crack of gunpowder, Damon collapsed.

I scrambled up off the ground, running toward the exit. *If I could just get to the entrance*, I thought to myself. Then someone would see us, and he'd have to stop, right? I kept my gun in a ready stance as I saw the daylight. I could hear people and cars; I knew I was close. I felt something grab me by the hair and throw me through the air. My gun flew out of my hand as I felt the side of a car make contact with my body. Glass rained down on me.

"I can still smell him on you."

I pulled myself off the ground and stood on the still shaking ground. He threw his body against mine, pinning me to the car.

"Why can I smell him on you?" He put his mouth dangerously to my neck. No more Ms. nice. I used all of my force and pushed him off me, sending him flying into the other car.

"Fuck off," I yelled at him.

He got up and tackled me into my car, sending the windows shattering. I squeezed my hand into a fist and sent him flying with an uppercut. I stalked after him and waited for him to get up. He rose with the whites of his eyes now covered with black. He swept his leg under my legs, bringing me to the ground. He lifted his leg to ready for a soccer kick that landed in my guts. It sent me flying across the cement, dragging the glass with me. I felt little pieces of the glass cut me as I slid, coming to a stop at the back of my car. I tasted my blood in my mouth, and I spat out a piece of glass.

I started to lift myself up, feeling the glass cut into my palms.

Damon wrapped his hands around my shoulders again, pulling me up. His fingers dug in so deep I could almost hear my bones screaming for help. I groaned helplessly. I knew I was no match for his strength, but I knew I would be able to get him. I looked into his blackened eyes. He stared at me for what felt like hours. He shoved his lips into mine, and he started kissing me. I felt a small amount of blood trickle from where the glass had cut me. My lips started kissing his back.

He let out a small groan as his tongue licked away a bit of the blood. He crushed his lips in deeper, pulling his body into mine. His lips started traveling toward my neck, slowly kissing each bruise he'd created. I felt the void rip me open again, all the pain that he caused. I pushed him away with all my force. He tumbled into another car, leaving a small dent like the one before.

I wiped the blood and the kiss off my lips. *"WHY ARE YOU DOING THIS TO ME?"* I spat at him. He looked at me with the eyes of a lusting priest. I felt my tears well up again. They ran free of their prison and mixed with the blood on my face.

"I can even taste him on your mouth." He whimpered. "Why?" He stood up straight. "WHY!?" he screamed. I could feel his anger crawl against my skin. He loomed over me in an angry sort of pace. He wiped the debris off his face with a careless hand.

I fell to my knees, feeling his Reaper powers crush me. The bones in my body began to move. My brain started to feel as if it were being crushed. Everything started spinning in rapid pace.

"Why do you care?" I said, squeezing the air out of my collapsing lungs. I carefully and secretly prayed that he didn't kill me. But then again, love was like a killing dance. I felt my bones cracking back into place as my healing process began. I lay down on the only spot that wasn't moving, the ground. I knew it was only a matter of time before he struck again. He stopped and looked at me.

"You just don't get it, do you?" he spat with filtered bitterness. That threw me off. But he was right, I apparently didn't.

"Get what? Speak normal! Crazy person!" I yelled at him.

He grabbed a fistful of my hair and pulled my face closer to his. Painfully, I was forced back on my feet. His lips were set in a hard line, his eyes pitch black, and I couldn't help but wonder if this was what people saw before they died. It couldn't be because even in his rage I could feel his lust. If this were six months ago, I would be thrilled—and hopefully less beaten up.

"Why can I still smell him?" he whispered close to my face. His other hand ripped my blouse off as his hands grew claws. Never in all my years had I ever seen a Reaper change this far. Physical pain was nothing to me, but I couldn't handle his lust, his love and his pain. What was I to say? I knew this time it was my turn to hurt him.

"'Because I fucked him, Damon." I laughed. "And it was awesome."

His fist came down on my face, throwing me into another car. More shattered glass and then darkness.

🦋 20 🦋

Beep, beep, beep.

My eyes fluttered open to the brightest lights of my life. My body was like dead weight in the realization that by some miracle I was still alive. The smell of bleach cleanser and the unforgettable cotton engulfed my senses. Where was I? Was I being held captive? No, No. I tilted my head to the side to attempt to see where I was. With the world spinning, I closed my eyes and lay back. I opened my mouth to ask someone to please stop the ride, but it came out like mush. Surrounded by white, I tried to move, but somehow I didn't care. Somewhere in the back of my head I realized that I might not survive, yet it didn't matter.

I floated in the white hazy mist. My eyes rolled back into my head, and I resisted the urge to swim back into the warm, forgiving darkness.

"Trin?" a soft male asked somewhere in the haze.

I let a moan escape my mouth. I felt the air burn like cold fire in my chest. I tried to move my legs, which didn't even acknowledge that I had wanted them to move. I licked my dry lips and surfaced to the top of the fog. I swam in this warm ocean of fog. I felt happy and free. I realized in that moment that this bliss was too good to be true. Battering my way through the cobwebs, I tried to surface through the clouds. I batted my eyes.

"Trin? Are you awake?"

A room came into view filled with light and flowers. Where the hell was I?

"Is she awake?" muttered a light female voice.

A dark shadow hovered toward me. I tried to focus, and the light blurred and focused again. I tried to move again, but my limbs hung like dead weight. *Keep it together, Trin, c'mon, get up.* A face came into focus with fire black eyes. A cold weight of realization set into the core of my chest. Damon. He was coming for me. I felt my pulse ripping through my head.

"Trinity! Calm down!"

A rapid beeping fueled the music of my panic. I had to get away.

I pulled at the blankets trapping me.

"We need a doctor," the female voice yelled. "I have to get a doctor."

The fog tried to capture me again, and I struggled against the tide. My legs finally got the message to move, and I tried to kick off. Damon reached his hand out to me. "Damon, No!" Clear tubing on my right arm made it hard to move. I pulled against them until I was free. "No!" I screamed. "Don't hurt me." A red sticky mess ran down my arms, making it harder to move. I threw my arms up to my face to protect myself and found myself once again drifting back into the darkness.

"Trinity!" the male voice screamed. "Please! Come back to me!"

A grassy field filled with light. "What's the matter?" I looked over to the man sitting across from me. His long red hair blew in the passing summer wind. I looked around and took a minute to figure out where I was. It was Iowa, and I was with Michael. This was the most beautiful sunny day I had ever seen. The purple and yellow flowers seemed to sigh with each wind.

"It was nothing. I just had the weirdest daydream." I shook the thought out of my head and readjusted my white summer dress. "It's so beautiful here."

"That's why I brought you here. Are you thirsty?" he said as he poured a glass of water with lemon. "It's unfortunate, you know."

"What is?"

"That we can't stay here forever. Like this." He mildly gestured to the vast grassy field nestled in the middle of a forest.

"Who says? We can stay." I took a long cold drink of water. "Why don't we go to our favorite fruit stand? You know the strawberries are perfect this time of year."

"We can't stay. You know you have a lot more work to do."

I felt the tears well in the back of my throat as I put down the glass.

"This isn't real, is it?"

He gently grasped my hand.

"No, my dear, I'm afraid it isn't, but I thought I would make it easier on you. After all, you've been through a lot over the last month." He looked out onto the expanse of the field. "This was the only time you and I would get a chance to speak privately."

I took a long cold drink, enjoying the water.

"Is there something wrong?" I studied his face, which was filled with wells of concern.

His chiseled jaw tensed, making his angular face seem so much harsher. "I want you to know that nothing is like it seems."

I knew that already; didn't he just admit this was all an illusion?

He released my hand and combed his fingers through his hair. "Damon didn't mean to hurt you that badly. He lost his temper."

A realization came upon me. Maybe it wasn't a bad dream. I couldn't have forgotten. I didn't understand.

"No kidding. Where am I? Really, where am I?"

"You're in a hospital, deep in a coma at this point. They almost lost you twice today. It's why I took you here to spare you that much."

"Great." I was happy here, content. "Why can't I stay here? With you?"

He took my hand and pulled me into a hug.

"Do I have to go back?"

He tilted my head to meet his eyes. I closed my eyes as I felt his lips brush against my forehead. This wasn't lustful, just unconditional love.

"If I could have you here with me forever, I would want nothing more. But you know you are needed there." He pulled out of the embrace and sat beside me. "I'll make things easier for you, I promise. You'll remember nothing of the fight or what happened afterward or even this."

I looked at the hem of my skirt, studying it. I wanted to ask why, but I knew the answer. It was the same answer I received every time I had seen Michael. "It's safer this way," he would say with undeniable conviction. I wanted to know why I was so easily a target for Damon and his anger, but then again I just wanted to stay here with my guardian angel, where I was safe and happy, but I knew that would never happen. I knew that the second this was over, I would forget him entirely. There was the ironic heartbreak within it all. He allowed the moment to consume us in its silence. The wind blew past us, throwing my hair in my face. His hands pushed it out of my face and tucked it behind my ear. His finger softly traced a line from my ear to my chin as he sighed. "Damon wanted something so bad that he would sell his soul, and when the devil saw this weakness, he exploited it."

"What?" I felt tears sting my eyes, but I swallowed them back. "Why? What could have been so precious? What was the cost?"

"Some people don't know how to accept who they are on the inside. They want to be like everyone else. Damon just wants to be like everyone else, and in order to have that, he gave them you.

He wanted a human wife, with human children and, in short, a white picket fence."

"He got what he wanted," I said with spite. "Why fight me?" Michael's voice vibrated with a throaty chuckle.

"Oh, he got what he wanted, but he didn't realize the price it would really carry."

"And that price is?"

"You."

"I don't get it, he sold me out, and now he can't handle giving me up?"

"The short version, sure."

I twisted my face in a frown.

He stared off into the distance. "Be careful of the people who come into your life. Including Jake."

I looked at him in disbelief.

"Jake? Why?"

"Jake is a good man on a bad path." He looked at me with intensity. "Damon takes for granted all you will become, and Jake realizes all you will be. The one who owns your heart will own your power."

"My power?"

"You're going to become something special. I'd ask you to stay away from Jake, but I think it is unavoidable."

I giggled slightly.

"I don't think it would be that hard. We have only been on one date. Far too soon to be thinking of anything further down the line, don't you think?"

"Sure, your first experiences with him but not his first with you."

I looked at him with a sinking confusion.

"I've told you too much already. Let's just enjoy the time we have left."

"How much time do we have?"

"We have only a few moments left." We both stood up. I took

a deep breath in with the wind. We wrapped our arms around each other, basking in the warmth of the sun.

"I'll never forget your kindness, Michael," I said as I buried my face into his chest. He nuzzled his face in my hair, placing a kiss that would be soon lost to the wind in it. I felt warm wet tears fall on my cheek.

"Yes, my darling, you will."

❧ 21 ❧

My eyes opened to a room of soft white. The perfectly clean, square room left a large window to the twilight of the night. The room was the dead quiet that only a hospital room could be. A dull throbbing in the back of my head was a full sign that the drugs had worn off.

"Trinity?" a soft female called.

I looked to my left, and sitting at the edge of her seat was a very tired-looking Autumn. Her normally bright blue eyes looked hollowed and rimmed with red. Her lips were thinned and skin color gaunt. If this was how she looked, why was I the one in the bed?

"You look like crap," I whispered hoarsely.

Autumn let out a loud bark of laughter that nearly broke the sound barrier.

"You're one to talk," she croaked. She picked up her chair and moved it closer to my bedside.

I lifted up my thickly bandaged left arm.

"You woke up and freaked out," Autumn said cautiously. "You tried to, uh, defend yourself and tore all your needles out."

Ugh, that sounded gross. I couldn't help but wonder if it was going to scar. Putting down my arm, I tried to remember what had happened to put me here in the first place. I looked at Autumn's face. Aside from the obvious worry, she carried no bruises or scratches. Whatever did happen, it was a good guess she wasn't involved.

"What happened?" I felt the dull probing in the side of my head rise. The ebbing of my pulse washing through each wound elevating itself. I clenched and unclenched my fists with each crescendo. In this ocean of hurt I felt a fog rolling in. A mixture of confusion and exhaustion mixed over my mind doing little to hide the blank spots in my memory.

Autumn's face grew confused.

"You don't remember?"

I shot her a sarcastic glance.

"I just figured you remembered something because of when you woke up."

"You mean when I tore up my arm?"

She nodded, and she looked around apprehensively.

"Is there something you aren't telling me?" I heard something crinkle in her hand as she shifted uncomfortably.

"Who is Damon?" Another crinkle. "You said his name when you woke up."

"An ex, but I haven't seen him in a while. Why?"

"Did he do this to you?"

I tried to think back to earlier today and could only remember the office and then darkness.

"No, I don't remember. What aren't you telling me?"

She shifted again, and another crinkle sounded. "What is in your hand?"

"I was the one who found you. I thought a car hit you. I called Jake after the ambulance had arrived. There was glass everywhere. I don't know how you survived, but you did." She took a deep breath. "Jake and I were sitting here waiting for you to wake up. For the last two weeks we have been taking shifts."

Two weeks? I chewed on the thought as Autumn continued, "In the first few hours after they had you stabilized, you woke up, and Jake came to your side. You called him Damon and asked him not to hurt you. You got out of the bed and managed to get to the door before you collapsed. I ran to get a doctor, and Jester was just outside the door and heard everything. His eyes." Autumn shook her head and cleared her throat. "He wrote this down and told me to give it to you when you woke up. He told me not to let anyone else see it."

"Wrote what?"

She slipped me the piece of paper she had been shifting in her hands. It read *quarantine relocation evaluation code orange level 88*.

"Fucking great." HALO, the wonderful bureaucrats that they are, had created a coding system. They considered the coding system a way for all operatives to get a message regardless of how or where they were. Jester was basically telling me I was to come into no contact with other agents unless absolutely necessary and that I no longer lived where I thought I lived. Which meant HALO had located me elsewhere. Level 88 was a botched assassination attempt. Damon wasn't the nicest to me—ever—but I highly doubted he would try to kill me.

Autumn looked hollowed out. Her eyebrows knitted together in concern.

"I don't suppose he gave you any other information, like keys, a map or a GPS tracker, did he?"

She shook her head. Great, Jester, keep the cripple completely in the dark.

A dull knock sounded from the door. It was if the person behind it didn't want to wake the person in the coma. "Come in."

Jake peeked his head through the door, and a wide smile spread across his face.

"Holy crap!" he shouted as he rushed to my bedside. "You're awake!"

I winced at the sound.

"I'm awake, not deaf. Mind toning down the sound level to the newly risen?"

He mouthed sorry.

"I'm not deaf—indoor voices, please."

Autumn and Jake laughed a hearty laugh. It reminded me of a laugh people use to break the tension at a funeral.

Autumn rose from her chair and stretched.

"I'd better go get the doctor. Trinity looks like she is getting back to normal," Autumn said as she exited.

Jake took her spot and slipped his fingers into my hand. His eyes intently fixated on my face. He studied it like an artist studies a painting. There was something fluttering behind his eyes that I couldn't touch. It glided across them like a shadow across a window. My knuckles were splattered with the former battle wounds of scabs that had left angry trails across my hands. Bruises were browning and trailed up my arms. Just looking at my arms alone, I was beginning to fear what the rest of me looked like. I guessed I wasn't going to even think about sex.

"What?" I said as I smiled. I felt more throbbing through my face. Something told me I wasn't as pretty as I should be.

He grinned slightly and tightened his grip on my hand.

"I'm alive and A-OK. See?" I gave his hand a squeeze, and he stared at my hand. "C'mon, Jake. Look, I'm fine. Not as pretty as I was on our first date but alive."

He shook his head.

"You are more beautiful than I ever could have imagined," he whispered as his lips brushed against my hand. His two hands wrapped around my fingers.

"Imagined? What's there to imagine? I'm right here, flesh and blood."

"Thank god for that much." He inhaled my scent, and I felt my skin tingle. Even with the pain, I couldn't help but feel aroused by him. I shifted uncomfortably as more pain shot through my body. I grunted with pain.

"The doctors are calling you a miracle, you know."

I laughed. A miracle? It was no miracle, it was HALO.

"You shouldn't laugh. They said that considering the damage to the other cars, it is a miracle that you had no broken bones."

"Uh, just lucky, I guess."

A smirk dangled on his lips that said he didn't believe me.

"Ah! Ms. Trinity!" a loud booming voice said with enthusiasm. "I see you are amongst the living and up. You're not jumping off the bed this time around."

His name tag said Dr. Mcviker. His face read that of a joyous life offset by an active-lifestyle body. He looked healthy, and that was even more comforting. His round face and full grin screamed that he'd had more successes than failures. Which was a good thing considering the situation. His salt-and-pepper hair complemented his ruddy complexion, offset by sparkling green eyes. "Vitals look great. Blood pressure is awesome. I'll be back in a moment. Your mother has been calling every hour on the hour, and I think she'll be happy to hear you're up and around." With that he turned and walked out the door, leaving the three of us in silence.

Autumn sighed and leaned against the doorway.

"Autumn, did J leave you anything like a phone? Or even a phone number?"

She blinked twice and reached into her back pocket for her cell phone.

"Yeah, he gave me his phone number." She shifted uncomfortably as if she didn't know what to expect.

"Okay, it is better than nothing. I'm guessing that he took the majority of my personal belongings."

Autumn nodded.

Jake's mouth twisted into a frown. I couldn't blame him. A man he never heard of had taken his would-be girlfriend's purse.

"I'll explain everything later. I promise, but until then, can I get some privacy to call him?"

Jake leaned back from my bed and folded his hands on his lap.

"I'm not going anywhere until the doc says you're okay."

"Me too," Autumn interjected.

I sighed, I wanted answers, and I wanted answers now.

"Fine." I flipped open the phone and searched for the number that he gave her. This wasn't his real number but a number that he used in these special circumstances. The phone dialed, leaving a trail of rings, a quick jerk of a pickup, and then a waiting silence. "Explain everything."

"Ah! You *are* alive," he jested with a sense of relief.

"That wasn't everything, but yes, I'm alive and apparently up the creek without a paddle."

"Yeah, about that—"

"I don't take well to waking up homeless." I felt Autumn and Jake literally jerk. "Guys, relax."

"You're not homeless; you just don't know where it is." He started laughing.

"Fucking semantics!" I shouted as a roar of laughter ensued.

Autumn's eyes kept flickering from me to the vitals monitor. "Trinity, calm down," Autumn cooed.

I could feel my body throbbing and pulsing with a weird mix of anger and pain. Jake's lips were tightening into a thin white line. Give the man brownie points for keeping his mouth shut. I took a deep breath.

"Okay, okay!" Jester shouted into the phone. "Don't have a heart attack, you damn cripple!" This was followed by another roar of laughter.

"*FUCK YOU, GODDAMN IT!*" I screamed into the phone. The monitor started beeping, and Autumn ran and got a doctor. "Jester! I swear to god!"

"Alright, alright, calm down. I'm glad you're alive. All of your things from your previous residence are now in your new residence. I'm en route to the hospital right now. After I stop and pick up your mother and brother."

Autumn, followed by a nurse and doctor, ran into the room. The doctor looked at the monitor and looked at Autumn with a raised eyebrow.

"It started to beep—um—a lot," she whispered softly. "And it was loud."

The doctor and nurse shook their heads and walked out the door. Autumn visibly wallowed in her own embarrassment.

"Thank you," I replied calmly. "What about clothing? I don't think that this has a back, and seeing as indecent exposure is a class D felony, I would really appreciate some pants."

"If Jake's there, are you sure you need any?"

"JESTER!" I shouted.

"Hey, you're wounded not dead."

I hated to admit it, but it was true. My eyes flickered to Jake. I never thought a man could look so hot when he's angry.

"Admit it," Jester chimed in. "You're thinking about it right now."

Jake raised an eyebrow, and I realized I had been staring. I cleared my throat and stared at my blanket.

"Like you said," I smirked. "I'm not dead."

"Yet, I have some bad news."

The smile dropped off my face.

"We haven't apprehended him, Trin. He's been really smart about staying off the radar."

"So the rumors are true," I whispered.

Jake jerked up from his chair and swiftly left the room. I couldn't blame him for that. Actually I found myself impressed with the fact that he stayed as long as he did.

"Our operatives obtained the security tapes from the garage. It—" He stopped and reflected. "I'm sorry, Trin, I should have been there."

"No one could have known." We sat in silence. "I'll see you soon, okay?"

"Yeah." We hung up without another word. I didn't think

either of us wanted to say anything close to goodbye. I passed Autumn back her cell and lay back down.

"Jake's pissed," Autumn remarked. "Wonder why."

"I noticed. I'm surprised he stuck around as long as he did. I think he doesn't like secrets as much as I do. Or it could be the homeless thing."

"You're homeless?"

"Not technically. As Jester so warmly put it, 'I'm not homeless; I just don't know where it is.'" I laughed as Autumn looked even more confused. "The people I work for have special steps for situations that are dangerous for their agents. This is one of them."

"What do you mean?"

"The piece of paper you gave me told me that I was being 'relocated' for my own safety. It also says that the situation that I was in is being considered an assassination attempt, although I couldn't tell you why."

"They think someone tried to kill you?"

I nodded.

"But why keep you in a hospital, where you are a sitting duck?"

"They take measures for that too, but I couldn't tell you what they are." I looked around apprehensively. I did feel like a sitting duck, and for the most part I was afraid for the people around me. What if Damon was so hell-bent on hurting me that he'd take down anyone who got in the way? I should hide. Drop off the face of the earth and never let anyone near me, but as I looked to Autumn's worried face, I realized doing that wouldn't be fair to her.

"Don't worry, Autumn," I said with a half smile. "I'll be well taken care of, you'll see."

Jake walked back into the room with a big pink plastic sack in his hand. I raised my eyebrow slightly. "If that's a severed human head, I'm going to be *very* disappointed."

Autumn started giggling as Jake let out a huff of discontent.

"Get over it, you big baby. I'm fine." Something in his stance told me he wasn't very happy.

"Autumn, could you give us a moment?"

Autumn's eyes grew wide as they flickered from Jake to me.

"It's okay, Autumn, there are no cars here." I started laughing again. Now that I knew I was alive, making jokes about it seemed like the next step. Autumn departed with a simple nod but kept her eyes on Jake. "Autumn, if it was going to happen, it wouldn't be like this. Trust me." I could tell by the twist in her mouth that she wasn't entirely convinced.

Jake closed the door behind her and sat with me in stoic silence.

I didn't have time for this. "What is it?"

He set the bag down, and he reflected for a few moments. His eyes met mine with burning questions.

"You're not being entirely honest with me in this situation, are you?"

"I think the best answer would be 'have I had the chance to?'"

He shook his head with irritation.

"I mean, let's think logically here. We have had one official date and two casual meetings, and I am not counting this right now as a date. Have we really had any time to talk except during our one official date?"

He rolled his head back and forth for a second.

"Okay," he said, letting out a pent-up breath. "You have a point there. But why not tell me why and how you are homeless?"

I rolled my eyes.

"My best friend is Jester. He moved my house and belongings. And technically, I have a home." I looked down at my arm, noting the bruises. "I just don't know where it is right now." Wow, that did not sound sane at all.

"It isn't like a set of car keys, Trin... you don't misplace it!"

"Yeah," I noted. "But this was an extenuating circumstance."

"This is where I get the 'not being honest with me' feeling."

"What makes you think there are any suspicious things going on?" I tried to give my best poker face, but he countered with the "you're joking" face.

"I saw the wreckage. After Autumn called me, I went to the garage. It wasn't a car wreck. So why don't you tell me what really happened?" His gaze bored into me like a stack of books.

"I honestly don't remember," I whispered. "And given the fact that I have been comatose for the last two weeks, I'm not sure I want to remember."

"Fine," he said unhappily. "Who is Damon?"

I thought I saw his eyes flicker black, and I shook my head. It still felt numb from the drugs.

"You screamed his name, who is he?"

"He and I..." I paused. I wasn't comfortable using the term *boyfriend* or *dated* for us being mated. "Were engaged, and things ended. I wouldn't say badly, but he really didn't care that I was ending things. Until now I guess, maybe." I paused slightly. I really didn't know, did I? "I just don't remember."

His eyes softened slightly.

"I wish there were more I could tell you, but I really don't recall much."

"I'm sorry." He cleared his throat. "I'm just not used to people keeping things from me because I tend to keep things to myself." He shifted in the hospital chair. I was beginning to think that those chairs were very uncomfortable. "I want a fresh start with you, and I guess I am being very hypercritical. I want things to work out with you."

If he only knew how much blood my life was bathed in; being the good guy and taking out the baddies was *always* a messy job.

"Cut me some slack, ok?" He smiled lightly.

"I got this for you the first few days you were under. I thought you might want something comfortable to wear." He lifted the pink sack onto the bed and started lifting out clothing. One was a pink jersey; the second item was a pair of the softest track pants I had ever felt. He then lifted out a new matching bra and panties. When I raised my eyebrows, he coughed and stumbled for an explanation. "Seriously I didn't think anyone would remember this, so, I, ugh."

I lifted up the black lace panties, "Actually, I'm impressed with the detail you went through. This is very sexy." He blushed, and it made me smile. "You're really cute, you know that?"

He leaned forward and gave me a kiss. I grabbed his shirt and drew him into me. I felt a tingling shoot from my lips to my chest, filling me with warmth. I pulled him onto the hospital bed, and he didn't fight me. I slipped my tongue between his teeth, feeling a sharp bite of deliciousness. I wrapped my arms around his neck, enjoying his smell. I felt his lips move from my mouth down my neck.

"Ahem."

Jake's eyes met mine, and in unison we looked to the door. Dr. Mcviker stood with his arms crossed over his chest. "Well, it looks like you are feeling *much* better."

Jake slowly moved off the bed and readjusted his clothing.

"Well, Doc, I'm in a hospital bed. Not dead." We both laughed. "I am feeling much better. When can I leave?"

"I'd like to run some tests to make sure there is no long-term damage, and I'd like to see how you operate under normal daily situations."

"Pardon?"

"Make sure you can walk alright, function normally, before I would feel comfortable letting you leave, and even then I would want someone with you at all times for at least twenty-four hours. I would also like to see you relax, but judging by your current demeanor, that is unlikely to happen." He noted the look of confusion on my face. "But on the other hand, a little exercise would do you a world of good."

I started giggling.

"Still, I want to make sure there is no brain damage, and I am dead serious about not being left alone."

"Don't worry, Dr. Mcviker," Jake said with a smile. "She won't leave my sight again."

"And the, uh, exercise? You'll see that she gets it?" the doctor said, grinning. Good to know that even though I was in the hospital, my sex life was still a joke.

"I think that's up to her, but I would be more than happy to oblige." Jake winked. Something told me he was here to stay.

❦ 22 ❦

I stepped out on to the sidewalk and looked up at the looming hospital. I let out a giant sigh of relief, happy to be out of a hospital room.

"So," Jake said, stepping beside me, "what would you like to do first?"

I zipped open my bag that Jester was kind enough to bring me, containing my keys to my new house, makeup, clothing and deodorant. Pulling out a manila folder with Jester's trademark smiley face, it occurred to me that I no longer possessed a car. Dang. I ripped open the top and pulled out a single white piece of paper.

2106 Barnaby lane. Take RR 228, follow it to the end. You'll know
the house when you see it.
    Enjoy, J

"Well, I would love some company to take me to my new house." I smiled at him.

He furrowed a brow.

"Like I said, I'm not homeless, I just didn't know where it was. Now I do."

He shook his head and offered his arm.

"You're not going to leave my sight for at least twenty-four hours."

I opened my mouth to protest, but he lifted a finger to my mouth and pressed it close.

"Doctor's orders, Trinity."

I let out a childish growl in protest.

"Nope, not going to bend. Now, you are stuck with me."

I laughed at him. I wouldn't say stuck, but that was just me. He walked into a parking garage, and I stopped. He walked two steps ahead before he stopped. A knot twisted in my stomach, telling me not to go any further. I took a step back, pulling myself away from him.

"Trinity, what is it?"

Danger! my gut screamed.

"Trin?" He turned to face me.

Why can I smell him? a voice in the back of my head screamed. I took another step back.

"I'm not going in there," I said as I stepped back. "There's something wrong." I took another step back to the bustling side-walk. "I'm sorry, but I can't do this." I couldn't ignore my gut any longer. I had to get out of here. I had no idea why; I just had to leave. Jake tried to grab me, and I picked up speed. I had to leave and survive. I felt my head start to throb. The buildings looked like they were getting taller. They started to waver with the wind. I stopped in place to catch my breath. I had to keep going. I kept walking at a brisk pace, looking forward to the horizon away from the buildings. A silver Porsche pulled up beside me as the passenger window lowered.

"Hop in, Trinity."

I bent down to see Jake.

"If you don't want to go in another garage, I will never make you step in another again."

I got in the car and buckled myself in.

"Where are we going?"

I prattled off the address and smiled weakly. He plugged the address into his onboard computer and allowed the computer to dictate the address. We drove in silence with the drone of the voice of the onboard computer.

"I'm sorry; I don't know what came over me." I saw his jaw tighten and then relax. "I just had this overwhelming feeling to not go in there, and I reacted badly."

He let out a sigh.

"It's alright. Now I *really* can't let you out of my sight."

"Listen, I'm okay, really," I said so weakly that even I was surprised. "After we get to my place, you'll see." I noted that we were coming to a dirt road. I looked at him. "Are you sure you have the instructions in properly."

"Yes, I plugged it in properly."

Dirt road? Nice touch, Jester.

"I just wanted to make sure you weren't going to take me in the middle of nowhere and rape me." I laughed.

A grin spread across his face like hot butter.

"Would I really have to rape you?" He leered.

"You're right, you can't rape the willing, but keep in mind," I said, straightening myself, "I'm a respectable woman."

"Right, gotcha." He leaned over close to me. "So if I'm going to rape you, I need to do it in a house." We both started laughing.

The GPS said to go straight until we reached our destination. "I don't see it, do you?"

"I swear to God, Jester, if this is a bunker, I'm gonna be pissed!"

Jake started laughing. Woods began to crop up around us.

"You know, you never did tell me who Jester is," he said coyly.

"He's an old friend. That irreplaceable person who always has my back and has a terrible sense of humor. I sometimes wonder if he makes a career out of bad jokes."

"Sounds like a keeper." I could feel him getting more uncomfortable.

"Before you get any ideas about Jester and my friendship, we did date once, but we realized we were just better friends."

He tilted his head as if to get more comfortable with the idea. Too bad for that, friends are forever.

"He's been a very good friend for a long time."

A white house peeked through the woods, which gave way to a winding driveway. "Is that it?" We pulled into the driveway that was pointed to an old Victorian house. The house was pure white with a finished porch. "No way," I gasped as the car pulled to a halt.

"This is some friend," he said with hints of spite.

I got out of the car and walked up to the red door with my keys ready to enter. I saw a white envelope was tacked to the door with a giant smiley face on it. I opened it up as Jake finally got out of the car.

Glad to see you made it in one piece. This is your new home. Everything in it is new and well taken care of, all at HALO's expense... Ha ha. The security system installed is state of the art, and there is a panic room equipped with all of the necessary and state-of-the-art weaponry that you could ever ask for. The code you need to enter in is 7777, and the panic room button is located behind the picture of Saint Michael defeating Lucifer. Press once to open it, and afterward tap it twice, and it will automatically dispatch operatives to your location. I will show you around when I get the chance. There is a new silver death-proofed car in the garage. The keys will be sitting on top of the mantel where the entrance to the panic room is. All the food is stocked, and take a look around to see that everything is to your liking. And since you get so angry when I know something you don't, keep your eyes peeled for surprises.

Don't die.

—J

"So what's in the note?"

"Just minor details," I said as I opened the door. After entering the code, I was amazed. The floors were cherry wood, and the smell of fresh linen floated through the white walls. As I walked in, I noticed that old Universal monsters adorned my walls. I was glad he at least kept a few of my things. I peeked into the living room, which looked like a living room a professor would have. The couches were leather, and the floor all hardwood, with filled bookshelves coating the walls. I was in love. Walking further down the hallway, I noticed a blue tile kitchen that looked like it came out of *Better Homes*. It led the way to a beautiful dining room filled with iron twisted furniture that seem small against the large windows that looked out onto a pond. There was a door to the patio. I opened the door to see a pool connected with a hot tub. I could barely conceal my happiness. How the hell did he convince HALO to spring for this?

I noticed the staircase tucked neatly into the corner. As I climbed the hardwood stairs, I noticed carefully aligned pictures with silver frames covering the wall. They were pictures of my family and friends. Rae and I during our trip to Germany three years ago, my mother with my grandfather, various memories that had had been all but forgotten, centered around a gold frame housing the cropped only photo of Jake and me. A white note stood out pressed against the glass, reading: To the future. –J. I had hoped Jake would see the note and wipe the moody look off of his face. A flicker of guilt ran across his face as his eyes rested on the picture.

Reaching the top of the stairs, I noticed four doors partially open. Peeking in through the door on my left, I saw the cleanest white bathroom in existence. A large six-foot claw-foot bathtub had a gift basket filled with my favorite shampoos, a bath towel, robe, slippers, and soaps that looked tiny by comparison. Another note was wedged in the basket: "A new house always needs new towels, Love Mom." The toilet and sink matched the same Victorian flare. In the two-paneled window sat freshly cut roses.

Walking out of the bathroom, I peeked my head into the next room, which had the same Victorian theme for décor, but this room was purple. Guest room, I thought. Moving to the next room, I noticed it was the same as the room beside it but blue. I would have to compliment the dream team of my mom and Jester, but when thanking Jester, I would have to make fun of him. *Such style and flare! Can you paint my nails too?* I giggled out loud.

The final room, on first look I knew was the master bedroom. A Californian king bed sat on a wrought-iron frame that reached to a billowing canopy of white silk. Three large windows shone a bright light inside the room, making the room glow. The bed seemed like a bed of soft clouds that roughly resembled a white fluffy comforter. To the right of the bed was a closet, and as I opened the doors, I noticed that it was a walk-in closet housing at least two dressers topped with clothing. I closed the closet doors and looked over the bed to notice two large doors. I opened them up to see a balcony overlooking the pond down below. I left the doors open and let the fresh air fill the room. I turned to Jake, who was leaning against the door frame with his arms crossed over his chest. He looked deep in thought. I walked over to him and slipped my arms around his waist. "You look so sad."

He looked at me with focused eyes. "I'm not sad." He unfurled his arms and wrapped them around me tightly. "I'm just not good at competition." I couldn't stop the grimace that crossed my face. "I wanted to be your hero."

"Who says you're not? If this is about Jester—"

"No," he said quickly. "It's hard to explain." He placed a kiss on my forehead as I floated in the warmth of his arms.

It was really difficult to think about anything negative, but somehow a creeping thought slunk into my head. Damon was still out there, he hadn't paid for what happened, and even though I wanted to believe that he didn't do something awful to me, it was hard to deny that HALO appeared to be on a warpath. I turned my head to the window and saw a storm brewing in the distance. If Damon wanted to kill me, I knew it was a matter of not if but when.

23

It began to chill me with how well Jester knew me. The house was one thing, but the food was another. How many people knew that you liked 2% acidophilus sweet milk? Looking in the fridge, I noticed all my favorite foods right down to the exact kind of ice cream I ate. The fridge contained my favorite beer! It felt like an eternity since I had cooked, and there were some things you just need to do to work the lead out. Jake was insisting that he order us some food, but after one day of hospital food, I was ready for something that wasn't wrapped or preprocessed.

Jake still had the stench of jealousy straining his every movement. When a man is jealous, he can never just stuff it down deep inside. It lingers above his head like a giant glowing sign. "How do you know he stalked you?" he remarked as he watched me shuffle through the cupboards in the kitchen.

I discovered a black apron with a Hello Kitty sticker and put it on. I continued to shift through the cupboards to discover an array of pots and pans. Setting them on the counter, I tried to think; if I were a pantry, where would I be?

"You ever meet any Hungarians? All we do is eat!" I put my

hands on my hips and looked around the kitchen. "Between Jester and my mother, I'm pretty certain one of these cupboards is going to burst." Seeing a large door beside the staircase, I opened it to reveal a walk-in pantry. Lo and behold, I was right. The pantry was stocked with enough food to fill a bomb shelter. "Aha!" I yelled to Jake.

He peeked around the corner with a twisted frown.

"See? Told ya." Looking through the shelves, I picked out all the things I would need for spaghetti. "Do you like veggies in your food or no?"

He shrugged indifferently while I brushed past him. I piled all the gathered cans on the counter and started to prepare the sauce. Jake paced for a moment and then stopped once he realized he'd begun. He wasn't very good at hiding the thoughts that seemed to float above his head. I could see why he was a very private person. If you got even one reporter that had a clue, he would be in some serious trouble. I opened the cans of tomato paste and dumped them into a saucepan. Now, if I could just find the spices.

"So," Jake said, pulling up a chair, "am I supposed to just sit here?"

I looked into his eyes and still felt some bitterness. When it came down to it, who would I keep around? I guessed that would depend on which one asked me to drop them.

"No, you can talk to me." I put the saucepan on a low heat and turned my attention to getting the large pot full of water. "I like company, you know." I smiled and put the pot of water on the stove. "Now, where the heck are the spices?"

Jake pointed to a rotating spice rack right beside me.

"Smart ass," I remarked. Looking for the right spices distracted me from the awkward silence that was filling the room.

"Okay, what's with you and Jester?" Jake blurted out. I guessed I wasn't going to have to wait too long for someone to get dropped. He attempted to straighten himself. "I mean, what's your history together? You two seem to care about each other a lot."

I looked at him cockeyed for a moment, and then it occurred to me that they had never met before.

"You never met Jester, did you?"

He shook his head.

"I thought with you in the hospital that you both certainly would have met. But then again, I can see how if this is what he was doing the entire time, he had his hands full." I looked around the kitchen and smiled. He did a wonderful job. I got fresh veggies out of the fridge and began to chop them. I looked to Jake and saw dashed hopes in his eyes. "There is no 'Jester and I,' at least not in the carnal sense. We are best friends, always have been, always will be. We stopped talking for a long time because of—" what name shall we give it? "—semantics." I cleared my throat and tried to think of the normal way to put it. "We both belonged to a club that we got into during high school and became friends."

"No one's story is ever that clear cut."

"The shortened version, do you like it?"

"I *like* details."

"Details? Okay. What *kind* of details?"

"Who, what, where, when, and how are all really good starts."

Alright, Jester was going to love this backstory.

"Jester and *just* Jester moved here from New York twelve years ago. He happened to be a Hello Kitty enthusiast like myself. Although, I will admit that he is far more the fan than I am. There was a club for it in our school, and since he and I didn't fit what Hello Kitty fans should theoretically look like, we naturally bonded. He met my family, and we constantly just kept in contact. My mother even calls him her second son, but she secretly suspects he's gay."

"Why?"

"He doesn't date often, and frankly neither *did* I," I said, pushing lettuce aside.

"Don't date?"

"People confuse things too often. I just have a lot to do and little time to explain it." Oh, if that wasn't the understatement of the century. "I just like my life, and I am picky about who I let into it. Friends I am picky about; having a boyfriend I am even pickier about."

"Is that supposed to make me feel better?"

"I'm not dating Jester, but we are best friends." We sat in silence for a minute as I kept the words "deal with it" caught in my throat. "Why is this an issue with you?" I put down the knife and focused all my attention on him. "I feel like I'm on trial here."

"How do you expect me to act? He took care of everything in this house and hung it all, decorated it, arranged it, and what kind of person does that without having a motive?"

I shook my head.

"I'm sorry, but most men I have met don't work like this out of the kindness of their hearts."

"First off, he is like family. Secondly, it was with my mother and people who love me all joined together to make sure this was taken care of. Thirdly, it's a little early to be getting right to the 'you're cheating on me' speech, isn't it?"

He crossed his arms over his chest, and I knew I had won.

"I like you. I don't date. That just makes you special, *very* special."

He looked out the window.

"I'm not as easily won as most women. So give me a break, okay?"

"I'm sorry," he mumbled. "My last relationship didn't end well; she cheated on me with Daniel."

I stopped chopping and stared at him. It made more sense now. Nothing seemed more torturing than the betrayal of a friend. I felt bad, but in this I had to stand my ground.

THERE WILL BE BLOOD

"I forgave Daniel, but I haven't started seeing anyone for six years." Six years of celibacy, I'd die. "I don't want to get hurt again," he remarked weakly.

I put down my knife and grasped his hand.

"Please understand, Jester and I are best friends and nothing more."

Letting go of my hand, he moved behind me as I began to chop vegetables again. Somehow, I didn't think that this conversation was over. Jake's hands found their way to my shoulders and began to rub them. I couldn't deny how wonderful it felt. "This doesn't get you off the hook, you know."

"I didn't mean to upset you." He pushed my hair out of the way and started massaging my neck. "It's been quite an intense day, and you need to be pampered."

I felt lips graze the back of my neck. I had to push down the delicious shudder that was crawling through my body. It was becoming very difficult to be mad at him.

"Are you sure you don't want to order out?" His fingers grazed underneath my collar, mingling with the sweet tendrils of his hot breath. I was seconds from being like a cartoon wolf in an old Warner Bros. cartoon after seeing a hot chick. Somehow my eyes popping out of my sockets while howling didn't seem like a good idea for proving my sanity.

"I'm not an invalid, and cooking makes me feel better." He traced my ear with his tongue. "You're not being very fair."

"Yet I don't hear you asking me to stop."

I let my body relax into his, feeling his hand start exploring under my apron.

"Are you asking me to stop?" His lips began to explore my neck as I let a gasp escape my lips. Jake's teeth grazed my neck, adding an undeniable mix of pleasure and pain.

"I want to... so I can finish cooking." He bit in deeper. "But you are making it *very* difficult," I moaned.

I felt a tug at the apron, and with little effort, it came undone.

His hand started to explore my back as it ventured under my shirt. How much could a gal take? I stabbed the knife into the cutting board and whipped around, shoving him into the cupboard. I threw off the apron and jumped on him. My lips found his with a ravenous hunger. He lifted me up with little effort; I wrapped my legs around his hips. A heard a clearing of a throat distinctly behind me.

We froze with our eyes wide open. I didn't want to turn around and find my mother or—even worse—Jester. I started praying, *Please don't be my mother*. I untangled my legs and sank my feet back down to the floor. *If you are a kind God, please let that not be my mother*. I turned around to find a giggling Autumn and Daniel. At least it wasn't my mother.

"Excuse me!" I shouted, putting my hands on my hips. "Neither of you can tell me you never once thought of skipping dinner for dessert!"

They both let out a roaring laugh. I turned to see Jake's face as he started to glower from embarrassment as the laughter echoed through the house.

"You two done yet?" Autumn started flicking away tears while her counterpart decided to point and laugh at Jake.

"I brought a housewarming gift." Autumn snickered. "It's dessert."

I shook my head and started laughing alone with her.

"It's pie!" she roared.

"Well, I was just about to make some food. Are you two hungry?"

Daniel managed to squeak out a yes while still laughing at a now very pissed-off Jake, while the wise Autumn just nodded.

"Okay, guys, out of my kitchen!"

Autumn turned around to leave.

"Hello? I said *guys!*"

Jake stormed out with a still laughing Daniel trailing behind him. Jake looked so cute when he glowered.

"So, what's new?"

"Not much," she replied as she took a seat and set her purse down. "Need any help?"

I shook my head.

"I have word from our employer, and he wants to get you out on those streets."

I rolled my eyes.

"His words—not mine."

"Ah, did you get your legwork done?" I said, throwing noodles in the boiling pot of water. I stirred the sauce and spiced it. "I hope I wasn't off the clock for too long."

She reached into her purse and fetched an envelope. Judging by the size of the envelope, she had been a busy bee.

"Nope, I even made you copies *and* pictures to go with it! Ain't I grand?" she remarked gleefully as I gave another eye roll. "These are all the spiritual people who will be speaking at the event."

Picking up the tightly packed envelope, I was so proud of how confident Autumn had become. She glowed with a grace better saved for golden Hollywood. I opened the envelope, which gave way to a heavy mass of paper. I set the papers aside to stir my sauce, and they gave way to a landslide. I knelt down the floor to pick them up, and I noticed something.

Autumn joined me on the floor, she quickly started picking up the mess, but I stayed her hand. "What?"

I picked up a single photo and remembered my assignment.

"Who is this man?"

"Oh, him? He's Reiki master Tennorman."

I gulped my revulsion. *Great, an all-you-can-eat buffet.*

"He is considered one of the best in the country." She looked at me as if I had vomited in front of her. "He is only a recent practitioner but has moved up the ranks quickly, becoming the fourth most popular authority in the country. Okay, am I missing the punch line, or are you just making funny faces for kicks?"

I picked up the rest of the file quickly and put it on the empty counter.

"Trinity? Come on, I was only kidding."

I fished out Tennorman's photo and handed it to her.

"He's my target," I said bluntly. It was her turn to gulp.

She slipped the photo back to me with a lingering look.

"You're not going to..." She let the sentence float in the air as if she feared to say what I hoped I didn't have to do.

I shot her an assuring smile.

"If all goes to plan, no." I was hoping that this could be a quick job. I was hoping I'd be able to slip into his house and fit an iron bar underneath his skin. The iron bar, a newly developed technology, was an iron bar with an electromagnetic pulse disabler chip in it. Suckers rely on harvesting electromagnetic energy from the area around them to suck off of other people; with the chip inside them they were rendered defenseless. Suckers are what I like to call a twenty-first-century vampire, and if it were up to me, they would die in a twenty-first-century manner. "You got an address?"

Autumn stood and watched me as I continued to keep an eye on the food.

"I don't want to be a part of this."

"Autumn, please. I'm not going to kill him, but I have to disable him from hurting other people."

"How do you even know he is going to hurt someone?" She spoke quickly. "I mean, you don't know for sure, right? It could be a mistake, right?"

I let out a sigh. How did you tell some people that some bad guys are just bad guys?

"Seriously, he does a lot of charity, helps rape victims—"

That one I snorted at. Helped? I'm sure.

"Would you listen to me; he's not a bad guy."

Silence filled the air. I didn't like my job, but it was my job. I looked at her with aged eyes, I remembered saying the same thing once. I remembered having hope that people could change until I realized that they couldn't help it after they started.

"What?" she said, breaking the silence.

"Autumn, do you know what a vampire is?"

She cocked an eyebrow at me.

"I'm serious."

"You mean like Dracula, creatures of the night, *Twilight* kinda stuff?"

"Well, kinda."

I turned all the pots on low and listened carefully to the boys. I asked her to give me a second while I whisked beers off to the men and flicked on the sports channel, claiming I was going to be a while longer making dinner. The distractions of beer and sports would be their undoing, but for now my peace and quiet. I walked back into the kitchen and noticed that Autumn still looked confused. "So we agree that vampires take something, right?"

"Yes, but I'm still not following you."

"Don't worry, you will." I cleared my throat and tried to think of the best non-nutbag way to put this. "They exist."

Now it was her turn to snort. Alright, not my best sit-down explanation. "Vampires take things from people, like blood, yes?"

"Okay, yes."

"Now, there are some people out there who start to take others' energy."

"Energy?" She shifted in her chair uncomfortably. "You're not going to whip out some funky-smelling candles and crystals, are you?"

"Only to beat you to death with, my dear," I leered. She didn't find it so funny. "Oh, relax, would you?"

I leaned close to her. "It starts out with permission. They ask in one way or another. They can be in a relationship with a person, and this unfortunately gives permission. It can be sex, it can be a fistfight, or even emotional prodding to get a person to cry; it all depends on the, ah—" I rolled around what saying would be more appropriate "—vintage the person prefers, but none of these ever lasts too long. Eventually the boyfriend or girlfriend becomes too weak to continue the relationship; many of them are hospitalized. And instigating fights only lasts for so long, one-night stands only last so long, and eventually they start looking for people who are in their weakest states. These people don't give permission, but they are easily fed off of." I remembered my first love, my first experience, and unfortunately my first sucker. I shook the memory from my head and decided to continue, "The people who at first enjoy it become dependent on the sucker."

"What do you mean? Weakest?"

"People who have suffered abuse, addiction, suicidal tenden-cies... people who get in a downward spiral. They look for any branch that will help them up, *any way* to get them out. They are so thankful that they don't notice that the branch is a snake." I could see her eyes wander a moment while she took this all in. "An out is an out, no matter how awful."

"That doesn't explain how or why he would choose them," she said skeptically. "And what the hell do branches have to do with spirals? What about quicksand? Wouldn't that be easier? Like you would reach for a branch while you were sinking?"

"Look, I'm not changing my analogy, okay?" I gave an eye roll. "Besides, think about lions picking off the weakest of the herd—"

"Now, why didn't you use that analogy?"

"Focus!" I snapped my fingers. "Anyway, what I am trying to say is that it may look like he is trying to help people, but what he is really doing is securing his food and making them dependent on him. It is truly horrific. Autumn, sometimes your enemy is just the enemy. There is no way to justify hurting people or, worse, killing them in a slow and painful way."

She stared at me while chewing this over; I knew this wasn't the last time we would talk about this. Looking over at the pot of noodles, I decided it was time to serve dinner.

24

The dinner was an enjoyable normal function. Autumn, to her credit, pretended that the conversation had never happened. Daniel seemed so happy with the meal that he took leftovers. Autumn and I finished off the dishes while the men finished off another drink. I felt like I was in the middle of being in *Leave It to Beaver*, but as I watched my friends leave, maybe it wasn't so bad. Maybe this was what being normal was all about? Jake and I entertaining dinner guests in a comfortable mansion, maybe I could get used to this.

I opened all the windows and let the fresh air dance through the house. I looked around and tried to figure out what I wanted to do. I walked on to the porch that connected to the kitchen and breathed in the air. I was amazed; it wasn't a totally bad day. The night sky was clear and crisp. It danced to the tune of the bubbling hot tub. I heard footsteps behind me, and the wood of the door gave a small groan. I turned to see him leaning casually against the door with his arms folded over his chest.

"What?" I said, turning back to the sky. It felt like he wanted to say something but couldn't find the words.

"This is nice, quiet but nice." Jake started walking toward me.

"You know," he said, wrapping his arms around me, "we could be in New Venture by 3 a.m."

"What's in New Venture?" I felt his arms tighten.

"What *isn't* in New Venture? I could take you to the best opera houses, carriage rides, concerts. We could climb the tallest building and watch the sun rise." He placed a kiss on my neck. "Let's go somewhere, just you and me."

"Novel thought, but I have to work." I attempted to weasel out of his arms, but his grip tightened. I turned around to face him. "How fair would it be to Autumn if I just up and left?" He brought his lips an inch away from mine. "You're making this very difficult and *very* tempting."

"Come with me; let's travel the world. Experience it together." He grazed my lips like a soft breeze. "Let's be together off somewhere exotic."

I broke off in a bitter laugh. How did I explain?

"Exotic!? New Venture? It's filled with pretentious tofu-eating yuppies who dress like hobo roadkill."

"But—"

"Not to mention it smells like urine downtown—"

"But—"

"And a lot of transvestites—"

"But—"

"Not that I have a problem with transvestites. Their beautiful clothing is a distraction, not to mention they have better legs than I do—"

"But I love you."

Gulp. I stared into his eyes to see if he was serious, and by the looks of it, he was dead serious. His eyes looked so clear and deep that I could dive into them. I could dive so deep that I could never find the bottom. My breath was caught in my chest. I didn't want to get hurt again, but I really wanted to be with him. I didn't know what it was about him, but I wanted to melt into him and never leave.

A strange look came over his face. "Ah, Trinity?" he said, sounding oddly concerned, "You're not breathing."

"Sorry, I have garlic breath. Excuse me." I twisted out of his arms and marched back in the house. God, give me one moment, I prayed. I popped a mint in my mouth and found Jake fast on my heels. "Hey, how about some wine?"

He shrugged his shoulders.

I found a bottle of my favorite wine and pulled the cork. I poured the glass and suggested we adjourn to the living room, where the fireplace was warm and toasty. I brought the bottle and tried to think of something—anything to say but *I want to be with you forever.* Maybe it was the pills. Maybe it was the only person aside from Damon who had ever flipped my switch like this. Maybe it was because he made me all fuzzy on the inside. I kicked off my shoes and plopped down on the leather couch. Jake kept twisting the glass in his hand as he watched me on the couch.

"I never really said that before," he blurted out. "I mean, uh." He coughed a moment and rubbed the back of his neck. "I've said it, but I never thought I meant it before I met you." He shifted his feet. "I mean, um, you know I'm not very good at this and, um, I don't really know what to say. I just want to say something suave, but I—"

I put down my glass and decided to throw caution to the wind. I rose to my feet and walked toward him. I took the glass out of his hand and set it down on the nearest table.

"I want to—"

I wrapped my arms around his neck and shut him up with a soft kiss. The second our lips touched, I felt an electric current zing through my body. I took my lips away from his.

"I want to be with you forever."

I looked into his eyes and took a deep breath.

"Because I love you."

Jake's lips crushed against mine with a delightful pain. I felt unfamiliar hunger wash over me, and I jumped on him as his hands explored my body. My hands fumbled with his shirt. His hands kneaded the back of my shirt, feeling up toward my hair. Upon finding it, he pulled forcefully back, exposing my neck to his hungry lips. His hands filtered through my hair, finding the collar of my shirt, and with a loud rip, my back was exposed. He groaned as he found my naked skin hot to the touch. We kept tugging on each other's clothing, attempting to shrug them free. I stumbled on the floor in front of the fireplace, attempting to free myself of my cumbersome pants.

As I was enduring my fight, Jake stripped quickly and was on top of me. "Allow me to help you with your problem," he said as he smiled widely. With remarkable ease, he ripped off my pants and underwear.

"Wow, that's a talent," I whispered breathlessly. His lips found mine again as he slid inside me. I wrapped my legs around him and enjoyed the moment. My hands explored his back hungrily, leaving small scratches in their wake. With each thrust, I felt the climax build. I felt like I was melting. His lips left mine, and he looked into my eyes.

"Marry me," he whispered. A wave of pleasure threatened to wash us away, and before I could even think the thought, it did.

"Yes, yes! Oh god, yes!"

25

I awoke the next morning to the smell of pancakes and coffee. My legs were twisted in the white covers, and I ached. I saw the sun filtering through the curtains and remembered last night. All three times of last night to be exact, but then again, who was counting. I felt through the bedsheets for Jake and realized he wasn't there. I sat up and realized the smell of coffee had to have been made by someone. I stretched out on the bed as I lay back down. I took a deep breath in and remembered Jake's timely proposal. I wondered if he meant it. I mean, some people say some crazy stuff during sex. My ex before Damon once called me his aunt Sally during our hot and heavy. I let out a small giggle at the memory. The look on his face was classic.

Regardless of whether he meant it or not, I was on cloud nine. I was now officially under the impression that no woman has lived unless she has had sex with a musician. I sat up and tossed my legs over the side of the bed. I wrapped the sheet around me as I stood up only to find out that my legs weren't working. My face met the floor with a very noisy THUNK. I groaned as heavy footsteps ran up the stairs. Jake's face peered across the room. "I'm okay, really," I mumbled, propping myself up on my arms. "I meant to do this, like all the celebs are doing it." I raised my right hand with a pointed finger. "It's called face floor yoga."

He started laughing as I crawled back to the bed.

I threw a pillow at him. "I can't walk, damn it!"

He picked me up and set me on the bed.

"Well, I'm sure we can find a way to get the feeling back in your legs," he remarked as he kissed me. "I *was* attempting to surprise you with breakfast in bed, but since you decided to exercise your face floor yoga, would you care to join me for breakfast?"

I rolled the thought around in my head for a moment and thought that maybe a shower would be best at the moment.

"I really want a shower."

A smile spread across his face as he leaned in for another kiss.

"I think we should wait until I get the feeling back into my legs, don't you?"

His bottom lip protruded, and he started to pout.

"That wasn't a no, it was a not right now."

He got off the bed and sighed.

"We aren't even married, and you are already denying me sex!" he said theatrically with his hand to his forehead. "Oh, woe is me."

I threw a pillow at him as he laughed out the door. I stumbled toward the bathroom with my gooey-feeling legs. Flashes of last night flew through my mind. I couldn't help but feel that everything was moving so quickly. I felt good. Actually, I felt great. I was loved by a man who wasn't rejecting me, and I was falling for him. Then it occurred to me, had I agreed to marry him? No. Wait, marriage, me? Never. I guessed I would wait for him to brooch the subject.

Finally making it to the bathroom, I took one look at the shower and decided to opt for a bath. I filled up the tub and crawled into the juicy goodness. I added some of my favorite bubble bath of lavender vanilla. Jester was going to be on my good side for a long time, which for him would add up to a whole five minutes. I grabbed my washrag. I wiggled my toes and enjoyed the warmth of the bath. I heard Jake's careful footsteps traveling up the stairs. I dunked under the water, enjoying the silence that only water could offer. I rose above the water to see Jake leaning against the door.

"Swimming?"

I giggled and sprayed water at him.

"Of course. What time is it?"

"Some time after eleven." He walked over to me and kneeled until he was facing me.

I yawned loudly and stretched.

"How long have you been up?"

"Quite a while."

"By quite a while, you mean?"

He just smiled that poster-boy smile.

"Would you like me to wash your back?"

I smiled and handed him the rag.

"You'd better be careful," I remarked, feeling the gentle caress of his hands.

"Oh?"

"I might get used to this."

"I hope so." He laughed. He quickly stripped out of his clothing and joined me in the bathtub. I made room for him as he wrapped his arms around me. "I have some bad news."

I had a sense of dread in my gut.

"I'm sorry, but Dan needs me back on the biz. So I will be leaving soon."

I sighed. Granted, it wasn't as bad as I thought it would be, but still it sucked.

"Bummer, when will I see you again?" I knew this had to end sometime, but at least it was great sex. I felt him shift, and he wrapped his arms around me. His hands found mine and entwined his fingers in mine.

"Don't worry," he said as he pulled me closer. "I'll see you sooner than you think." He placed a kiss on the back of my neck.

I smiled and closed my eyes. I felt a tugging on my left hand and then the feeling of cold metal. My eyes flickered open to see a ring on my finger. I let a gasp slip out of my mouth as I looked down at a large square diamond surrounded by smaller diamonds. I stayed silent, looking at the ring on my finger.

"Don't you like it?" This was no heated-moment-of-passion delusion. This was the real deal.

"Golly," I remarked.

He started to laugh.

"So... I mean, um." I found myself encased in a case of the stupids. I felt rumbling laughter in his chest. It felt like a wonderful wave flickering through my soul.

"Yes, Trinity. I want you for my wife."

I smiled and felt like my happily ever after had arrived.

"Just say yes again."

"Yes."

He tightened his arms around me.

"Definitely yes."

He kissed my neck again and slid out of the bathtub and grabbed a towel.

"Where are you going?"

"Breakfast of course," he said, tightening the towel around his waist. "Or did you forget about that?" he said with a grin.

"Then why come up here in the first place?"

"I had to make sure that last night's proposal wasn't a pleasure-induced hallucination."

I laughed as he disappeared down the stairs. I sank into the tub, daring not to look at my ring that graced my finger. I lifted my hand out of the steaming water. No one had ever given me a diamond let alone told me that they wanted to spend the rest of their life with me. Was this really happening? In such a short amount of time? I poured shampoo on my scalp and gave it a quick scrub before dunking back into the water.

I smelt pancakes and thought I was in heaven. I stood up in the bathtub and felt good about the feeling back in my legs. I pulled the plug and grabbed a towel. Was it so bad that I finally got a chance to fall in love? I wondered what our lives would be like. I flipped my hair in the towel and walked to my bedroom. Opening up my closet, I discovered a whole range of traditional black and white clothing with matching shoes. I picked out a white dress shirt, black vest, black tie and black slacks. I threw them on the bed. I looked down at the ring he'd put on my finger. What would the world be like if I lived normally? Did I have to keep doing this forever? Maybe I should quit and live out my days with Jake.

I threw on my clothing and walked back to the bathroom to put on some makeup. Maybe I should really quit. I had a life of my own too. Maybe I could stick around and write or travel. I finished up my makeup and started to head down the stairs to the kitchen. Jake stood over the stove top with slightly messed-up hair and flipped another pancake.

"Those smell amazing," I remarked.

His face looked at me and smiled.

"Not as good as you."

"Flattery will get you everywhere." I saw the file on the counter, picked it up, and started going through it.

"I wanted to ask you last night, what is the file about?"

"For the assignment, I wanted to know about my subject. Get into his head." I grimaced. "Helps for better shots." I rubbed my shoulders as I felt a chill come over me.

"You don't seem very happy about this."

"That obvious?"

"Yeah, it is." He looked at me intently.

"I think he is a manipulator. I think he takes advantage of the people who come to him for help. I can't stand people like that."

"Some people are like that," he remarked.

"There is something wrong with melding the weak to one's will. But I think this is the last time I will do this."

His eyebrow rose in question to me.

"I think I might just shoot some pictures and leave it at that."

Jake flipped another pancake.

"Whatever you want to do, it's your choice. I'll stand behind you regardless."

I smiled.

"You're right, you know."

He shrugged and smiled. He had a wonderful smile. It lit up the room like stage lights.

The phone rang and snapped me out of my trance. "Hello?"

"Hey, girlie! It's me," chirped the happy voice of Autumn.

"What's going on?"

"Not much, I got a call from Tennorman's office and Mr. Tennorman wants to meet us in his office."

"Oh, that was quick."

"No kidding." She laughed. "Did you get the chance to read over the file?"

"Yeah, it was very informative. So when is the appointment and where?"

"Four o'clock at the Bennington building."

I looked at the clock: 12:15 p.m.

"Bring your equipment."

"One thing I have to ask you," I said with apprehension. "Don't go in without me."

"Yeah, yeah, I know," she said, brushing away my fears.

"No, Autumn. Listen to me carefully."

Jake stopped what he was doing and listened to me intently.

"Do not, under *any* circumstances, go in without me. It is dangerous. He is not what he seems and is dangerous."

"Okay! Yeesh! Relax, girlie! I won't go in."

"I mean it." I sighed. "Please give me your word that you will not go in without me."

"I won't, I promise," Autumn said with a moody tone. "So I'll see you there?"

"Without a doubt. And I have something to show you when we meet up." I looked down at the ring. "You're not going to believe it."

"Okay! I'll see you soon." Autumn hung up with a click. Even her hang up sounded happy-go-lucky.

"Is there something you need to tell me?" Jake asked as he poured some batter on the skillet.

"I wouldn't know where to start."

His lip twitched.

"It's a long, long, very long story that I promise to tell you after this assignment is done."

He looked at me with a thinking look.

"Neither of us have time to listen to my sob story, do we?"

"Okay," he said reluctantly as he pointed the spatula at me. "But you are not off the hook."

"I know. But let's enjoy the time we have together."

He smiled and nodded.

"I want to spend as much time with you as I can. After this tour is done with, you won't be able to get rid of me." He flipped the last pancake and shut off the burner.

"I look forward to that problem."

"I hope you're hungry."

"After last night, I'm starving."

❧ 26 ❧

I sat in a chair with my foot tapping against it. I didn't like it; I didn't like it at all. My eyes flickered to the door that sat across from me, guarded by the vulture-like secretary. She reminded me of the woman from *American Gothic* who just hopped out of hell. The office was a rich red trimmed with gold that only made me angrier. She was even wearing a red suit. I didn't see red, no. I saw blood. The blood of his victims painted the walls of his empire. He had the top floor in this building, and I started to think about the exits. I started to shake my leg harder. Autumn was with him, alone. I looked down at my watch to see that it was 3:45 p.m. I had even come early. The room was beginning to bother me.

I looked down at my camera bag; I should be in there right now. It wasn't safe. There was a gold plate on the door that read *Frank Tennorman*. I couldn't take it anymore. I rose out of my seat with my camera bag. "Excuse me, miss?"

The secretary's silver-framed glasses slid to the end of her long nose as she narrowed her black eyes at me. I gave her a half smile. "I—sorry to bother you, but I was wondering if I could join my counterpart yet."

She scoffed under her breath.

"He said no visitors and no interruptions when he was being interviewed." She pushed her glasses up her nose. "And that means you will have to wait while he is doing God's work."

I gulped.

"I'm sorry, we are supposed to be interviewing him for the upcoming events. What does that have to do with 'God's work'?" I heard her stifle a laugh.

"That's what's wrong with *your* generation, you can't be healed." She turned her attention to her computer.

I wanted to pull the smug right off of her. "But Autumn's soul isn't interested in bein' healed." I gulped. *Please tell me this is a lie. Autumn, tell me you're not going to fall for it. Okay, calm down, Trinity. Think logically. How do you get her out of this?*

"You know, it's great you guys are all, like, spiritual and stuff." Yep, that always irritates fanatics. I loved playing dumb. "But Autumn can *totally* get fired if she is, like, getting any raking done while she is on the clock."

"It's Reiki," the woman muttered with disgust.

I gave her a vacant look while I nodded my head. Her thin lips twisted into a contemptuous smile.

"If she wants to do it on her own time, that is totally cool, but I just don't want her to get in trouble."

"Well, that's her problem," she muttered, paying no more attention to me.

Fine, I tried to be nice. I went to the chair and sat down calmly. I flipped open my phone and sent a text message to Jester.

"J-man, I need a favor." I only had to wait a moment before I got a response.

"Hello, oh mostly injured one! Aren't you blunt this afternoon? Whatever could you need, considering you are SUPPOSED to be home and resting?"

I rolled my eyes. I wasn't in the mood for this.

"You knew I couldn't just stay home! I'm on assignment, and Autumn is in trouble."

"Now why didn't you say that in the first place? Need I mention to you that you are not supposed to BE on assignment until Damon is caught? Going up against a sucker when you are still weak is dangerous, and you should know better!"

"Are you done with the lecture yet?"

"Until I see you tonight, sure. So what is the emergency that shouldn't be happening right now?"

"Somehow, Autumn is being 'healed' by the sucker, and I can't get in the office without causing a scene. Long story short —HELP!"

"Alright, I'm on it."

"Already? Damn, that was fast. Where are you?"

"The seventh floor."

"What the hell are you doing on the seventh floor?"

"When the doctor told you to rest, you didn't actually believe that *I* thought you would, did you?"

I could almost hear his mocking laughter from here. At least he was consistent. He was like a rogue guardian angel who had the habit of driving me nuts.

"Alright, smarty pants; do you know what's going on?"

"I attempted to stop her from going into the building, but the target had spotted her and asked her to enter the building."

"Crap! She's in there with him alone, and he is 'healing' her! I don't care what you come up with, just do it."

A moment later, alarms sounded, and water started to pour down on my head. The secretary let out a shrill and annoyed scream that brought a smile to my face. Autumn came rushing out the mahogany doors that led to Frank's office. I picked up my camera bag as water beaded on the vinyl, thankful for springing the extra cash for waterproofing.

"Where the heck have you been?" Autumn said accusingly. "I

have been waiting over an hour for you!" Her face was flushed and her eyes glazed over.

I looked over at the vulture lady and grinned.

"Blame Whistler's mother. She said that her boss demanded not to be interrupted."

Autumn rolled her eyes in an uncharacteristically snotty way and stormed past me. She flipped her hair and kept walking. A large man with short wavy hair wearing a black pinstripe Armani suit walked with a long stride. He watched his well-finished meal stride out to the beat of the alarm. He didn't seem to notice the water beading on his expensive suit. The tail end of a grin flickered on the end of his mouth as his black eyes traveled to meet mine. I let all expression drain out of my face.

As his eyes flickered to me, I knew he was already thinking about dessert. He reached his hand out and with a ravishing soap-star smile said, "Ah, you must be Trinity."

I looked at his hand.

"I'd shake your hand, but I think we need to get out of the building. You know, fire and all."

His eyes narrowed slightly, and then he walked out of the building with this secretary quickly on his heels. I was going to thank Jester after I was done taking care of this situation.

The fire trucks had pulled up with men piling out of them as I made my way outside. The sky was clear and sparkling with the magic only an afternoon could offer. I approached Autumn, who was covered in a business jacket. Always keep your food safe, right? Her eyes glistened with childlike admiration as Frank spoke to her. I wondered if I should even go over and talk. In all honesty, I didn't even want to be here right now. I wanted to be home with Jake. As I walked over to them, I saw Jester in a plumber's outfit in front of them. He winked at me, and I gave him a nod in acknowledgment. I pushed past him to get to Autumn. A small, wet crinkled piece of paper made its way into my hand. I pretended not to notice.

"I'm glad to see that everyone made it out okay." I smiled. "Anyone know what happened?"

Whistler's mother's mouth twitched slightly. "They suspect it came from the cafeteria on the fourth floor, but then again they say they have found several fires."

I turned to Autumn, who was shivering in the warm afternoon sun. Whistler's mother started to storm off in fury, and Frank turned to follow her.

"Are you okay?"

"Fine," she said with a cruel edge to her voice.

"Good," I said, mimicking her tone. "Because I don't want to be bothered to ask again."

She looked at me as if I had hit her.

"Don't like a taste of your own medicine, do you?"

"What's that supposed to mean?" she said, placing her hand on her hip.

"You're not being very nice right now," I pointed out as I swallowed the remnants of my anger. *Temper, temper, Trin.* I started to examine the polish on my nails.

"So?" Autumn remarked, flipping her hair. "You were late!"

I calmly lowered my hand, and whatever look was on my face made her take a step back. So much for keeping my temper in check.

"Don't you dare pull that shit with me, you said four, remember?" I hissed sharply through my teeth. "Are you fucking deaf? Did I not tell you not to go in alone? Did I not tell you it's dangerous? You have no right to be pissed at me."

The color drained out of her face, and she looked down at her feet. Every essence of the Autumn who was in Frank's office leaked out of her face, and the old Autumn returned.

"I don't know why I—"

I forcefully grabbed her chin so her eyes met mine, and I let the fury in my eyes fill her.

"No. Fucking. Shit." I let her go because I didn't want to see the tears stream down her face. "Did you start the interview without me?" I turned my attention back to my nails.

"Yes."

My eyes flickered to her with a raised eyebrow.

"I mean no. I don't know. Kinda."

I turned back to my nails.

"Either you did or you didn't. Which is it?"

"He wanted to show me what he did, and, well, it wasn't bad. I feel great."

"Yeah, you do *now*, but wait until later." I knew she was trying to make me feel better, but I had seen this before and knew the horrors that could happen. "We need to focus on our job."

Frank sauntered back over to us and clapped his hands loudly.

"So," he said, happily amused, "I would love to continue this interview, and since our lovely photographer has joined us, I would love to entertain you at my penthouse."

Autumn smiled widely and nodded. I gave a small nod.

Frank led the way to his lavish apartment. It was across the street from his business building. As we ventured up the elevator, I noticed a pattern emerging. It was gold and red much like the décor in his office. Black mirrors were used as decorative pieces, and it made it look as if the hallway would go on forever. I stared forward into the black mirror only to see Frank studying me with a strange look on his face. He was sizing me up and for what, I didn't understand.

"So what did I miss?" I asked as a general question.

He broke his stare and set his eyes on Autumn.

"Oh, you missed a lot," Autumn began. Her words went in one ear and out the other as I watched Frank watch Autumn like a wolf watches their meal. I couldn't risk revealing myself as I felt him tasting her energy. Then it came to me. I took my camera out of my bag.

"Hey, Autumn! I got some awesome shots of the churches I want you to look at!"

She smiled and moved closer to me.

I shut off the screen. "Oh dear, let me look at it in a different light." I moved between her and Frank and blocked the connection. "Ah, much better. Can you see it okay?"

She nodded and leafed through the photos. I caught a glimpse of Frank out of the corner of my eye, and he didn't look happy. The elevator opened, and I felt like I was able to breathe again. I stuffed my camera in my bag as Frank stepped out first. Autumn and I stayed a little behind to follow him. His apartment was at the end of a long black mirrored hall. Giant doors of solid wood stood gallantly at the end of the hall. Frank paused to open them. There was no sound other than our breathing.

A large rush of air burst forth as he opened the doors. We stepped into the vaulted ceiling entryway that held statues of Roman women. The room looked like one out of a temple in Rome. Red marble lined the walls. Lamps that looked like torches lit the room. "Welcome to my home." We entered his round living room, and we took our spots on one of the two couches in the room.

"You have a very lovely home," I said politely.

He smiled brightly.

I looked around his living room to see visages of a beautiful woman draped in red and green silk. A snake was wrapped around her body. Her eyes were sad and downcast as she proudly held the snake. "I really like your statues."

"I glad you appreciate them." He snapped his fingers loudly, and his secretary appeared with drinks and small sandwiches. "They are images, or at least presumed images, of Lilith." I took out my camera and started taking a few shots. "She was the first wife of Adam, or at least that is what Jewish folklore claims."

"I'm afraid I'm not familiar with it."

"According to the lore, Lilith was the first woman out of three that he created for Adam."

I looked to Autumn quickly. She looked as if under a spell. He gave his undivided attention to me, and I felt uncomfortable with his attention, but I dared not show him.

"One day Lilith and Adam got into a dispute."

"What was the dispute over?"

"Who got to be on top during intercourse."

I giggled at that.

"Seriously?" I questioned him.

"Yes, most certainly," he said with a twitch of his mouth. "Adam refused to give in, and Lilith left. Shortly after, Adam asked the angels to convince her to come back and be subservient."

"I'm guessing that didn't go over well."

His eyebrow rose slightly.

"What makes you say that?"

"Because according to the Bible, it was Adam and Eve who got kicked out of paradise not Lilith and Adam."

"You make a very good point," he said, pausing. "She refused to comply to subservience and was cast out among the demons."

"That must have hurt greatly."

"She made the best of it," he remarked half-heartedly.

"Oh?"

"She became the most feared creature in the world."

We sat in awkward silence for a second as I chewed on the thought. Autumn broke the silence with more questions for the interview. His eyes never left my face as he spouted each answer. I started shooting pictures and felt haunted by his eyes.

The interview fluttered by quickly, and I couldn't wait to leave. Autumn barely said a few words to me, but then again I was more set on leaving. As soon as we were out of the building, I took a huge deep breath. The sun shone brightly, and I felt the warmth fill me.

"So what was that all about?" she remarked bitterly.

"What was what all about?"

"He was staring at you. He wanted you."

"I don't know. I wanted to leave as soon as we got in there."

"So," she said and crossed her arms, "you don't want me to spend time with him because you want him. Is that it?" Her eyes narrowed, and she glanced at me sideways.

"What?" I said, returning her suspicious gaze. "What are you talking about?"

"He—"

"He is a fricking sucker I couldn't care less about. Can we go now?"

"No, it was more than—"

"No," I said, cutting her off again. "It's the addiction doing this."

"What addiction?" she spat bitterly.

"The one I warned you about, remember?"

"Listen, I don't need this crap. I'll talk to you later." With that, she harshly walked away.

I stared after her. I looked down at my feet, shuffling them uncomfortably. I reached my hand in my pocket and felt for the piece of paper Jester had shoved in my hand. I pulled it out and unfolded it as it crinkled. As I read the words, my world stopped. Damon had been caught.

🕷 27 🕸

I arrived home in time to see the one and only Jester waiting for me on my stairs. He had a wide smile on his face. I ran up to him and gave him a huge hug. "Is it true? They caught Damon?"

"You'd better believe it," he said, letting out a deep breath.

"When did you find out? Did he say why he did it?"

He stepped back from me and looked at my face. "I have one better for you, if you are ready for it?" He grabbed my hand and took me into the living room. "Sit down, please."

"You are beginning to scare me. What is it?" I felt a deep pit of cold form in my stomach. That cold that tells you something bad is just around the corner. I sat down reluctantly and watched Jester tower over me.

"I could get fired for this, or worse."

"Okay, you are still not telling me anything. They caught him and are going to try him, right?"

He walked over to the flat-screen to the Blu-ray player.

"When they brought Damon in, they didn't tell me anything other than he was caught. They didn't talk about a trial or anything." He paused and reflected. "I got suspicious. As you know, they are all about paperwork and documentation."

"What organization isn't?"

He looked at me with a half smile on his face.

"Very true as always, Trin." He cleared his throat. "I naturally started searching for answers. When there was no paperwork, not even processing papers, I started hacking through the files."

"That *is* dangerous."

"I did find something, and I took a copy." He fished a disc out of his pocket and put it in the player. "I watched it, and I think it has some information that you need to hear." He had a very sober look on his face as he said this. When Jester got serious, it was time to start worrying.

"You're beginning to scare me," I said, trying to swallow the lump of panic crawling up my throat.

"Watch this, and we'll talk afterward."

He pressed play and took his seat beside me, fixing his eyes on the television. I looked at the scene unfolding in front of me. It was a typical interrogation room. Gray room with matching table and chair, single hanging light and Damon staring down the camera. I flinched at the sight of him. His eyes were the color of coal.

"*State your name and rank for the camera, please,*" said a deep gravelly voice behind the camera.

"Damon Slate, fifth-tier Reaper of HALO."

"*State your offenses for the camera.*"

"I am accused of the attempted murder of my mate, Trinity Smith. I am also accused of thieving classified documents and other information pertaining to my mate."

"*She is no longer your mate, Damon.*"

"She'll always be mine."

"*Why is that? If she is your mate, why attack her?*"

"I didn't mean to attack her. She started dating another person, and I lost my temper."

"*You put her in intensive care and in a coma.*"

"It was an accident; I didn't mean to hurt her." Damon shifted uncomfortably in his seat. "I just wanted to talk to her." He attempted to defend himself.

"*Agent Jester informed us that you were no longer interested in her and became engaged to a straight. Is this correct?*"

"Yes, I mean no." He ran his hand through his hair. "It's complicated."

"*Why not tell us why it is complicated?*"

"I don't have to do shit." He spat bitterly at the narrator.

"*You forget, this is HALO law you are going up against. We have enough evidence to put you away right now. We will shove you in a dark hole and NEVER let you out. There is no one on your side after what you did,*" reminded the voice condescendingly. "*What we want to know is where the file went and why you did what you did. If you don't want to tell us, fine. You'll never see the light of day again.*"

Damon crossed his arms over his chest and stared at the person behind the camera.

"As you are aware, I was trying to go into retirement, and I was finally able to get the cushion to do so. I wanted to be normal. So I picked out the perfect girlfriend, and I was going to live a normal life."

"*Where did you get the cushion?*"

"I was offered a substantial amount of money to get information on my mate for surveillance purposes."

"*Who offered you the money?*"

"They never gave their name; I only spoke with a female representative."

"*A representative of what?*"

"A representative of HORD."

"*Are you aware of what HORD is, Mr. Slate?*"

"No." Damon analyzed the look on the person behind the camera. He shifted uncomfortably, and he looked like someone was going to get eaten.

"When did you receive these funds?"

"Last week, before my last meeting with her. They finally had all the information they needed on her, and my services were no longer required."

"What were the services?"

"To find out any and all information on her and her family. But mainly her." He coughed slightly and readjusted his chair. "They seemed very interested in her personal habits. Where and when she sleeps, her clothing sizes, personal thoughts, where she likes to go on her time off, passions. It got really weird toward the end."

"What do you mean weird?"

"Her favorite things, like songs and stuff. What she ate day by day, how many hours she was sleeping, how she wore her hair that day, hairdresser's name. Video of what she does when she was alone. Really personal details."

"You were paid for surveillance?"

"Yes and no."

"What do you mean no?"

"I was given a bonus for my last task."

"What was the last task? How much money were you given?"

"You're not going to believe me what the task was for a five-million-dollar bonus."

I mouthed, "Holy shit." That was a lot of money.

"Just answer the question, Mr. Slate."

"To leave her alone, don't talk to her, don't see her, don't date her, and most importantly never be her mate again."

"You agreed to this?"

"Five fucking million to never see her again. I could have everything I ever wanted if I just backed out of her life."

"Then why didn't you stay away?"

"I saw this magazine, and I lost it. It could have been anyone in the entire world but *HIM*."

"To whom are you referring?"

"That bastard Jake." His lips pressed into a thin white line. "Why him? It could have been anyone else but him."

"*You left her. Why do you care?*"

"You and Jester talk often?" he said with a sneer. I heard Jester muffle a chuckle. "I never thought I cared about her. She was always there, so whatever," he said with a shrug. "I never dealt with being a Reaper well, and she reminded me too much of my place. Even with that, I still loved her. She was perfect for me and only me." His eyes turned black again. "Not Fortinbras, never for him."

My eyes flickered to Jester. His eyes grew dark with concern.

"*What is your issue with Jake Fortinbras?*"

"You know the answer to that question; it's in my file."

File? What file? There were files on us? I took a deep breath and filtered it all in.

"*Fair enough. Why hurt her? She didn't know.*"

"Like I said, I lost my temper. I smelt him on her." He rolled back his eyes, remembering something. "She smells like sunshine, delicious free sunshine. When I smelt that dirt bag mixed with my sunshine, I needed to know why and—" he shook his head free of the thought. "I love her; I guess I didn't know until she was gone."

I felt an ache in my chest. *It's too late,* I wanted to say to him.

"*Then why sell her out? According to our records, she was always good to you. Never said a single word of complaint when you dated other people. Or even when you left her alone on assignment.*"

"I figured since I wanted my own life, on my own terms, when an opportunity to get a shit ton of cash for just letting her leave me without a fight, I took it."

"*How did you know she was going to leave you?*"

Damon had a huge smile on his face.

"It was in her journal."

In all the confusion, I had forgotten about my journal. I didn't misplace it; he took it.

He smiled contently at the camera.

"Why are you smiling, Mr. Slate?"

"None of this matters."

"None of what matters?"

"This. All of this. I'll get my standing back, I'll be found innocent, I'll get Trinity back, and she'll be mine." Damon straightened his clothing and picked off an invisible piece of fluff. "Then I think while I'm at it, I will kill Jake." He folded his hands in front of him and stared at the camera with his black eyes. I felt as if he knew that I would be watching. He seemed so sure of himself.

The tape went black, and we sat in silence. I sat still, trying to take it all in. I wasn't sure what I was more concerned about, Damon, Damon escaping, or Jake dying. I sat back on my couch and tried to clear my head. I had a lot of questions, but the answers wouldn't come easy.

"Trinity, talk to me," Jester said in a sober tone.

"What do I say to this?"

"How much do you know about the organization we work for?" he said, leaning to face me. "I mean seriously?"

"I never really thought to question it, you know? We are the good guys; we stop the bad guys. We all have been chosen from prior members' offspring."

"Noted. Have you ever heard of HORD?"

"Never."

"I didn't think so. I have worked for HALO for almost ten years as a seventh-tier Reaper, and I have never heard of HORD. This worries me. Who are they, and why did they want information on you?"

"No clue." I took a deep breath. "We have to find out what HORD is. That is not the only thing that bothers me."

"I think I know what you are thinking."

"What do Jake and Damon have in common?"

"Exactly." He shifted slightly on the couch. "Something about this bothers me. When Damon was brought in, there was no evidence. It all poofed. Why? No one is talking. Why?"

"I think I am going to stop. I'm done with all this shit."

He shook his head.

"What are you talking about?"

"When it comes down to it, I want Jake. I want a normal life." If there was one thing I could always do, it was be honest with Jester. "I mean it. Where am I going with this? What is my future? Am I doing anything?"

"We've saved hundreds of lives." He grabbed my hand. "Don't have any regrets for what we've done. It's all been for the better. Why are you saying this?"

"Jake proposed to me, and I accepted."

His face melted into a blank look.

"I started to think about the future, and maybe I want a happily ever after."

"Do you even know this person?" Jester said with blackened eyes. "You guys just met; how are you even going to explain who or rather what you are?"

I looked away from him and took my hand out of his.

"Sorry to be the voice of reality here! But seriously, and the past with Damon?"

"I love him, okay? I don't know why, I don't know how, I just know he makes me happy. Why is it so wrong for someone to love me for me?"

"Trinity, think about it. Please," Jester said painfully. "I know you are in love, I'm happy for you, but after watching this video... how do we know who he is?"

My cell phone rang. Upon seeing it was Jake, I ignored the call.

"Please think this over."

"I deserve love too. Why should I have to sit around and wait for someone to come to their senses and maybe just maybe love me? Jake doesn't make me feel like any less of a person. He wraps his arms around me and I feel safe. I look at him, and I don't want to stop touching him." The phone rang again, and I ignored it.

"Why not wait? Just put it off or give it a long engagement until you know."

"We haven't even thought it out that far. I'm not ready to pronounce him guilty without a fair trial." I stood up and stepped in front of him. "Sure, I just met him, but there is something about him that I love more than anything I have ever felt before. Maybe it is his strength or his smile, but I love this man, and I am not letting him go easily."

His eyes met mine.

"I need to meet him." He ran his fingers through his hair. "If you feel this way, who am I to stand in the way? But let me do more background on Damon and find out what the past is."

I nodded. Whether I liked it or not, he had a point.

"How about you and I have some coffee?" he said as he got up from the couch.

"Sounds delightful." I followed him to the kitchen.

He knew where everything was, so I just started to open up all the windows, letting the fresh air in. I wanted to be out in the fresh air, so I stepped out on the porch. I leaned against the banister, looking down at the beach area that I hadn't noticed yesterday and smiled. I smelt fresh hazelnut coffee brewing. I was hoping that I could wrap myself up in the smell. But even more I wished that Jake were here to wrap me up in his warmth where I could live forever. I closed my eyes and felt the fresh air blow through my hair.

"Have you gotten any rest? And not that eight-hours-of-sleep crap, I mean real sleep," Jester said, bringing me a cup of coffee.

"Not really," I admitted as I took a sip. "I got caught up in, ugh, stuff."

He raised an eyebrow.

"Stuff? Riiiight." He giggled. "More like my girl got some action."

I shrugged easily.

"Hey, doctor recommended it." I heard my phone go off again.

"You'd better answer that."

"Hi," I answered.

"Are you okay?" Jake said quickly between the noises in the background. I heard many people talking loudly and glasses clinking together.

"Yeah, would you believe tough day at the office?" Dear god, not even I believed myself.

"Yes, I guess I would." He paused for a moment. "Why did you ignore my calls?"

Crap, I should have ignored this call too. I took a second and thought, *What wouldn't be considered lying?*

"I was in the middle of a heated discussion that I had to win."

Jester gave me a twisted face.

"I won, and that's what is important."

"I'm glad to hear that. I was calling to tell you I missed you."

"I miss you too. When are you going to be able to see me again?"

"Well, we aren't really sure yet; might be upwards of three weeks. We aren't really certain yet. Um, I was thinking..." There was another influx of noise.

"Yes? Are you in the middle of something?"

"No." He coughed. "Okay, yes, but it concerns you."

"What? Concerns me how?"

"I told my bandmates, and they are celebrating." He laughed. "I was thinking about it, and we should probably sit down and plan or something."

"We just got engaged last night. We don't have to have a date set, do we?"

"No," he said, sounding disappointed. "I was just thinking, and the guys..." He trailed off. He was a diehard romantic. How many guys are so quick to get to the altar?

"How about this," I started. "When would you like to get married?"

He was quiet for a moment.

"I have always liked fall weddings. What do you think?"

"It sounds good to me. Is there a date you were thinking of?"

"Yes, actually. How about October twentieth? It falls on a weekend."

"The leaves will be brilliant then, shouldn't they?"

"Yes, they should!" he nearly shouted ecstatically. "It will be perfect."

I could almost see him smile that playboy smile.

"You sound really happy."

"How could *I* not be? I'm in love!" He started laughing loudly, and I heard cheering behind him. "I just called to tell you I love you and I missed you. And most importantly, I can't wait to see you again."

"I know this sounds corny, but me too. Try to come home soon, okay? Please be safe."

"Yes, I will, I promise. I love you, darling."

"I love you." We left the conversation at that, and I had to come back to reality with a leering familiar Jester with a very wide smile. "Go ahead, say it."

"I get it now, it took a while, but I get it."

"Oh," I said with irritation. "And what is that?"

"You are completely head over heels in love with the guy, so much so that you are retarded for him!" He started laughing.

"Oh yeah," I remarked. "What are you going to do about it?"

The next two weeks were lonely without Jake, but between Jester coming over every night to play cards and working on assignments for the paper, the weeks went by in a blink. Tim had me doing photo editing for other projects from home while Autumn did interviews and legwork for the rest of the headliners for the Fair of Faith. Tim claimed he wanted me at my sharpest before the events. Yet even when the events had occurred, she avoided me. Not that I could blame her. I tried to call her, but the conversations last only a few words before she had to do something else. Or maybe she was still mad at me.

Jester had been searching for Frank's home but was unable to find it. We had been up for many nights attempting to pinpoint the exact location. He seemed to be in the middle of nowhere. Jester kept scoping out his apartment, but as fate would have it, he never slept there. It became useless to try to find his real place of residence. I was kept out of the loop for the simple reason I wasn't supposed to be working, period.

The plus side of being a Sentinel is unusual healing speed. I could now move without too much pain. Only light bruising remained, and I felt confident in my looks and my ability to cover it up with makeup. I had a lot to think about over the last two weeks. I wished for it to be over. I wished I knew why Damon could only love when I'm not around. I looked forward to a second chance. I was happier than I had ever been in my entire life. Jake made me feel whole and like I was normal.

Jester was working to change my mind about quitting the organization for good. Jester made me take the bed rest whether I liked it or not. He made me stay in my pajamas and watch horror movies. Jester decided to wait at Frank's office to see if he could catch him. He had to finally go off to see if he could implant the chip without me.

I kept wondering what the rest of my life would be like with him. However, I knew Jester was right about one thing. I needed to wait. I should sincerely think this out before I tied my life to him. What kind of past did he have with Damon, if one at all? I wished to call him and demand answers. I sat at my kitchen table with a cup of coffee and tried to think it all out. What did I know about Damon? I didn't know much about him at all. I needed to talk to Phipps. I wanted answers. Any answers.

I wanted to think about something else. I couldn't help but be excited. Jake called three times a day and was already planning the wedding. I found it funny how a man with such a reputation about commitment could be so ready to settle down. He was excited to get back to me, and it seemed that every day I was more and more excited for his return.

I started to get an onslaught of headaches that nearly sent me to the hospital. I started to get these waves of nausea. I never thought the concussion was that bad, but it kept getting worse. My entire body was sore; even my breasts started to hurt. Even though I thought I was healing quickly, some things didn't seem to do what I thought they were going to. I spent most of my time in the bed with sheets that Jake and I had lain in, watching old episodes of Scooby-Doo.

I was lucky I wasn't a normal human being or else I would be in a wheelchair. I had my fill of getting rest, and I desperately wanted to get out of the house. I got out of my pajamas and slipped into an old faded AC/DC tee shirt and jeans. I decided now that I was left to my own devices, I'd go out for a cup of coffee at the Demeter Cafe. At the very least out of the house and doing something other than sitting in my bed. After a quick trip to the bathroom to put on some makeup and a quick call to Autumn, thankful that she agreed to meet, I was on my way. I knew I had to talk to her. I really wanted to talk it out.

Upon arriving at the coffee shop, I barely recognized Autumn. She stood up and gave me a smile that seemed to drain her of all her energy. She plopped down on her chair with a sigh as I ventured to pick up a cup of coffee for both of us. Her black, silky, ringlet hair had been fluffed in a frizzy mess. Her brilliant gleaming alabaster skin had turned a papyrus olor of yellow better left to rotting corpses. Even though we were both the same size, she looked as weak and frail as a ninety-year-old. I felt as if I was towering over a wilting flower that was clinging desperately to life. She was in a wrinkled red dress shirt and jeans that only made her look sicklier. She slouched over the table while I placed the steaming cup of coffee in front of her. "Would you like some cream or sugar?" I said so quietly that I was afraid that anything louder might break her.

"What? Huh?" She shook her head as if to try to break herself out of her trance. "Yeah, sounds good."

I placed some sugar and cream in front of her. Her eyes danced with red among the pale blue. I didn't know what to say to her. She wanted so badly to believe the best of people. I knew she was sick.

"How are you doing? I haven't been able to..." She trailed off, and I snapped my fingers in front of her face. She blinked forward. "Uh, sorry, I haven't been sleeping."

"I noticed." I took her mug and mixed in two cream and two

sugars. I pushed the mug back to her, which she graciously took. "Listen, I don't mean to be rude, but you look like shit."

She rolled her eyes and took in a big drink.

"Well, I'm sick," she proclaimed in a nasally voice. "You know, you didn't look so fantastic a few weeks ago." Well, she had me on that one. "I'm fine, really." She took a big gulp and brightened up a little.

"I'm sorry to hear that. What are you coming down with?"

"The doctors don't really know, but they have been testing." She stared into her cup.

"I got a strange question for you," I said, leaning in. "When was the last time you saw Frank?"

Her eyes narrowed at me, and she shook her head.

"For the love of god! Not this again!"

I held up my hands in surrender.

"Just a question. You don't have to answer it if you don't want to."

"You really think the worst of people, don't you?" She slammed down the cup of coffee and glared at me.

"I really try not to, but—"

"How does it feel to be so fucking petty?" She got up abruptly. She was getting really upset.

I saw her eyes water. I reached out my hand to her.

"Listen, I didn't mean any—"

She held up her hand and cut me off.

"I don't care!" she yelled. "I know that maybe I don't want to speak to someone who is a giant judgmental piece of shit like you."

My hand dropped away. I felt the sting of her words as she turned to walk away.

"Autumn!" I shouted. "Wait!" I got up and started to walk after her.

"I don't want to talk to you!" she shouted.

I stopped in my tracks and watched her walk out the door.

She took five steps and started to sway. I took a step forward as she started to grab her head. I stepped out the door.

"Autumn, are you okay?" I said lightly. She fell to the side, and I ran to catch her. "Autumn?"

"I don't feel so good," she croaked.

I knew what I had to do.

"Okay, honey. I'm going to get you some help, but I need you to trust me."

Her eyes blinked at me twice and rolled in the back of her head. I put her arm around my shoulder and started to carry her into the back seat of my car. My phone rang, and it was Jake. I flipped open my phone. "Hi, can I call you back?"

Autumn started shaking, and I walked over to my trunk to get a blanket.

"Trinity, what's wrong?"

I popped the trunk and fished my blanket out.

"You sound upset."

"Very astute observation." I put the blanket on Autumn and tucked her in. "Autumn is sick."

"Yeah, Daniel told me. How sick is she?"

I got in the driver's seat and started up the car.

"I am bringing her to a specialist right now. She started to act really funny, and then she kinda passed out." I looked in the rearview mirror to see a very passed-out Autumn. I backed out of the parking space. "She's not doing so hot." I pulled out of the parking lot and started speeding.

"Oh shit. Okay, call me back and let me know what is going on."

"Can do." I ended the call with him and immediately dialed a HALO safe haven for injured operatives. They picked up on the first ring.

"Hello, this is *Touch of Healing*. Gina speaking," a polite and bubbly voice sang.

"Hi, it's Trinity." I looked at the speedometer and prayed that I didn't get pulled over.

"Trinity, I haven't heard from you in—"

I made a sharp turn.

"I know, and I have an emergency. Are you open?"

"Yes, yes. Of course, who is the operative?"

"It's not an operative, it's a civilian." I heard a hushed pause. "Please, she's passed out and is very sick right now. I don't know how she is going to make it."

"How did this happen?"

"Long story. Can you have a room ready?" I pulled into the back of the building and stopped the car to a screeching halt.

"Yes, I—"

"Good because we're here." I hung up the phone and jumped out of the car.

Gina rushed out of the back of the building as I was fishing Autumn out of the back seat. Her finely tuned brunette hair bounced as she took Autumn from the other side.

"Ready?"

Gina nodded, and we dragged Autumn inside to a private room. I lifted up her on the table. Autumn let out a small groan.

"You're lucky it's a slow day," Gina scolded me as she walked out.

Hair fell over Autumn's face as her breathing started becoming more erratic. I brushed the hair out of her face. Two practitioners quietly walked in. I recognized the smaller redhead with the wide sprite-like smile as Homa. She was a tiny, bouncing pile of life. Her triangular face offset her warm eyes. She smiled at me brightly as she got ready. The second practitioner was taller than Homa. She had long brown hair with sparkling blue eyes and a warm grandmother's essence. Kristie gave my shoulder a warm squeeze as she went to join Homa.

I stepped out of the room and let the healers do their work. I turned to see a very concerned Gina.

"Mind telling me what happened?"

I gave her the shortest version I could conjure up while she took me into the break room. She listened intently as she brewed some tea. The break room looked like an old darkroom/kitchen. I leaned against the sink area.

She handed me a cup of the tea. "Sounds like you've had quiet the case."

"No kidding," I murmured. "Thank you for helping her. I don't know how she got so bad."

"These things happen. It's not unusual."

"It's been a rough case," I said. "There is something wrong with this case, and I can't put my finger on it. My gut is nagging at me, and I can't understand what it is that is getting to me."

She leaned next to me.

"Who is the case?"

"A typical sucker, Frank Tennorman." I took a sip of my tea and noticed a weird look come across Gina's face. "I have read any information I could get my hands on, and I come up with nothing, but maybe there is something I'm missing. Mind telling me what's going on?"

"Well, nothing that's solid."

"What do you mean?"

"I heard rumors, but there was never any official proof."

"What kind of rumors?" I asked curiously.

She reflected on her words.

"You know that there are lists of HALO candidates."

I nodded.

"Over the last six years, candidates have gone missing."

"Missing? Do you mean HALO lost track of them or—"

"No, I mean completely disappeared off the map."

I felt my skin crawl, and I rubbed my arms.

"The candidates all attended a church service that he was heading, and then after all the children disappeared, he decided he had a calling elsewhere."

"Sounds suspicious," I said with an edge to my voice. I didn't like to see adults push around kids. "Anything ever come of it?"

"Not really, no one could find any proof as to what happened, and at that time no one really knew about him." Gina stared at me for a second and smiled. "Someone has made you very happy."

I nodded. I looked down at my ring and showed her.

"I already know," she said, giggling. She shoved an open magazine my way and flipped it to a story. It had a picture of Jake looking over rings, smiling.

I started to read the story, which confirmed our engagement. I laughed and wondered when he'd had time to get a ring. I looked at the picture of Jake and automatically missed him. Jester was right about one thing, I didn't know him that long.

Despite the short time we'd known each other, he made me feel very loved. It was like he knew me inside and out. I felt as if I didn't have to constantly explain myself or make up excuses. I loved the way he smelled, his smile, and I didn't know if I could ever be without him. I felt like a seed in the soil that had its first taste of sun.

With a quick stab of pain, I remembered Damon. This was how I had always imagined it would have been with him, but I was glad he had been replaced by Jake. From the outside, what did he have to offer me as a person? He was aggressive and violent. He wasn't that smart, and he never bothered to get to know me at all. Not to mention attempted murder was not a turn-on. I felt bad for him, but in the same sense I knew that he deserved everything he got.

I felt warm just thinking of Jake. My heart grew with the memories of him. Forget how long I had known him! He made me the happiest I had ever been. I met Gina's eyes with a wide smile.

"He is," I said as I took a big breath, "amazing."

She gave me an even wider smile with a warm laugh. She

wrapped her arms around me for a hug. She got stiff for a moment.

"Oh," she said with a bright spark of surprise. "I didn't realize." She stepped out of her hug and looked at me.

"Huh?" I said with shock caught in my throat.

"The baby, silly!" she said with a smile. "When is it due?"

I paled.

"Oh. You didn't know?"

I shook my head. I felt a dozen feelings wash over me. I felt panic that was washed out with waves of joy. Homa walked into the break room with a chipper bounce, humming a happy tune.

Gina rubbed the back of her neck and looked away from me. "Oh," she said, stepping back. "You didn't—"

"Ah, no," I said awkwardly.

"Hey, Trin! Your girl is feeling much better." She poured herself a cup of herbal tea. "Oh, honey, it wasn't pretty. That must have been one hell of a sucker."

I snapped my attention back to reality.

"The worst I have ever dealt with. Why, what happened?" I said with concern. Poor Autumn had been through enough for one day, and I wasn't up for any more surprises.

"There was this thing on her that kept drinking her energy."

"Seriously?" I said, surprised. "I didn't think that was possible."

Homa looked a little uncomfortable and exchanged glances with Gina.

"What's wrong?"

An uncharacteristic darkness shadowed her eyes.

"I have never seen anything like this," Homa started. "At first it looked like a white mist, but as we started peeling back layers of dirt, I noticed something weird." She glanced at Gina again and flashed her eyes back to me. "We noticed something wrapped around her legs, and as we started to unravel it, it was tightly coiled around her body, and as we got to her neck, we noticed it was wrapped tightest around her neck." She paused and took a breath. Looking into her cup, she continued, "It was wrapped around three times. That was when we noticed that the head was lodged in her neck."

"Lodged in her neck? What the hell was it?"

"It was a giant snake. I have never seen anything like it. It was coiled around her like nothing I had ever seen before."

I thought about it for a moment.

"Wasn't the snake Lilith's animal?" I asked.

"Lilith? Who is Lilith?" Homa looked at us with wide eyes.

"According to Jewish theology, she was believed to be the first wife of Adam, but she fell from grace when she failed to comply with Adam's sexual wishes," remarked Gina.

"Sexual wishes?" repeated Homa.

"Basically, he wanted to be on top, but she wanted to be on top. Adam demanded she comply, and she didn't want to. So she left him."

I sipped my tea as I listened to the conversation.

"Just like that?" Homa asked.

"Yup, angels tried to get her back. She said no and became demonized. Or that's the rumor. She has connections all throughout history, even in Zoroastrianism. Although she is named Adri Anahita, it is pretty much the same concept," Gina said as she poured herself some more tea.

"So what does that have to do with the girl you brought in, Trin?" Homa asked. "You are being awfully quiet."

"When I visited Frank at his apartment, he had visages of Lilith all over the place. Original ancient artifacts and paintings. I suppose I shouldn't be that surprised." I paused for a moment and reflected. "Something isn't right; this isn't a routine sucker job."

"It doesn't seem like it," remarked Gina. "What else could it be?"

"I have the feeling maybe there is something big in the works. Lilith was the murderer of children and seducer of men."

Gina shrugged.

"There is a lot of theology behind the enigma of Lilith. She is also called the Queen of the Succubae."

We all stood in silence for a moment, all thinking but getting nowhere due to the confused looks on our faces.

"Is Autumn going to be alright, Homa?" I asked, eager to change the conversation.

"Yes, I think so. As a matter of fact, she is healing already, and she'd love to see you." Homa started to lead the way to the private room.

As I entered the room, I saw Kristie warmly rubbing Autumn's back. Autumn's hair created a veil over her face, but it couldn't hide her crying. I carefully stepped in the room. She was already looking better.

"How are you feeling, honey?" I whispered quietly.

She rushed off the table and hugged me.

"I'm so sorry!" she cried. "I didn't mean those awful things I said."

"Autumn, it's okay," I said, patting her back.

"I didn't believe you, I thought... I don't why I thought these awful thoughts and—" She broke down with a sob. Kristie walked over to us and wrapped her arms around us. Gina and Homa joined in too, creating a warm cocoon of love.

"Keep an eye on her for a day," Gina whispered to me. "She needs time to heal."

I listened to Autumn sob, and I knew it was a part of the healing process. She'd been victimized by someone she had been attempting to prove wasn't a victimizer.

❦ 29 ❦

I gingerly helped Autumn through the door. She still looked tired. There was a big difference between looking like you need a few hours of sleep versus looking like you are on your deathbed. I helped her up to the guest room closest to the bathroom, with a set of pajamas.

I held a crinkled drugstore bag, wishing that I didn't have to go through this gut-wrenching moment. I stood in my bathroom, staring at a little white stick. *It's just a stick, right? I can't be pregnant. I'm on birth control, and I haven't even missed a period.* I paced a moment in the bathroom. What could hurt about this? I mean, I couldn't be pregnant, so what was the issue with checking? I peed on the stick and walked out into the hall.

After she was dressed and comfy on the guest room bed, I started the waiting game. She sat on the bed facing me as I stood comfortably in the doorway. "Jester did all this decorating?"

I nodded with a smile.

"Then it is official," she said a matter-of-fact voice.

"What?"

"No man who picks out a bed this comfortable can be evil." She giggled. "Seriously, the whole house?"

"Right down to my wardrobe. I got to admit, the man has taste."

We both laughed at the thought. The laughter dwindled off and left us in an awkward silence. She was looking at me sideways as if she wasn't certain what to say.

"So how about them Yankees?"

Autumn shook her head.

"What?"

"Always the witty one under pressure. Do you ever react normally?"

"I react normally when I have to poop."

Autumn's face contorted with rapid disgust.

"OH! Gross!" she yelled. "Why did you share *that* with me!?"

I shrugged as I glanced down at the test. Thank god no lines yet. I checked my watch; okay, only a few seconds had passed.

"You asked."

"Ugh, so not what I meant."

"So what *do* you mean?" I said with a smile.

"Do you really think you're preggers?"

I thought about it for a moment, did I believe I was?

"No, I think maybe Gina saw I was bloated and looked pregnant."

"Isn't Gina like a big super psychic or something?" She definitely caught me on that. "Like, how often is she wrong?"

I tried to think of the last time I had ever even heard of her being wrong.

"Judging by the look on your face, I will take that as a big no."

"I think that is a safe assumption." I chewed on the thought for a moment. "But logically speaking, it's not very likely. I mean, I am on birth control."

Autumn blinked and hesitated for a moment.

"You do remember you were out for two weeks, right?"

I felt a sinking sensation in the pit of my stomach. Oh, right, the whole coma thing.

She studied my face with an awkward look on her face. "I'm judging by the look on your face, that might not have crossed your mind."

I looked at the white stick, and a single pink line appeared. "Maybe it is not that big an impossibility." I tapped my foot against the floor.

"Fuck! Has it been three minutes yet?!" I checked my watch. Only one minute and I was already feeling panicky.

"See? Now that is a normal reaction!"

I sent her my best fuck-off look.

"Okay, let's talk about something else." She thought for a second. "Why does Gina want me to rest for a while? I feel much better."

I took a breath and tried to think about it.

"Well, I know you are beginning to feel better, but you need some rest. Also the first twenty-four hours are always the most sensitive for healing."

"I still don't get it," she said with confusion. "Like, what's the big deal?"

"Okay," I said, clapping my hands. "Think about it like this: you are a mosquito."

Autumn shot me a weird look.

"Bear with me. Anyway, you find a juicy young blood donor and start sucking their blood, and it is the best blood you have ever had. So you keep sucking and sucking. All the sudden, your donor disappears... what would you do?"

"Go looking for more food?" she remarked coyly.

"Remember," I reminded her. "Best meal of your life."

"Go looking for the donor before I lost them?"

"Right! When suckers find someone they like, they are not likely to give them up. They will do anything to reattach. You have your phone on you?"

"Yup, why?"

"Pass it to me."

She passed me her cell phone. I turned it off and took out the battery. She looked confused.

"Even if the phone is shut off, GPS can track you. Don't turn it on until after the twenty-four hours have passed."

"Okay, but I don't understand what happened to me."

"You are just a very juicy young meal."

She huffed a moment and looked down at her toes.

"You trusted him and tried to give him the benefit of the doubt, and he proved you wrong. It's no big deal. You will get better now."

"But that still doesn't explain why I have to be under surveillance."

"Everyone has this aura around them, and in order for a sucker to take energy from you, they have to rip open a hole in your aura. Twenty-four hours, disaster pending of course, allows the hole to start closing and continue healing."

"What happens if the hole stays open?"

"Then the sucker can start drinking off you again without permission."

"Permission?" she said with hints of anger lacing her voice. "I didn't give him permission to kill me."

"I know that, honey, but you gave him permission when you allowed him to touch you. Just be careful whom you allow to touch you. You never know when someone might try to hurt you."

She looked at me with serious eyes, and I knew she understood.

"It's over three minutes," she remarked. My eyes grew wide, but I didn't know if I wanted to look. The white stick felt heavy in my head. I felt my hand begin to shake. I looked down and saw two pink lines staring at me.

"Oh my God, I am pregnant!" I said in shock.

Autumn jerked up sharply.

"Oh my God, Trinity!"

I looked up at her and saw she wasn't looking at me. She was looking behind me. I slowly turned around. Jake was standing behind me with a wedding dress in his arms. His eyes were glassy, and his face showed nothing.

"Jake..." I whispered.

He blinked twice and looked at me.

"Does this mean I'm going to be a daddy?"

We all stood in silence. We were at a loss for words. I heard footsteps coming up the stairs behind Jake. Daniel bounced up the stairs with ease and a smile. He looked at Autumn with a leering grin.

"So!" he said, clapping his hands. "What'd I miss?"

❦ 30 ❦

Jake and I lay wrapped warm and naked in our bed. He played with my hair as my head rested on his chest. My arm was thrown across his chest. I felt imperfect lying next to him, but I felt whole around him. I felt his heart beat loudly, and I placed a kiss over his heart. He squeezed me tighter. We were swimming in silence as the sounds from the beach lapped against the shore.

"I know this sounds like a total chick thing to say," I started, "but what are you thinking about?" I found his fingers lacing in with mine.

"I'm thinking about the future." His gaze fell on the wedding dress that he'd brought with him. It was a dress that had a poufy skirt, corseted around the waist, and sleeves that fell off the shoulders. The dress looked as if it fell out of the eighteenth century. Apparently his outfit was going to look out of the same period but pure black. I loved it. Not because I was a bride but because we are happy together.

"Oh? I hope it's a good future." I looked up at him with hopeful eyes. He was smiling.

"It's better than anything I could have hoped for." He kissed my forehead lightly. "I'm happy."

I smiled.

"Why did you come back? I thought you weren't done yet."

"I wanted to surprise you by coming home early. Also, I kept trying to call you, and I didn't get an answer. I thought I would just pop in and see if you and Autumn were okay." He kissed my forehead again. "I didn't think that I would come back to such lovely news."

"I just found out as you did. I didn't expect you to, um..." I held my breath, attempting to find the right words.

"Be happy?"

"Yeah," I said, exhaling.

"Why wouldn't I be?" he said, arching an eyebrow.

"I don't know. Maybe you weren't ready for the commitment."

He started laughing at me.

"Not ready for commitment?" He stopped to laugh some more. "I'm going to marry you! How much more committed can a guy get?" He started laughing even harder.

"Okay, good point! Can you stop laughing at me now?" I said, pouting.

He squeezed me tightly.

"The baby growing inside you is a piece of both of us, and I love it as much as I love you."

"I don't get it. Why do you love me?"

He rubbed the side of my face, tilting it upward. His blue eyes looked into mine.

"I fell in love you before I even met you, and when I met you, I was blown away." He leaned in to kiss me. His lips were soft and warm. His kisses reminded me of pure sunshine. "I'm very happy to be with you right now." He paused a moment. "I got the perfect dress for you. I know things have not really been that fantastic, but I'm still the happiest I have ever been."

I looked up at him and smiled. I heard a heavy thud and giggle come from the guest room.

"I think it is safe to say the same about Daniel."

"I'm glad that you are happy," I said, snuggling back into his chest.

"There is something that is bothering me."

"What is bothering you?"

"How do you feel about everything that is going on?"

I reflected for a moment.

"How do I feel?" I rolled off him and lay on my back. "I'm happy, concerned, a little bit worried, but it's hard to tell what or how I feel right now. Nothing feels real." I took a moment to reflect. "I mean, think about it, just two months ago my life was completely different. Now everything has completely changed." I rolled onto my stomach and sighed. "It will take some getting used to, but at the same time, I'm just happy with the way things are."

He faced me, and he looked very serious.

"What's wrong?"

"Nothing," he said as his finger traced my face. "I was just thinking..." His regular smile returned, and he traced his way around my lips.

"About?" I kissed his fingertips, and his grin got bigger.

"How about you and I get married in someplace exotic?"

I laughed a little.

"Seriously?" I giggled. His hand found its way to my hips and pulled me closer. Goosebumps popped all over my body, causing me to shudder. "What is with you and going exotic places?"

He leaned close to my ear and whispered in a husky voice,

"Because I want to do things to you that you've never experienced." He nibbled on my earlobe. I let out a little gasp of pleasure. "I want to take you places you've never been," he whispered roughly. "And watch you enjoy every moment of it."

I placed my hand on his well-muscled chest and pushed at him lightly. I looked deep into his blue eyes.

"You don't really think you are going to get out of this discussion that easily?"

His eyes sparkled and seemed to dance.

"It's never going to be easy with you, is it?" He placed a kiss on my lips as his hands moved to my hips.

I caressed his arm and pulled closer to the warmth of his body. I was warm and happy.

"No, sorry. But hey... it could be worse, right?"

He gave me a huge grin and went under the warm cotton blankets. I felt his kisses laid gently over my stomach. He crawled on top of me and spread my legs with his knee. I felt his tongue move from my navel to my throat. I felt his teeth graze my jugular. His tongue kneaded my pulse, and I felt a burst of warmth as his skin touched mine. I let out a sigh as I absorbed his weight. He lay on top of me with his fingers lacing in my hair. We stared at each other eye to eye.

"I suppose you're right." He placed a kiss on my lips. "But let me choose a beautiful location." I could feel him against me as he relaxed. "I promise it will be lovely and perfect and everything you ever wanted."

"That's not a bad deal." I grinned. "To be perfectly honest, I'm not so good at the whole being giddy over wedding planning kind of thing."

He pulled me tighter against him.

I released a pent-up moan of pleasure. "Actually," I said breathlessly, "I'm pretty sure you could talk me into anything in this position."

He bit his bottom lip.

"I'll have to remember that." He placed another kiss on my lips. "I have everything in my car, awaiting your eye."

"Everything?"

"Everything we'll need to finalize the wedding plans."

I couldn't hide the confused look on my face.

"I want you to take a look at everything to make sure you are happy with what I have in mind."

I wanted to ask him when he'd found the time to plan everything, but he leaned into me, and the thought began to drift away. He wore a smug smile as he watched my face. He knew the effect he had on me. I wanted to ask myself what the hell I was thinking, but that was washed away by another kiss. I wrapped my arms around him and drew him in. I felt him slide inside me, and we both sighed together. This was heaven.

🦋 31 🦋

The morning flew by with a rush. Autumn, Daniel, Jake and I indulged in a grand breakfast of rich pancakes. I came down in a V-neck white tee shirt and jeans. Autumn was herself again and cuddled up to Daniel. After the noises coming from their bedroom all night, I was surprised to see them both perkier than we were. I cleaned the dishes as Autumn and Daniel disappeared again.

Jake went to his car to fetch the wedding plans. I had never thought for a moment that he would bring in two gigantic boxes of paper. I kept my eyes on the dishes and thought about the impending sense of doom about the wedding planning. He put the boxes on the table. I turned around to meet his eyes. He was wearing a grin of a little boy at Christmas.

There was something in the way he talked and moved that made him seem too real. I noticed that his features were so sharp that I could see him clearer than anyone else. I turned my attention back to the dishes. I put my hands in the warm, soapy water, watching the sunlight reflect off the multicolored bubbles. I heard the shuffling of papers behind me and felt the weight of Jake's gaze. I finished the dishes and gazed out the window into the fresh rays of light that now filtered through the sky, promising a beautiful day. A day Damon wouldn't be able to see.

I tried to remember how I'd felt about him before he decided to kill me, before Jake. I hoped that the memories that came to my mind would remind me of good times together. I had been seventeen when we first met. We spent every hour that we could manage with each other. I remembered before we were mated, I would go over to his house to wake him up for school every day. I climbed up his trellis, climbing over all the carefully manicured roses, to reach his unlocked window. I slowly opened the window and stepped in. I took off my shoes and padded over his soft bedroom carpet. He would hide under his covers, and the second I got close enough, he would grab me and shove me into the covers with him. I would giggle and laugh while his body wrapped around mine. It was the best way to wake up.

I felt fingers push my hair away from the base of my neck. "What are you thinking about?" Jake said, snapping me out of my memory. He placed a warm and loving kiss on my neck. My hands lay listless in an empty sink of warm water.

"Old memories," I said wistfully. *Dead memories* was more correct. I emptied the letting the colorful bubbles wash away. The day after it was announced that we were to be mated, Damon had torn down the trellis and refused to speak to me. "It doesn't matter anymore," I said with a heavy heart.

Jake wrapped his warm arms around me. I watched the left-over mystical bubbles down the drain. The happy bubble seemed without sorrow as they went to their death.

"It has to matter if it has caught your attention." He kissed my neck again.

"What plans have you made?" I said, duly noting the boxes that now cluttered up the table. He took a step back, allowing me to turn around. He had a suspicious look on his face. "You were so excited about them last night; do you not want me to see them?"

A half smile dangled on his lips as he turned his attention toward the table.

"You are going to love this!" he said with enthusiasm.

I hated to tell him that I wasn't enough of a girlie girl to really appreciate the wedding plans he was so excited about. Personally I figured we could hit up a drive-thru wedding chapel in Vegas and I'd be happy. I could picture it now, a creamy frosting cake of a building with a happy bride and groom sitting on top—madly in love of course. I would be wearing some corny veil hastily put together with a hot glue gun. He would be wearing a tee shirt and jeans, with some obscure sauce fermenting on his pants. The two of us would be sitting in some old beater car, leering at a screen, waiting to be pronounced man and wife. I giggled at the thought. Like Mr. perfectly dressed all the time could bear to have some bizarre stain on him, doing things very much untraditionally.

His face gave way to a twisted look. "What?"

"Oh, nothing," I remarked nonchalantly. "So... what's in the box?"

He stood waist deep in the piles of white fabrics and papers. He looked like a child in the middle of Christmas wrap.

I walked over to him and pulled out one of the chairs. "What's all this?"

"Wedding planning!"

"Yeesh! This is what all goes into it?"

"Yes." He took a moment to cough. "Well, it looks like a lot, but it's all about choices, and I have narrowed it down to three different choices."

"Oh?"

"Yes." He piled three giant books in front of me with a loud thud.

My eyes grew wide with shock. Did he really expect me to look over this all? That drive-thru was beginning to look better and better.

"I wasn't expecting to be reading three different versions of the Bible."

Before he could reply, a squealing voice came from behind me.

"Oh my god! Is that what I think it is?!" Autumn plopped beside me and grabbed one of the books. The second she flipped it open came another squeak of delight. "It is! Oh, and it is soooooo beautiful! You put all this together? It is so incredibly romantic!" she gushed loudly. "How did you come up with such ideas?"

He smiled brightly. Daniel came in and started shaking his head. Boy, did I ever know how he felt.

"At least someone can understand!" he said, sticking out his tongue at me. I went over to the fridge and grabbed a beer. "I want the most perfect romantic wedding."

Daniel's eyebrow perked, and I grabbed another beer. While Autumn and Jake were talking, I motioned to the patio door, and Daniel nodded in agreement. I passed him a beer as we made it outside.

"I swear to God." Daniel sighed. "If I hear one more thing about the wedding, I'm going to explode!" He leaned against the banister, facing the warm lapping water.

"You're going to explode?" I laughed. "I'm not into this whole thing."

He raised an eyebrow as he took a sip.

"I want to marry him, but I'm not usually the type to be making wedding plans. I never really got the whole romance concept." I leaned next to him and gazed at the water.

"What?"

"Before Jake, I thought romance was something you read about in corny dime-store novels." I took a sip and enjoyed the bitter taste. "It never really occurred to me that I would be getting married this soon let alone at all."

He grinned and nodded in agreement.

"I'm kinda a tomboy."

"To be honest, we all had a pool going on poor ol' Jakey boy," he said with a mischievous voice.

"A pool?"

"Yeah, well, he never dated anyone or at least anyone too seriously. He never let anyone get close."

"But he seems..." I gazed back into the kitchen, where he and Autumn were laughing over the books. "So warm."

"Yes." He tilted his head. "And no. He is like this around his friends but never any woman. You must be something special."

I wanted to laugh. *You have no idea.*

"Not really, just some normal ol' gal who got lucky." I shrugged lightly.

"Ah, I'm not gonna buy that one for a second, but the important thing is that he is happy."

"Something to agree on." We took a moment to enjoy the air. "So where did you guys meet?"

"We met through some friends at a party. This was before we all got famous. Just two guys out of college and ready to take on the world." He looked at me curiously. "He was always really quiet but not like shy quiet, just quiet about himself." His look continued to linger.

"What?" I said, pushing my hair behind my earlobe. I took a swig of my beer, attempting to escape the weight of his gaze.

"Why you?"

I got drawn back by the question.

"Don't you think that's a question for Jake and *not* me?"

He shrugged lightly.

"Yeah, that had occurred to me, but I would rather ask you."

I sighed and shook my head. He was blunt, I'd give him that.

"He said I was honest and genuine."

"I've slept with..." He trailed off and started counting in his head. I gave him a few minutes to consider it all.

"Geez," I remarked, overly getting his point. "I get the idea already!"

He laughed and took an enjoying sip. "So why do seem so shocked? Did he never settle down before?"

"Nothing personal but—" He looked as if he was swallowing what he really wanted to say.

"Just spit it out. I hate when people fluff things up."

"We have a lot of women at our disposal, and Jakey never really had any interest in them. He was there but on autopilot... you know?"

I knew all too well. It was like being on assignment. You had to do your job and play your part, but you always had to have your eye on the ball. I nodded in agreement.

"He is smitten with you." He took another swig and coughed slightly. "I'm glad to see him happy. I don't think I have ever seen him happy." He looked at the skyline, chewing things over for a moment. Maybe it was time for a change of topic.

"I'm sorry we haven't been able to talk, but I have been meaning to ask you how you are doing."

"You mean since the concert?"

I nodded.

His face lost the childlike glow, leaving behind a despondent look. Dark circles appeared around his eyes as they flickered to me. "I don't really know." He put down the beer and started rubbing behind his neck. "Physically, I feel fine." He shook his head. "But, spiritually..." He trailed off.

"Are you an atheist?"

He gave a sorrowful nod.

"But I don't think I am... anymore." He stood up straight. "I mean..." He started to pace. "Like, there is something out there? Right? There has to be." He stopped and changed direction. "Maybe there is something I'm missing or something I can't see." He looked more troubled.

I stayed still, as still as I could hold myself. A part of me feared what he might say, and another half knew that he had to get out what was bothering him.

"What is bothering you?" I took a deep breath in. "After all, you are alive and well."

"I saw something," he said cautiously.

I exhaled very quietly. I had a feeling this wasn't going to be pretty.

"What did you see?"

His eyebrows drew together as he looked at me with a sideways glance.

"If you don't want to talk about it, you don't have to, but I'm an ear if you need one." I half smiled at him. He looked uncomfortable in his own skin.

"It's crazy." He wrapped his arms around himself and looked down at the ground. "It doesn't make any sense."

"I won't tell anyone." I reached my hand out and touched his shoulder.

"When I was on the stage on the ground, I thought I was going to die. I saw a white light cover me, and it was warm and safe." He took a deep breath. "An angel came out of the light, and all my pain went away." The corners of his mouth twitched as if he wanted to smile. "She had a beautiful smile, but to my right there was this pitch blackness... it was like it was threatening to take my life." He paused and mulled over what he wanted to say next.

Then something occurred to me. A suspicion danced in the back of my head. I removed my hand and shoved it in my pocket.

"Blackness? Like what kind?" I asked.

"It was a hot darkness, like the kind you'd imagine coming out of the pits of hell. It smelt like roses." He laughed loudly. "Fucking roses? Can you imagine? I'm dying and I smell roses." Suspicion confirmed. I had been looking in the wrong spot. I had been searching in the crowd, not onstage.

"What else happened?"

"The darkness just disappeared. Then shortly after the angel did too."

"What did the angel look like?"

He looked at me with a raised eyebrow as if checking to see if I was messing with him.

"I'm not screwing with you or anything. I honestly just want to know."

The look dropped from his face, and he shrugged his shoulders.

"I didn't really get a good look. All I saw were her smile and her eyes."

"It's okay, Daniel. What you experienced was not unusual. It has happened to a lot of people." I smiled at him happily. I took my hand out of my pocket and offered him a hug. He wrapped his arms around me and squeezed me tight.

"Hey!" a voiced yelled behind us. We turned to see Jake. "No groping the bride until AFTER she's married." He laughed.

"I just wanted to see what the fuss was about," Daniel said as he resumed his typical confidence. They both laughed. "I wanted to give my approval via hug." He grinned.

"Okay," Jake said, crossing his arms. "Let's keep it that way."

32

It was getting close to sunset as Jake and I enjoyed a candlelit dinner on the beach. I laid a light kiss on his cheek. This was wonderful. It smelt of the tendrils of a summer campfire with the happy, childhood smells of roasted marshmallows. We had just finished a wonderful meal, and now it was just time for him and me. I laid my head down on his lap, facing him, and felt his fingers brush through my hair. We smiled warmly at each other. I felt nice and clean in my white sundress. I stretched out my bare feet so that they were touching the sand.

He moved his other hand over my lower abdomen. "So what do you think for names?" he said quietly.

"I haven't really thought about it. I mean, I'm about a month along."

"I know," he said with a sheepish smile. "But I was thinking maybe Christophe or something along those lines."

"It sounds good to me." I cuddled up to him and kissed his elbow.

He lifted me up closer to him.

"Why don't you and I go to Paris."

I started laughing.

"What is it with you and large cities?"

He chuckled lightly.

"It's not so much the large cities," he whispered.

"Oh? Then what?"

"I want to take you places. Anywhere and everywhere."

"Haven't you been everywhere?"

He looked confused for a moment and then smiled.

"Not with you."

I started laughing.

"SO, Paris it is!"

"You know what? Why not, let's do it!"

He reached into his back pocket and pulled out a phone. He quickly dialed a number.

"Geez! You're serious?!"

"Yup!" he said, grinning widely. "Hi, Rachael? I need you to do me a favor..."

I sat up and shook my head. I heard my phone ring and reached into my pocket to fish it out. It was Jester.

"Hello, Jester."

"Trin, you need to get to your panic room now."

"What? Why?"

"Damon broke out today, and chances are he knows where you are."

"OH, fuck me."

Jake turned his attention to me.

"When did this happen?"

"No one knows. All that was left behind was that stupid fucking tabloid that broke your engagement. I'm in my car now and on my way. Is Jake with you?"

"Yeah, he's here."

"Good, get a gun and get inside."

"I'm on it."

"One last thing," he said carefully. I heard a horn honk in the distance.

"What?"

"Stay alive."

"Count on it."

We hung up, and I looked at Jake. "We have to get inside. Now."

He shook his head. I got to my feet in a flash.

"Why?" He slowly rose, looking at me sideways.

"This was going to come out sooner or later. The short story is I'm a secret operative for an ancient organization that saves the world."

He didn't look very shocked.

"My ex-mate is on his way here to kill us. We have to get into my top-secret panic room." I grabbed his hands and tried tugging him off the blanket.

"Trinity, wait. I have to tell you something."

"Can this wait until we are in the panic room?"

"No, I—" The crack of a gunshot burst through the air. I looked down to see a blossom of blood on his white dress shirt. His eyes were frozen on me. Another crack came through the air, and I tried to pull him, but he fell to the ground. Damon came out of the woods with a silver Beretta dangling from his hand. Bullets screamed forward.

"Damon! No!" I screamed, but it fell on deaf ears. Damon's cheeks were hollowed out, and his eyes were black. He just stared at Jake as he lay dying. He pulled the trigger, and a hollow click sounded.

"You stole her from me," Damon remarked calmly. He pressed a button to release the empty magazine. "You knew, and you stole her from me." He pulled another magazine out of his pocket and loaded the clip. "She can't possibly love you."

I threw myself at him to try to get the gun, but with a single swoop of his arm, I flew back and hit the ground.

Damon didn't even seem to notice me as he kept his attention focused on Jake, who lay gasping for breath. He pulled back the slide and aimed it at Jake's chest. I tried to pull him up, but he couldn't move.

Jake turned to me; blood spurted forth out of his mouth. "Trinity," he sputtered. "Run." He coughed again. "I'll be okay. Take care of Christophe." He gave my hand a lingering squeeze and pushed me away.

Damon calmly pulled the trigger as I scrambled to run up the hill. I looked behind me to see that Damon finally saw me. Shit. I suddenly regretted not wearing any shoes.

"It will be easier if you don't run." He walked swiftly.

"No, get away from me!" I said weakly. I made it to the top of the hill. My foot slipped on some dewy grass, and I fell with a heavy thud. With a few simple strides Damon caught up with me. As if in a daze, his gun rose. I raised my arms to protect myself. "Please don't. I'm pregnant."

His face twisted with raw anger.

"No," he said, his voice rough with anger. "You can't be." Damon twitched and shook. From his neck protruded a dart with a red feather.

"Actually," a voice said behind us. I turned to see Frank smiling gleefully. "I'm counting on it."

I opened my mouth to reply, but a sharp pain in my neck cut me off. I fought against the clouding darkness, but it came too fast.

❧ 33 ❧

I swam through the velvety darkness. I tried to move, but my limbs didn't want to. I floated through a haze, hearing voices echo. I tried to force my eyes open, and they decided to flutter instead. I caught a glimpse of red marble surroundings. I forced my eyes shut. *No, I'm home, with Jake.* I tried to move, but my limbs stayed fully asleep.

I forced open my eyes to see Frank Tennorman speaking with a nervous-looking man in a lab coat. The man looked like a crazed twitchy Jewish doctor from Auschwitz. Round-framed glasses sat perched on the end of his hooked nose as his eyes shifted about the room. Whatever was bothering Doktor Auschwitz didn't seem to bother Frank at all. He wore his dazzling wide easygoing smile. I looked at the room, and it was unlike any room I had ever seen before. I was lying on a chaise, looking at a very round room made entirely out of red marble.

It reminded me of a Roman temple with its red pillars and large fireplace. Across from me was a high-backed chair that matched the chaise I was stretched out on. I blinked hard to get out of this bad dream. I tried to open my mouth to scream. My mouth stayed shut. Frank Tennorman's shoulders were slumped, and his hands stuffed easily into his suit pockets.

"So, is she...?" Frank said with a nonchalant wave of his hand.

Doc Auschwitz took a hand and forcefully rubbed the back of his neck while his brown eyes flickered to my face. The doctor paled once he met my eyes.

"Ah, she's awake," Frank remarked as he turned his attention back to the doctor.

"Yes," Doc replied mournfully.

A loud clap sounded from Frank's hands.

"Marvelous!" he exclaimed as he turned to face me. "How long does this stuff last?"

"At her metabolic rate, I would roughly say an hour and a half. After the doze we just gave her, it's a miracle she is even blinking. I gave her enough to kill a large horse."

Frank's face darkened with a malevolent grin.

"That, my dear doctor," he said, moving the high-backed chair to right in front of me, "is the wondrous thing about the children of Mazda."

The doctor's eyebrows furrowed together as he eyed me with a sorrowful look.

"Are you sure this will work?"

"Oh, yes, it will."

"But if we're wrong—" he pushed.

"We're not," Frank said to end the debate. "Leave us."

Doc Auschwitz left without another word.

Frank sat down and stared at me. "I hope you don't mind, but I took the liberty of changing your clothes."

I tried to move my head, but it was too heavy. My eyes swept over my body, which I could see to view a red and white silk Grecian dress.

"I hope you like it. This is a very special occasion, after all."

I looked at his face. Wait, Damon. Where was Damon? My eyes flickered around the room desperately. I had to save him. I had to get the hell out of here! I tried to gather as much strength as I could to move.

"I wouldn't bother trying to move if I were you. I dosed you with a high neurological sedative. Meaning your limbs are going to be useless."

I forced a growl out of my throat. Good, at least one more thing was working.

"Well, well, well, that isn't friendly at all."

I shot him my best go-fuck-yourself look.

"Ah, yes, you do have a reason to be upset with me. That's why I want to talk to you. I really respect you. I mean, I have seen a lot of your type before."

My type? I thought as I brought my eyebrows together. Make that three things that were working.

"I have seen many Sentinels in my time, but you—you are something else, you know that?"

How did he know? I felt a pit of dread sink into the bottom of my stomach.

"You're not just a Sentinel. When I first started watching you, I thought that there was something completely undefined about you. You are the last in a very long line of..." He paused, tilting his head briefly to reflect on it. "Well, let's just say angels," he said wistfully.

If I'd had the use of my mouth, I would have asked him to let me in on the joke.

He focused back on me with a questioning look.

"You have no idea what you are, do you?"

I gave him my best deadpan look. I wished he would just get this over with.

"Isn't that something?" he whispered privately. "My dear, you are... well, were supposed to save the world. But I'm terribly sorry, but I need you for other things."

Oh, how thoughtful. Remind me to send you a fucking thank-you card and a big ol' fuck-you fruit basket (just for good measure, of course).

"I hope you don't mind." He folded his hands over his lap.

"I bet you are wondering where your precious Damon is?"

I blinked.

"He is in the courtyard, nice and sedated. I like him better when he is sedated, but I thought you deserved an explanation as to why you are going to die."

How polite. I tried to move my big toe.

"I am a follower of the temple of Lilith and the high priest."

I felt my toe move; chalk that up to four.

"When I was studying in Iran, I uncovered an interesting find. Did you know that every culture ever since the beginning of time has a 'Lilith' myth?" he said proudly. "Neither did I at the time. I came across an interesting find, one that no one else had ever seen before."

I moved my other toes.

"It was midnight in the desert, and I decided to dig alone to get ahead. That was when I found a tomb that allegedly belonged to Zoroaster. Do you know who Zoroaster is?"

I blinked twice. If I could just keep him distracted enough to get my body back working.

"Long story short; he was the main prophet in a very old religion called Zoroastrianism. It's the first monotheistic religion." He shifted into a more conversational pose. "I had opened the door to the tomb, and I had to go in. I walked for what seemed like hours until I came to an open chamber with a large book written purely on hematite. It was the conjuring spells to bring Lilith, or as they called her Uhuru, into our world. But there is a catch. It needed a child of Mazda, child of Ahriman, and a child who was from both lines but had yet to be given a destiny to which he or she would be. The first step was easy, find followers, and wouldn't you know it? She had worshippers all over the world! Followers give the will to power the ceremony; it really worked out nicely. But finding the children," he reflected briefly. "That was the tricky part."

I tried to move my tongue in my mouth. I felt as if my tongue had been replaced with a giant slug.

"At first I became a reverend and began searching for children HALO was interested in. HALO never sends different people. So it became easy to pick out those who were Reapers and Sentinels. But who of those had yet to choose? So after—" he paused and briefly tallied the number up in his head "—over two hundred dead candidates, I decided to reresearch."

I got my tongue to move but sluggishly.

"That's when it occurred to me! It would have to be an unborn child of both of them. That was when I came across you. The second I saw you, I knew it had to be you. I saw the life growing inside you."

My baby, my unborn child and the last piece of Jake that I would ever have, would be gone soon. I felt tears well up and fall.

"Oh! Please don't cry."

I moved my lips slowly. My limbs started to feel.

"Wh-wh-wh-why m-mmmm-me?" My tears poured over my face. This baby did nothing wrong; it had no right to die by the hands of this monster.

"Your child is from a Reaper. The doctor confirmed it just moments ago." He smiled gently and patted my head. "Don't worry. You'll be ushering in a new era of Lilith! You'll die a hero and so will Damon. Be proud!"

A knock sounded at the door, and a man in a long red cloak came in with gold engraved shackles. "Oh dear," he remarked wistfully. "It is getting close, isn't it?" He nodded to the cloaked man.

The man came over to me and shackled my arms and legs.

"OH! Before I forget, Jack, I noticed her toes had gotten the feeling back in them. Could you make sure that she is tied up nice and tight?"

Jack nodded and turned to Frank.

"Wonderful! You are such a lifesaver!" he said with a wave of relief. "And one last thing, would you be a doll and slit the good doctor's throat?"

Another sharp nod.

"Oh, thank you so much, Jack! I'd do it myself, but I really MUST get ready." What an asshole. "This will be a night to remember," he said with the enthusiasm of a sixteen-year-old girl. He walked out of the room as Jack threw me over his shoulder with remarkable ease.

The courtyard was a large circle imbedded with red marble. There were two pillars in the middle of the courtyard. Damon was tied lazily to one and clearly still very much out. I was quickly regaining the ability to move. Small blessings, right?

Jack tied me up with expert precision and left quickly to find the good doctor. He tied my arm away from the rest of me. He tied me wrist to wrist with Damon. I saw people in the same red cloaks take their places surrounding Damon and me. One by one they began chanting. At first it was quiet, but then it grew with each person joining the crowd. I saw Jack enter the circle. How did I know it was him, you ask? The robe covered in bloodstains and tears was a big hint. I got some joy out of the fact that the doctor had put up a fight.

Jack stepped in front of us as he pulled a large dagger out of his cloak. He raised his arms to the sky, chanting other words, then the surrounding crowd parted. Another cloaked person came forward with an engraved bowl and set it beneath our tied hands. I heard a groan from Damon as he floated somewhere in the darkness. He felt warm against my skin. A month ago I would I have killed to be able to touch him. I wished Jake were still alive. There was nothing more I yearned for than a happily after with him. But my precious Jake was now dead, and our baby was next on the menu.

I felt my mouth get feeling back into it, and I smiled. *At least I am going to die,* I thought to myself. I felt relief knowing that I was going to die soon. I had lost everything today, and I didn't have to live the rest of my life with the pain. Jack stepped back to reveal a naked blond woman. She looked thin and skinny like a super-model. Her cupid's-bow lips revealed a large tooth-filled grin. She bent her long neck forward. Jack revealed a long golden knife, and with a flick of his wrist, he slit her throat. She kept her smile as her blood spattered all over us. Damon twitched when the blood hit him.

The feeling had long gone out of my blood-spattered arms Pins and needles shivering through my arms warned me that they waking up. I looked to the right of me and saw Damon's eyes flutter. I had to save him. Sure, he was an asshole, neglected me, tried to kill me. I blinked for a moment. Actually, I didn't think I could think of a reason to save him. I had to try. The air became thick with sage smoke. I coughed lightly. I had to find a reason to live. I opened my mouth. I saw Damon's head roll, and a groan escape his lips.

"Damon," I said, nudging our tied arms. "Wake up. C'mon. Wake up!"

His brown eyes flickered. The chanters' arms rose toward the sky, beckoning some invisible force. Their arms were swaying in a rhythmic motion.

A sharp breath beside me escaped from his lips. "What the fuck..." Damon said with disbelief. The circle parted, and a tall figure cloaked in blue stepped his way through but froze only a few feet in front of us. The figure stepped in the center and raised his hands to the sky. A male voice boomed out over the chanting, reciting a separate incantation. Fear filled Damon's eyes.

"We're in trouble, aren't we?"

"Yup."

"This is going to be bad, isn't it?"

"Yup." The chanting got louder as if it were the thunder in the sky.

"We've had bad before, Trinity," he attempted to assure me.

"This is worse." Even through the thunder of the voices, I heard him gulp. I began to think about all the things I was going to miss out on, all the things I hadn't done. My eyes began to water. But then again, I had experienced the deepest love. *Oh, my dead beloved,* I thought sadly. *We will at least see each other soon.* The chanting stopped as if frozen in motion. Out of an unknown place, music began to ensue.

"What's going on?" I felt Damon struggle harder. The followers lowered their arms and turned toward us. I stared at the darkness that hid their faces.

"Why am I covered in blood?"

I narrowed my eyes and swung my head to face him.

"Oh, what? You forgot murdering the love of my life in cold blood."

He shook his head in a sarcastic fashion. The cloaked figures began to sway and dance.

"No, I meant the fresh stuff," he said bitterly.

I flicked my eyes downward.

"Oh, I see. I take it by the smile she was... willing?"

"Oh, well, now that your conscience is clear, we can die happy."

He smiled at me. Out of all the things he could do, he smiled.

"Why the fuck are you smiling?" I shook my head. "Out of all the miserable assholes I have to die with, I just *had* to be stuck with you!"

The smile fell off his face.

"Since I'm going to die, I figured I should tell you something."

"If you're looking for a confessional, you can just wait a few minutes. I'm pretty sure you'll be meeting God soon."

He shot me a look.

"Jesus! Always with the smart-ass comments."

"And you deserve better... why?"

"Goddamn it!" he cursed under his breath. "I love you, Trinity."

"Wow, it have killed you to tell me this, I dunno, a couple of months ago? Or wait, I don't know, not treat me like a piece of shit or try to kill me." I started to struggle harder against the restraints. Screw the ceremony, if I got free, I'd kill him myself. "Or how about killing the man of my dreams."

"I did you a favor by getting rid of that piece of shit."

I struggled harder against the restraints.

"So let me get this straight." I started feeling my blood boil. "You treat me like crap as soon as you find out we were mated. All the sudden you want me because I'm dating Jake. You fly into a jealous rage, try to kill me—almost succeed, might I add—then you kill the father of my child. And now—" I started laughing "—now you love me. Go fuck yourself, you selfish son of a bitch!"

He looked down. A look of sorrow crossed his face.

"I deserve that, and I'm sorry." He looked at my face with knitted eyebrows. As if I am supposed to take pity on him for what he did.

"Great, we're about to die, and you're sorry. Good to know," I remarked bitterly.

"You don't get it. Jake Fortinbras isn't who he says he is," he said in a harsh whisper.

"Like you know." That sounded weak even to me. "Not that it matters anymore."

"Jake works for an organization called HORD. Reapers once they reach a certain level are sent on missions solo against HORD. Jake works for them. Long story short, he is the bad guy."

"The only bad guy I know right now—is you."

"We're going to die soon, so I'll tell you this. I wanted out of HALO."

I didn't want to look at him after what he'd done.

"Jake approached me and promised to make all my dreams

come true. He gave me a large sum of cash to gather all the information I could on you, and I did."

"You just don't know when to shut up, do you?" I felt the sting of tears.

"Just listen, months went by, and one day he offered me a huge bonus." He nudged me. "Trinity, look at me, please."

I brought my eyes to meet his.

"He offered it in exchange for me staying away from you."

I looked at his face. The face I had so badly loved, and to some extent I still did. The dancing froze, and the music stopped.

"What's going on?"

The man in the blue cloak lowered his hands from the sky and seemed to stare through us.

"Didn't you know?" I remarked wryly. His face turned to me, pale with fear. *I regret nothing, nothing.* Suddenly this was all so funny. "It's showtime." I giggled lightly. The perfect ending to a shitty day.

"This day we offer a gateway to the mother of us all," said Frank, speaking from behind the cloak. "We offer to our goddess Lilith the life of a child who has yet to choose." He approached me with slow deliberate steps. A deep, tonal language rumbled from his throat as he reached his hand out, just hovering over my lower abdomen. The language grew louder, and a pain began to grow.

I felt my guts lurch forward. A fire started in my ovaries. It kept building into a blaze. I felt hot and dizzy. Pain ripped through me like a knife. *Please kill me. This is it, I'm going to die.* I tried moving my arms to protect myself, but it was useless. I felt the pain crushing me in its crescendo, using my screams to fuel its music. I crushed my eyes shut, praying that this was a nightmare.

"Leave her alone!" I heard between the waves of pain. I was being carried away in the flames, and the voice faded in a burst of blood running down my legs. "Trinity! Stay with me!" Damon became silent.

I opened my eyes to see Jack collecting my blood with a golden dish. I looked at Damon, whose face was completely blank. My scream left me hollow, and I was unable to say any more. Not that I cared anymore; I just wanted it to be over with. Beyond the fact that he was summoning a demon, it seemed sick and twisted to keep us alive. The followers began chanting.

"I offer you, Lilith, the blood of the unborn." Jack placed the golden dish underneath Damon's and my tied hands. "I offer you, Lilith, the blood of a child of Mazda." Frank then produced a blade, and with a single slice he opened my vein. I looked at the dish and saw the blood pouring out of my wrist. "I offer you, Lilith, the blood of the child of Ahriman." With a quick slice, he opened Damon's vein. Our blood entwined together as it flowed into the golden bowl. Frank threw off his cloak to reveal that he was naked. Jack handed him the golden bowl, and Frank walked to the center of the circle. I felt so tired, my knees gave out, but I was tied so tightly I didn't fall.

Frank faced us as he spoke.

"I, your high Priest, offer myself as your vessel. I drink this blood and leave myself open to your power."

I felt the air get colder and prickle. I lowered my head. I shook with the cold moving through my soul. I smelt something warm float in; it smelt like hot vanilla, with notes of sandalwood and lavender. Maybe Jake was waiting for me. I felt something tug on my chains and thought that my spirit was trying to get free from my body.

I raised my head to see Jake walking through the crowd of followers. His form still had the bullet holes and blood. He was coming for me, and I felt a pang of hope. He was going to bring me home. I saw a silver gun in his hand. Frank didn't seem to notice. I strained to focus my eyes; Jake's eyes were black. I shook my head. I didn't understand what was going on. Jake raised his hand, and in one strong wave of his hand, all the followers collapsed.

Frank, startled, turned to face Jake. He gasped, "A true child of Ahriman..."

Jake raised the gun to Frank's head.

"Wait, no!" he said, fear filling his voice. "You're a Reaper... this isn't what you do..." he begged.

I felt the chains loosen, and someone caught me. My head swam. I looked over to my side.

"You're going to be alright, Trin. I got you," said Autumn with a weak smile. Her eyes were red with tears as we looked toward Jake.

"You piece of shit," Jake said in a bitter cold voice. His face was contorted in way that blurred out the Jake I knew and loved. I was looking at a different man. "That's the good thing about being the bad guy, we don't fucking give a shit."

"N—" Frank attempted to scream before Jake pulled the trigger and splattered his brains everywhere. The echo of the gunshot rang through the air, and Damon blinked as he snapped out of the trance.

"Trinity?" He looked over at me with tears in his eyes. "Are you okay? I'm so sorry."

Jake stepped over Frank's body and walked over until he was right in front of Damon. Jake raised the barrel of the gun to his head and pressed it into his skin.

"Fuck off, Fortinbras."

"Give me one reason not to fucking kill you."

Damon clenched his jaw, and black ink filled the whites of his eyes.

"Jake!" screamed Autumn.

I staggered, attempting not to pass out. Jester appeared between Jake and Damon. Autumn let out a squeak.

"So," Jester said with a smile dangling on his lips, "you must be Jake."

Jake's eyes flickered to Jester, then back to Damon.

"I'm Jester," he said, taking a bow. "As much as I would like to see Damon get his comeuppance... I think you have some explaining to do."

Jake pressed the gun into Damon's head harder.

"That can't be Jake," I whispered.

Jester ducked under Jake's arm.

"What was that?" he said, putting his arms around me to help Autumn with the weight.

"He can't be Jake. Jake's dead."

He squeezed me tighter.

"I'm afraid he is." Jester turned his full attention to Jake. "I think you have something to explain to her that is more important than the vengeance of blood."

Jake lowered the gun, and the ink drained out of his eyes as he came toward me.

"Is it true?" I croaked out. I heard the ripping of fabric. I looked over at Autumn to see her tying a piece of my dress to my wound. Jake tried to reach out and touch me. I took a step back. "Answer me."

Autumn walked over to the next pillar and untied Damon. He walked away from Jake.

"Yes," he said with tight lips. "I can explain, please. Just give me a chance."

I stopped being able to breathe, and I started to cry. I tried gasping for air.

"I love you, Trinity, please. I've quit it all. I love you."

"I quit. I'm done. I'm done with HALO. I'm done with pain... I'm just done." I looked at Jester. "Take me home."

"What a great idea," Jester said with a smile. "I'm with Trin, Damon. I quit."

"Trinity," Jake started.

I raised my hand to stop him.

"I need time," I croaked. "We lost our child, I'm bleeding to death, and I need to be alone to heal."

Jester picked me up and started to carry me away. I fell asleep on the way to the hospital. As I looked over Jester's shoulder, I saw Jake crying silent tears. I wanted nothing more than to wake up yesterday and start all over again. But life doesn't have a rewind button, does it? As I started to pass out on the way to the hospital, I kept wondering how Little Red Riding Hood got out of the woods alive. Especially when she couldn't tell who the big bad wolf was.

ABOUT THE AUTHOR

E. C. Hinrichs was born in Canada and moved to the United States. She spent most of her college career writing and studying literature. After college, she spent her time working in different careers before settling into human services. She has spent the last seven years working with children, the elderly and persons with disabilities. E. C. Hinrichs spends her free time reading Tudor history, paranormal nonfiction and fiction.

www.ingramcontent.com/pod-product-compliance
Lightning Source LLC
Chambersburg PA
CBHW052046240626
47153CB00006B/2237